A SILENT STABBING

Books by Alyssa Maxwell

Gilded Newport Mysteries
MURDER AT THE BREAKERS
MURDER AT MARBLE HOUSE
MURDER AT BEECHWOOD
MURDER AT ROUGH POINT
MURDER AT CHATEAU SUR MER
MURDER AT OCHRE COURT
MURDER AT CROSSWAYS

Lady and Lady's Maid Mysteries
MURDER MOST MALICIOUS
A PINCH OF POISON
A DEVIOUS DEATH
A MURDEROUS MARRIAGE
A SILENT STABBING

Published by Kensington Publishing Corporation

A SILENT STABBING

ALYSSA MAXWELL

KENSINGTON BOOKS
www.kensingtonbooks.com

KENSINGTON BOOKS are published by

Kensington Publishing Corp.
119 West 40th Street
New York, NY 10018

All Kensington titles, imprints, and distributed lines are available at special quantity discounts for bulk purchases for sales promotion, premiums, fundraising, educational, or institutional use. Special book excerpts or customized printings can also be created to fit specific needs. For details, write or phone the office of the Kensington Special Sales Manager: Attn. Special Sales Department. Kensington Publishing Corp, 119 West 40th Street, New York, NY 10018. Phone: 1-800-221-2647.

Library of Congress Card Catalogue Number: 2019951395

Kensington and the K logo Reg. U.S. Pat. & TM Off.

ISBN-13: 978-1-4967-1742-9
ISBN-10: 1-4967-1742-2
First Kensington Hardcover Edition: March 2020

ISBN-13: 978-1-4967-1744-3 (e-book)
ISBN-10: 1-4967-1744-9 (e-book)

10 9 8 7 6 5 4 3 2 1

Printed in the United States of America

To my readers who found me through my Gilded Newport Mysteries and followed me across the sea to Little Barlow to meet Phoebe and Eva and the rest. Thank you for your kindness, your support, and most of all, thank you for reading!

ACKNOWLEDGMENTS

I always say it takes a village to write a book, and that doesn't change whether it's the first book or many books later. I feel incredibly fortunate to be a Kensington author. My deepest thanks go out to my editor, John Scognamiglio, Robin Cook and the copyediting department, the amazing people in the art department, publicist Larissa Ackerman, who never fails to light a promotional fire under me with each new release, and so many others who transform a manuscript into a book worthy of the shelves. And, always, many thanks to my agent, Evan Marshall, who is there to see that all goes well.

A SILENT
STABBING

CHAPTER 1

The Cotswolds, September 1920

Her arms full of fresh cut flowers, Eva Huntford entered her parents' kitchen and yet again caught her mother studying her reflection in the window above the cast iron sink. Eva went to the scrubbed pine table and set down the bundle of feverfew, primroses, and violets she'd snipped from the front garden. Soon the flowers bordering the house would be gone as brisk fall winds chased the last of summer away.

"Do stop fussing, Mum," she said with a tolerant smile and a shake of her head. "You look lovely." She meant it. Her mother's health had taken a turn for the worse during the last year of the war and had remained a concern for Eva until recently. Now, the color had returned to her cheeks and she no longer huffed with every physical effort or wheezed to catch her breath. At fifty-four Betty Huntford might no longer be a young woman, but surely she still had many good years left, not to mention three grandchildren on whom she doted. "Besides, it's only Alice and the children coming."

"Just the children, you say." Her mother turned and leaned her back against the edge of the sink. "It's been months and months since they've seen me. What if they think their poor grandmum is getting old?"

Eva stifled a chuckle. "They're three, five, and seven." The oldest had been born right before the war; the other two, during, the result of Oliver's rare trips home on leave. "They think *I* look old. Besides, all they care about is getting a warm hug from their grandmum, being told how big they've gotten, and sitting down to an extra-large piece of your lardy cake."

She sniffed the warm, spicy scents rising from the oven. Her mum's lardy cake, made with freshly rendered lard, plenty of sugar, currants, and raisins, was the best Eva had ever tasted, and that included Mrs. Ellison's at Foxwood Hall. It was a trifle expensive, of course, and Mum only made it for special occasions. "Smells wonderful."

"To tell you truly, Evie, I didn't expect this visit, it came so out of the blue when Alice wrote to say they were coming. It's left me the tiniest bit addled, having to get the house ready for them on such short notice." Mum cast a nervous glance at the old coal-fired range, cast iron like the sink, but black rather than white. The house dated to the early decades of the last century, and the range had been set into the cavernous hearth that had once served for cooking meals. "They should be here any minute. Provided, that is, Old Bessie doesn't break down again. I do wish your father would spend the money on a new truck."

"Even if he had the money, he wouldn't spend it on a new truck, Mum. Not while Old Bessie still has a breath left in her."

"Yes, yes, that's true. I'll just . . . I'll set the table. Oh, and I'll put those flowers in a vase. You go keep watch for them."

Eva didn't argue. If setting the table and seeing that every little detail was just so helped her mother expend some energy and feel less jittery, then Eva would leave her to it. In the parlor, she took up position by the front window that overlooked the road. Across the way, the poplar trees flanking the Pittmans' farmhouse were already glowing brightly gold, while the oak beside the Huntfords' barn retained most of its summer green, tipped only here and there in licks of flame.

The dry autumn air intensified the blue of the sky and the sharpness of the sunlight, making her squint a bit to see down the road. She did indeed hope Old Bessie, Dad's prewar motor wagon with its flatbed for hauling farm equipment, made it to the train depot and back. Poor Bessie had been making odd, grunting complaints lately that didn't bode well for her future.

"It was ever so good of Lady Phoebe to give you the day off," Mum called from the other room.

Eva nodded, though Mum couldn't see it. "It feels almost sinful not to be working on a Tuesday." Officially, she had time off only on Sunday afternoons, after church. But she happened to work as a lady's maid for a tolerant and thoughtful mistress, not to mention that Eva had helped Lady Phoebe's sister, Julia, now Lady Annondale, out of a particularly doleful situation earlier this year. Phoebe and the entire Renshaw family were only too happy to grant Eva the occasional favor, though she would never take advantage of their kindness.

Outside, movement caught her eye. There, down the road at the fork that led either west, to the village of Little Barlow or north to the train depot, a little cloud of dust stirred in the air. A moment later Old Bessie's snub, rust-stained bonnet came into view. Soon, through the open windows, Eva could hear the truck's creaking and groaning and the *chug-chug* of her engine. "They're here, Mum!"

Although it must have been a tight squeeze to fit Dad, Alice, and three small children into the cab of the motor wagon, Eva was glad to see none of them rode in the bed. She always grimaced at the sight of local children riding in the back of open lorries. But then, Eva didn't believe any seat in a motorcar to be completely safe; they went too, too fast for her comfort, and all that jostling at high speeds couldn't possibly do a body any good.

Mum shuffled into the room, realized she held a dishrag in one hand and still wore her apron, and doubled back into the kitchen. When she appeared again she was smoothing her cotton frock—her second best—and patting stray brown hairs peppered with gray into place. Outside, Old Bessie puttered to a halt in front of the house and let out a hiss. Mum ran to open the front door, grabbing her shawl off the back of a chair on the way.

When Eva expected her to hurry across the threshold, her mother instead went still, rather like Old Bessie with her tires gone flat. Eva peered out the window to see into the truck; there, just inside the passenger door, was her sister's profile. Just then Alice turned, spotted Eva, and waved enthusiastically. She opened the door to hop out. Eva heard a sigh from her mother. "Mum, what's wrong?"

"Where are the children? Where are my Hannah, Lizzie, and Ollie Junior?"

Indeed. Three small children should have poured out the door after their mother, but there was no one left inside. Alice went round to the back of the wagon and slid out her overnight satchel. Dad joined her there and hefted her larger portmanteau. Together they came up the front path.

"Mum, Eva, it's so good to see you both," Alice cried. She smiled broadly. "It's so jolly to be home."

Before stepping outside, Mum cast Eva a look over her shoulder, and in that instant Eva saw her effort to bring her features under control, to hide her disappointment. Eva felt a sense of letdown, too. She had so looked forward to playing the indulgent auntie to her nephew and two little nieces. As her mother had said, it had been months and months since their visit at Christmas.

"Here she is, all safe and sound." Dad shifted the weight of the trunk in his arms, and Eva noticed that he, too, worked to keep his expression amiable.

"I didn't expect you to be here today, Eva," Alice said after Mum had embraced her, inspected her appearance from head to foot, and declared her "looking lovely though a smidgeon tired."

Alice and Eva hugged and then stepped back to admire each other. Alice, Eva's senior by three years, had their father's eyes and Mum's dark hair, as did Eva. And like Eva, Alice's features drew from both parents. People had always said the Huntford sisters looked very much alike, but Eva was taken slightly aback now to detect the beginnings of crow's-feet beside Alice's eyes and lines that spoke of weariness around her mouth. Those lines deepened to brackets as Alice grinned. "How spiffing of the Renshaws to let you out for the day. You must have them wrapped around your little finger. They say a good servant eventually becomes the master, and the master the servant."

"Do they? I've never heard that."

"Well, let's not all stand outside for the neighbors' entertainment." Their father led the way into the parlor. With a grunt, he set the suitcase down against the wall. Dad had trimmed his beard short for the summer and sported a bit more of a paunch between his braces than he had last winter, a result of Mum's talents as both a cook and a baker. He gave his stomach a pat now as he scented the aromas coming from the kitchen. With a sideways glance at his elder daughter, he said, "Little Ollie loves his lardy cake, doesn't he, Alice?"

When her sister didn't reply, Eva decided there was nothing for it but to ask the question quivering in the air between them. "Alice, why haven't you brought the children?"

"Yes, Alice." Mum closed the front door; turning, she clasped her hands at her waist. "Surely you didn't leave them in Suffolk with Oliver. How on earth is he to tend to them and the farm at the same time?"

"Don't be silly, Mum." Alice set down her overnight bag, collapsed on the sofa, and let out a weary sigh. "No, they're with their Ward grandparents, well looked after, I assure you."

Mum's frown etched deep lines across her brow. So much for concealing her true feelings. "You do realize they have grandparents right here who would have adored looking after them."

"Yes, but they have school now. Surely you didn't expect me to take them away from their lessons." Alice patted the cushion beside her, an invitation for Mum to join her. After bringing Alice's larger case into the room she and Eva had once shared, Dad lowered himself into his favorite easy chair. Eva crossed the room to lean against the mantel. "The truth is," her sister began, and sighed once more, "I needed a bit of a holiday. I've earned one. You remember how it can be sometimes, don't you, Mum?"

"I'm . . . not sure what you mean." Mum's forehead knotted more tightly. Dad tilted his head and narrowed his eyes as if perplexed by a difficult math problem.

"All the demands of children and husband and farm

life." Alice held out her hands. "It's all so consuming sometimes. I just wanted . . . no, I *needed* some time to myself. And time with my family."

Mum's frown deepened still more. "How is Oliver? Is everything all right with . . . him?"

Eva guessed her mother's hesitation stemmed from her being about to ask if everything was all right with Alice *and* Oliver, meaning had they quarreled? Because that was exactly what Eva suspected.

"Oliver is just fine, Mum." Alice smoothed a nonexistent wrinkle from her skirt. "He's very busy now harvesting the wheat and barley."

"And he doesn't need your help?" Dad asked.

Alice looked up, her gaze shifting from parent to parent. "No. He's got day laborers."

"Oh. He can afford laborers? Isn't that a frightful strain on his profits?" Mum glanced over at Dad. "Why, your father almost never—"

"Do I smell lardy cake?" Alice made a show of lifting her nose into the air. She rose suddenly and hurried into the kitchen.

Her lips pursed, Mum gained her feet a good deal more slowly, with Dad rising and coming over to lend her a hand. "What in the world?" she whispered to him. Dad shrugged. "Time with her family? Her husband and children are her family. And she certainly didn't seem eager to answer our questions and put our minds at rest. Vincent, I'm worried about that girl. This isn't like her."

The oven door whined on its hinges. "Mmmm," Alice sang out with appreciation. "I'd say it's almost ready. Mum, have you any perry on hand?"

"In the pantry, luv," Mom called back, but her gaze never left her husband's.

"Is it Ripley's?" Alice's footsteps could be heard crossing the kitchen.

Her mother said impatiently, "Of course it is."

"Alice is no girl, that's certain," Dad murmured. "And we've no cause to pry simply because she's come home for a visit. Maybe it's as she says—she needed a holiday."

"Yes, but *why*?" The conversation continued in hushed tones, giving Eva the impression her parents had forgotten she was still in the room. "I tell you, Vincent, there's something wrong. And I intend to find out what it is."

"Ah, here it is." Alice's muffled voice drifted from the pantry. "How has Keenan Ripley's yield been so far this year?"

No one answered the question about the local farmer whose family had long ago cultivated the species of pears that made Gloucestershire's unique cider, called perry. The Ripley perry was considered some of the Cotswolds' best. Even Eva, who only rarely drank spirits, was known to enjoy a pint on occasion.

"Would everyone like some?" Alice asked, her voice louder now as she apparently reentered the kitchen.

"Not for me, Alice," Mum said, her impatience once more conveyed by her rising voice, and Eva was certain her mother couldn't have cared less just then what she ate or drank. To her husband she whispered emphatically, "I'll soon know what's going on with that girl."

"Now, Betty . . ."

"No, I'm her mother, and I've a right to know when things aren't right with one of my children—" Mum's voice had begun to rise again, then suddenly choked off. A tide of red flooded her face, and her eyes filled, a sight that brought a sting to Eva's own eyes. Her mother's sudden wretchedness wasn't about Alice. It was about the one child she hadn't been able to help, to save. The child who had perhaps needed his mother, but he had been beyond her reach at the time. Eva's brother, Danny, who died in the war, whose body still lay in an unmarked grave in France . . .

The oven door again creaked open. "It looks ready," Alice called. "Shall I take it out?"

"I'm coming." With a last determined glance at Dad, Mum hurried into the other room. That left Eva and her father staring at each other. He looked apologetic and at a loss. Poor man, outnumbered by his womenfolk and often unable to puzzle out what were, for him, their mysterious ways. Eva blinked away the moisture in her eyes, went to him, and smiled up into his kindly face.

"Don't worry, Dad, I'm sure Alice is just fine. But if there *is* something wrong, I'll find out what it is, and I'll fix it."

The tables lining the stone walls of St. George's basement fairly groaned beneath their burdens, a circumstance that brought great satisfaction to Phoebe Renshaw. Her autumn charity drive for the Relief and Comfort of Veterans and Their Families, or the RCVF, had proved an unmitigated success, and by this time next week deliveries would be made to the wounded veterans of the Great War who resided in Gloucestershire, and to the families of those men who never returned.

"A job well done, my lady." Eva, Phoebe's personal maid, carried an armful of children's clothing, which she added to a pile on the nearest table. It was the fifth load she had carried down from the vestibule of the church above them in the past ten minutes. Eva had had the day off yesterday to welcome her sister, who was visiting their parents in Little Barlow, and it seemed she was determined to work twice as hard today to make up for it. Dearest Eva.

"The parish truly stepped forward this time, didn't they?" Phoebe continued scanning the goods piled high on each table. Besides clothing, there were linens and bedding, pots and pans, dishes and cutlery, tinned and jarred goods, sacks of flour, farming tools, and so much more. Toward the back of the room, two volunteers were sorting toiletries. Elaina Corbyn, the wife of a local sheep farmer, and Violet Hershel, the vicar's wife, spoke quietly together as they organized items and jotted down an inventory of goods.

Phoebe joined Eva at the children's clothing table and began separating boys' garments from girls'. "Now the real work begins," she said. "First the sorting and then the matching of donations to the requests we've received from the families who need our help."

"I'm happy to lend a hand, too, my lady." Eva's sister, Alice Ward, came down the steps from the sanctuary and set a box on the table marked *Cleaning Supplies.* A carton of Fels-Naptha soap peeped out over the edge of the corrugated cardboard container. Mrs. Ward so resembled Eva with her dark hair, trim figure, and small, even features, that often Phoebe had to look twice to know to whom she was speaking. Except that Eva, approaching thirty but not quite, still retained the bloom of youth, while time hung a bit more heavily on Alice Ward.

"I don't like to see you laboring during your holiday, Mrs. Ward," Phoebe told her with a laugh.

"This is pleasant work, Lady Phoebe. And with three children at home, I'm not used to sitting about all day."

Phoebe heard a little sigh from Eva. What was that about? Before she could ponder further, booted footsteps sounded on the stone stairs from outside. Two men made their way precariously down to the basement, one backward, the other facing front, carrying a large crate between them. A chilly draft from outside followed them down, prompting Phoebe to tighten her cardigan around her.

"Morning, Lady Phoebe," the one facing backward said. "I've got pears for you. They're a little overripe for perry making, but perfectly edible, and there's no use in letting them rot. Make excellent pies and turnovers, I expect." Farmer and owner of a local brewery, Keenan Ripley continued taking small backward steps while his older brother, Stephen, guided him to a vacant spot on one of the tables. Unlike Eva and her sister, the brothers could not have looked more different. Keenan sported dusky red hair that curled over his collar, while Stephen's close-shorn locks were as pale and straight as straw. The brothers set down their load, and Keenan wiped a sleeve across his brow.

Phoebe went over to inspect the contents of the crate. An assortment of red, green, and gold pears met her gaze. "What do we have here?"

That they were pears was obvious, but Mr. Ripley knew her question involved specifics. "Some Barlands, Helen's Earlies, and Blakeney Reds, mostly."

"Are you sure you can spare all these, Mr. Ripley? There are a great many here." She couldn't help wondering if the fruit was truly unsuitable for brewing Gloucestershire's unique blend of pear cider, or if Keenan Ripley was in an exceedingly generous mood. She glanced up at both brothers and smiled. "Or should I say, Misters Ripley? I didn't know you'd returned to Little Barlow," she said to the elder brother, Stephen. Though she had been a young schoolgirl when he moved away from the village, Phoebe remembered him because he had worked at Foxwood Hall, assisting the head gardener, Alfred Peele. She remembered her grandfather once commenting that Stephen hadn't seemed at all interested in the family orchard, but would make a fine gardener someday. He had left a couple of years before the war started and hadn't been back since.

"Only just back, but you're right to address your concerns to my brother." Stephen Ripley shoved a pair of spectacles higher on his sunburned nose. "I've not joined him in the brewing business. In fact, Lady Phoebe, I'll be working at Foxwood Hall starting tomorrow."

"Will you? I didn't know." What came as a surprise wasn't so much the news that Stephen Ripley would be joining the staff at home, but that her grandfather hadn't informed her of the fact. With his heir, Phoebe's brother Fox, still a boy in his teen years, Grandfather had taken to confiding in Phoebe when it came to matters of estate business. He said she had a good head for figures and organization, and she considered it of no small consequence that he showed such confidence in her abilities. She couldn't help wondering why he had omitted to mention a new employee. But she carefully schooled her features not to show the slightest smidgeon of perplexity. "Will you be assisting Mr. Peele again?"

Stephen Ripley's self-satisfied grin revealed a row of well-formed if uneven teeth. "No, my lady. I'm going to be your new head gardener."

"Head gardener . . . ?" She trailed off, once again unwilling to reveal her thoughts. Alfred Peele had served in the capacity of head gardener at Foxwood Hall for nearly two decades. Yes, he was getting on, but the man still stood as straight as the hedges he kept trimmed to such perfection that, from a distance, they appeared to be solid walls of emerald and jade. Phoebe had heard no talk of him retiring—not so much as a wisp of a hint. And obviously Eva had heard nothing belowstairs, or she would have said something.

Then what had happened? She wouldn't ask Stephen

Ripley. No, it wouldn't do to question the man directly, not when he had already reached an understanding with her grandfather. It wasn't her place. But she *would* ask Grampapa the moment she returned home.

From the corner of her eye she noticed Alice Ward hovering close by, and realized she might very well wish to chat with the brothers. Eva as well. All of them being of an age, they had grown up together, attended the village school right here in St. George's basement before the permanent school had been built next door, and before Eva had won her scholarship to attend the nearby Haverleigh School for Young Ladies.

But they would not exchange more than a few words until Phoebe moved away and busied herself elsewhere. For them to do otherwise would be considered impertinent. Oh, not to Phoebe—she never minded about such things. But the others had been raised to show deference to the Earl of Wroxly and his family, who had presided over the village and its surrounds these many generations.

"It's good to have you home, Mr. Ripley," she said to Stephen, and with a shift of her gaze, said to Keenan, "Thank you so much for the pears, Mr. Ripley. Your donation will bring a welcome as well as wholesome treat to many of our families who could not afford it otherwise."

She moved several tables away and began sorting kitchen gadgets: whisks, peelers, crimpers, mashers, etc. Meanwhile, the others did as she expected, with Mrs. Ward and Keenan Ripley appearing to become quickly reacquainted, and Eva and Stephen Ripley trading pleasantries. Mrs. Corbyn and Mrs. Hershel, older than the others, greeted the newcomers briefly but kept on working. Phoebe caught Eva's gaze and compressed her lips, and Eva nodded in the kind of comprehension they had become adept at over the past couple of years. With any luck, her lady's maid might unravel the mystery of Foxwood Hall's new head gardener.

"I heard from Keenan that you'd fought in the war," Eva said to Stephen. From the corner of her eye, she noticed Alice and Keenan move several table lengths away, just out of earshot. She frowned slightly as Elaina Corbyn, working in the back of the room, took notice, too, and followed the pair with her gaze. Eva turned her attention back to Stephen. "He said you weren't with one of the Gloucestershire infantries."

"That's so. I was living in Dorset at the time, and joined up with one of their units."

Eva found that odd. One would think that at such a time, a man would seek the fellowship of longtime mates, and most especially one's own brother. But then, Keenan and Stephen Ripley had never shared the kind of closeness Eva and Alice had enjoyed as children. She remembered the boys falling to fisticuffs so often in the churchyard during lunch recess that their schoolmaster, Mr. Thornton, had taken to ordering them to stay on separate sides of the building until it was time to return to their lessons. Perhaps that was typical of brothers, but even now, she felt rather sorry for them.

Then again, the bond she had shared with Alice seemed oddly frayed of late. Try as she might, she could wring no further information from her sister about why she came to Little Barlow alone, other than her claim of needing a holiday to herself.

A peal of laughter drew Eva's attention back to Alice and Keenan. Alice stood with her arms crossed in front of her, her hips askew, her head tilted in interest at whatever he was saying. In rapt attention, one might say.

Need they stand so close? Especially when, before the

war, and before Alice had met Oliver, she and Keenan Ripley had shown a budding interest in each other. Funny Eva thought of that now. Alice had had several beaux before meeting Oliver. In those days, young men and women didn't step out together as they did now. Mutual affection then was conveyed by much more subtle means. A quiet conversation beneath the canopy of a shade tree following church services, smiles traded in the market square, or a turn or two on the dance floor during a very proper cotillion on a Saturday evening. A pang struck her. How innocent they had all been before the war. How unaware of the upheaval to come.

"And you, Eva." Stephen reclaimed her attention. "Have you never left Little Barlow?"

She sighed and released the memories. "Not for any length of time. Only with Lady Phoebe and her family. So I've traveled round England well enough."

"Have you? Always at your mistress's beck and call, seeing little but whatever rooms you're relegated to in whatever big houses you're visiting? Haven't you felt you were missing out?" He rubbed a palm against his chin. Despite his fair hair, he sported heavy stubble that would quickly become a beard if he allowed it to.

"I've been content," she told him hotly—more so than she'd meant to. She didn't like anyone criticizing her choices, especially when they were in no position to understand how her regard for the Renshaw sisters—Julia, Phoebe, and Amelia—had shaped not only her life, but the person she had become. Alice was a mother, and at times Eva, despite being not many years older than her young ladies, felt herself equally so. "And anyway," she said, "here you are back in Little Barlow, where you began. And working for one of those big houses. Won't you be missing out on more exciting opportunities?"

His eyes flashed acknowledgment of her sarcasm, but he smiled. "The head gardener's position is different. I'll be at the beck and call only of the outdoors—the gardens, the hedgerows, the trees."

His blithe answer made her dubious. "Yes, but what really brought you back?"

Stephen compressed his lips as if to prevent a secret slipping out. The impression persisted as he slid a glance to his brother and then back again. "I have my reasons, which will be clear soon enough."

"How mysterious." Eva did her best to ignore another peel of laughter from Alice. The two women sorting toiletries, however, made no such effort, and watched Alice and Keenan with raised eyebrows. "Tell me," she said to Stephen, "how did you manage to be hired on at Foxwood Hall without any of the rest of us knowing about it? Why the secrecy?"

"Ah. That was at Alfred Peele's request. He decided to retire and didn't want anyone trying to talk him out of it. So he wished nothing said until a replacement was found." He pointed a thumb at his chest. "Me."

"But if you wish to live here again, why not work the orchard with your brother? I've never understood your leaving. The orchard is your birthright. The farm and brewery have been in your family for how many generations now?"

"Too many, if you ask me. There's nothing particularly charming about picking pears and crushing them into pulp for cider. It's backbreaking, boring work and I've no interest in it. I learned from one of the best gardeners in Dorset, before and after the war, and I've the chance now to use those skills."

This time it was Keenan who expressed his merriment with a deep, rumbling roll of laughter that cut short any further inquiries on Eva's part. Stephen's answers had left her unconvinced. Had he escaped trouble down in Dorset? Her attention once more shifted to her sister. Eva's eyes widened. Alice had taken a handkerchief out of her skirt pocket and was using it to wipe a smudge off Keenan's cheek. To hold his head steady, she cupped his chin with her other hand. Mrs. Corbyn and Mrs. Hershel stared openly now.

Eva couldn't blame them. This was altogether too familiar, especially for two individuals who hadn't seen each other in years. Or had they? Her back stiff with indignation, Eva stepped away from Stephen. "Alice, are you ready to go? Lady Phoebe said she would drop you back at the farm on our way to Foxwood Hall." Eva only hoped Lady Phoebe might be persuaded to leave now, rather than later.

Alice regarded her and wrinkled her nose. "Mum and Dad's place is not on the way to Foxwood Hall, silly. In fact, from here it's in quite the opposite direction."

"I could give you a ride," Keenan offered.

Eva felt a twinge of alarm. "No, we wouldn't dream of inconveniencing you."

"No inconvenience at all. In fact, I need to visit the Corbyn farm out that way." He paused to nod at Elaina Corbyn. "If your husband's in," he said to her, "he and I need to talk about extending the lease terms for your grazing rights to our northeast pasture."

"I'm sure you'll find Fred somewhere about the place." Mrs. Corbyn held her spine and her upper lip with equal stiffness, her disapproval of the past several minutes obvious.

A low chuckle came from Stephen. He'd taken on a look Eva didn't like—a snide and once again secretive look. She wasn't the only one to notice.

"What was that for?" Keenan challenged him.

"Nothing, brother. Never mind."

Keenan studied Stephen another moment before turning back to Alice. He offered the crook of his elbow. "Shall we?"

Alice slipped her hand through his arm and showed her most brilliant smile. "Let's."

"I'll go with you," Eva blurted.

Alice and Keenan had started for the basement steps. They halted, Alice looking mystified. "Why on earth would you?"

"I . . ." What could Eva say? She had been given time off yesterday in anticipation of Alice's arrival, but she had no good reason to shirk her duties today—other than to play nursemaid to an older sister who was perhaps showing a want of good judgment. Her shoulders sagged. "Never mind. Tell Mum and Dad I'll be home for Sunday dinner."

Alice nodded and started to turn away, but Keenan lingered. "Mrs. Corbyn, would you like a ride home?"

Eva's surge of hope was quickly doused. "No, thank you." The woman's chin lifted a sanctimonious inch higher. "I'll wait here for school dismissal and walk home with my boys."

Once at home, Phoebe decided against asking her grandfather about the sudden change in the head gardener's position, at least not right away. Eva had told her what Stephen Ripley said about Alfred Peele not wanting anyone to know about his retirement until it was too late to urge him to change his mind. His fears were not unwarranted, for Mr. Peele was a popular man on the estate and many individuals, both above and below stairs, would be sorry to see him go. Phoebe would be one of them.

But surely there would be some form of send-off—a reception or a tea in the servants' hall, with Phoebe and her family making an appearance to wish the man well. Gram-

papa would shake his hand, discreetly transferring an en-
velope of cash into his palm. But Eva had heard of nothing
of the sort being planned. It was all very odd.

The person to speak with, she decided, was Mr. Peele
himself. To that end, she changed out of her pumps and
into a sturdy pair of Wellingtons, traded her lighter cardigan for a thick, cable knit to ward off the late afternoon
chill, and made her way across the parterre gardens, past
the brook, the pond, and the old, decorative folly.

On the way, she noticed the fallen column at the front
of the folly, and the crumbling top step that led inside the
small interior. Moss grew along the Greek-inspired structure's north wall, and ivy crawled over the roof. While
some follies were built to simulate a Greek or Roman ruin,
such was not the case here. No, the once pristine, minia-
ture temple had fallen into disrepair during the war years,
when extra funds went to supporting the soldiers and
there had been no men to spare for such trivialities. Even Alfred Peele, well into middle age though he was, had served as
an ambulance driver for much of the war. She wondered
whether Grampapa had any intentions of restoring the
place, or would have it cleared away.

At last she came to the two-story gardener's cottage set
snugly into the edge of the wood just beyond the manicured portion of the property. She knocked at the blue-
painted door loud enough to be heard should Mr. Peele be
upstairs or at the back, in his kitchen. She didn't think
he'd be working, not when he was leaving tomorrow.
When a minute passed in silence she knocked again. Surely
he hadn't left yet, without saying good-bye. Stepping back,
she looked up at the golden stone façade and saw that an
upstairs window stood open.

"Mr. Peele?" she called out. "Are you in? It's Lady
Phoebe."

The front door opened, startling her with its abruptness.

She nonetheless offered up her friendliest smile. "There you are. I wanted to—oh. Mr. Ripley." Indeed, the man standing on the threshold bore no resemblance to the gray-haired, stocky, aging Mr. Peele. She and Eva had left Stephen Ripley not an hour ago at St. George's. How on earth had he gotten here so quickly? "What are you doing here?"

His wheat-blond eyebrows went up in amusement as he regarded her through his spectacles. "I believe I mentioned starting work tomorrow, Lady Phoebe. So . . . here I am."

"Yes, but what about Mr. Peele? Are you sharing the cottage with him until he moves out?"

His amusement increased, bringing a chuckle to his lips. "My lady, Mr. Peele left yesterday. The cottage is mine now."

"Yesterday? But that's impossible. He never said good-bye. The rest of the staff didn't have a chance to wish him well. Why, I'm sure they'd have wanted to present him with a keepsake to remember them all by. And my grandfather would surely have wished to speak a few words of gratitude and send him off with monetary recompense for his years of service, and . . ." She left off. She'd made her point, yet this man seemed unimpressed.

Standing a good head taller than she, he flexed a bicep and rested his hand on the door latch. "Lord Wroxly may indeed have settled some reward on old Alfred, but as for the staff, as I told Eva at the church, my lady, this is what he wished. I'm sorry if anyone is disappointed, but there was nothing I could have done to change it."

"No . . . I don't suppose there was. . . ." With a niggling sense of she didn't quite know what, she began to back away. "I'm sorry to bother you."

"No bother, my lady. And if there are any special requests concerning the gardens, I'll always be happy to hear them."

"Yes, thank you, Mr. Ripley. Well, I'll let you get on with your unpacking and settling in. Er . . . welcome to

Foxwood Hall . . . Call up at the house if you need any-thing."

He propped a hand on the door frame and leaned out over the top step. "Thank you, my lady. It's my pleasure to be here."

She frowned all the way back to the main house. Odd. *Exceedingly* odd. Upon reentering through the French windows in the drawing room, she trekked determinedly across the Great Hall, onto which all the rooms of the ground floor opened. Outside Grampapa's study, she gave two firm knocks before letting herself in.

CHAPTER 2

The next morning, Mervyn Giles, Foxwood Hall's long-time butler, shuffled into the servants' hall murmuring to no one in particular. Beyond the high windows set at ground level, the first blue tinge of morning seeped through the foliage. "Alfred Peele would not have left without saying good-bye."

Like the rest of the staff, Eva stood before her place at the long, rectangular table. A lump of sadness sank in her stomach as Mr. Giles continued muttering. Of similar age to the Earl of Wroxly, the years had added inches to Mr. Giles's torso and lines to his face, had robbed him of a good amount of hair, and traded handsomeness—so essential if a footman was to rise in the ranks of the staff—for the dignified authority needed to run a house like Foxwood Hall.

What time had also done, tragically, was to steal into his mind and leave conflicting impressions of past and present, often rendering the poor man at an utter loss. Some mornings he strolled into the servants' hall practically bouncing on the balls of his feet in his eagerness to start the day. Other mornings, like this one, he wandered belowstairs until someone pointed him in the right direction and told him, typically more than once, what needed doing. In a tribute to how well-liked the man was among his underlings and employers alike, a friendly conspiracy had grown around him, from the earl himself down to Josh, the young hall boy, to gently guide Mr. Giles in his proper role whenever needed.

He glanced now at the dozen expectant faces staring back at him and frowned in puzzlement. "What are you all standing around for?"

Down both sides of the table, the servants darted looks of uncertainty back and forth at one another. Eva found herself biting her lip to keep from cueing the man as a stage director cues an actor who has forgotten his lines. It wasn't her place. Rather, George Vernon, the head footman and a young man very much in possession of those physical and mental attributes that had paved the way for Mr. Giles's rise up the servants' ladder, leaned in from his place to the right of the butler. "The prayer, sir," he whispered. Though everyone heard, they all pretended they hadn't.

"The prayer?"

To Mr. Giles's left, Mrs. Sanders, Foxwood Hall's housekeeper, raised an eyebrow meant to ward off any urges to grin or snigger at poor Mr. Giles's confusion. Her efforts proved unnecessary. The staff didn't secretly refer to her as Old Ironheart for nothing. Her word was law belowstairs at Foxwood Hall, and Eva had yet to meet a servant willing to defy her. Thus assured of proper discipline, the woman leaned to whisper to the butler, "Grace. For the meal, sir."

"Ah, yes. Yes, of course." He bowed his head, hesitated a moment, and began intoning mealtime grace. The servants obediently bowed their heads and listened, and when they all said amen it was with a sigh of relief.

Mr. Giles once more glanced around the table. "Where is Alfred? He often joins us for breakfast."

Eva's appetite waned; the prospect of swallowing Mrs. Ellison's scrambled eggs, black pudding, and baked beans seemed an intolerable chore. Once again, Vernon came to the rescue.

"If you'll remember, sir, Alfred Peele has retired."

Someone from lower down the table muttered, "Just up and left in the middle of the night, without so much as a tip of his hat to the rest of us."

Vernon shot the mutterer a warning look, but otherwise ignored the comment. "We have a new head gardener, sir. His name is Stephen Ripley."

"Ripley, eh? He any good?"

"Apparently. His letter of recommendation says so, sir. Besides, he worked here years ago, before the war."

"Humph. We'll see what he can do now, won't we." Not so much a question as a statement of doubt. Mr. Giles again scanned the faces round the table. "But where has Alfred *gone*?"

"Actually, sir . . ." The gardener's first assistant, a dark-haired youth named William, spoke up from the end of the table. Other young men from the village were often called in to assist with the large jobs, but William, training to one day assume a head gardener's position himself, resided at Foxwood Hall. "He's gone to live at his sister's house outside Cheltenham. Leastwise, that's what he told me."

"His sister's house? To live?" Vernon looked mystified, but said no more—for to say more might be perceived as insolent. There were strict rules belowstairs about gossip and speculation. Not that such didn't occur. It most certainly did. But not in Mr. Giles's or Mrs. Sanders's hearing.

Eva, too, felt mystified. Why would a man retire and go to live with his sister? Hadn't he put enough by over the years to purchase or at least lease a pleasant cottage of his own somewhere, where he might enjoy his retirement years? Otherwise, why retire at all? He had a good situation here at Foxwood Hall, and he certainly continued to enjoy good health, as far as she could tell. Was his sojourn at his sister's home merely temporary?

"Then where is this Ripley character?" Mr. Giles spoke with his mouth full, once again reminding Eva—reminding them all—of his decline.

Mrs. Sanders gently said, "The head gardener has the option of eating at his cottage, Mr. Giles."

The butler raised his coffee cup and grumbled into it. "You'd think the man would want to show his face and meet the rest of us. Simple common decency."

Eva couldn't agree more. And then unexpectedly, that very man poked his head in from the corridor. He held a plaid wool flat cap in his hand and wore an angry scowl. "You there, boy. William. What are you doing? I've been waiting for you."

The sharp tone startled the lanky, broad-shouldered youth into dropping his fork with a clatter. He came to his feet with a shrill scrape of his chair legs. "It's not yet six-thirty, sir."

"Do you think I care about the time? There's daylight enough to start on the hedge behind the hothouses. Now come along."

"Yes, sir."

His breakfast less than half eaten, William scrambled after his new superior, nearly tripping over his large feet in his efforts. Eva hoped the boy might slip away later for a slice of bread or cheese, or he'd surely run out of stamina before lunchtime. Or perhaps she might take a walk out by the hedge and bring him something. Meanwhile, Stephen Ripley rather plummeted in her regard. William was little more than a boy. Taking food out of his mouth prior to putting him to work seemed unnecessary, not to mention a bit cruel.

"That was rude." Mrs. Sanders glared at the empty doorway as if William and Stephen Ripley might reappear. A tight ridge formed above her nose. Was she attempting to conjure them? "Not so much as a *good morning*? A *how do you do* after all these years? It's been so long since he worked here I wouldn't have recognized him."

Though she basically echoed Mr. Giles's sentiment, he appeared not to notice her comments. Instead, he went on busily consuming his breakfast as though the common-place food held his fascination.

"First time I've heard of anyone complaining about a man wanting to get to work." Dora, Foxwood Hall's kitchen maid, carried in a fresh pot of tea. At a severe look from Mrs. Sanders, the girl's thin shoulders shrank inward and she lowered her chin. Dora's rank among the servants was only marginally higher than that of the hall boy's, but that rarely stopped her from expressing her opinions. She said under her breath as she set down the earthenware teapot, "I'm only saying. Can't a man get on with his work without everyone thinking ill of him?"

"Dora, that will be quite enough." Mrs. Sanders pinned her with the stare known for making even seasoned foot-men tremble. "Back to the kitchen with you, you impertinent girl."

Pouting, Dora took up the empty teapot and retraced her steps. Eva heard more murmurs from her, but couldn't make out the words. Mrs. Sanders lifted her teacup and shook her head.

"She's one to watch, Mrs. Sanders. Impertinent, as you said." Mr. Giles barely glanced up as he spoke, his interest in the other servants apparently having waned in favor of Mrs. Ellison's sultana scones and blackberry preserves.

"What's the world coming to?" Mrs. Sanders said with a note of accusation aimed at all of them. Even Eva, whose position among the upper servants usually rendered her immune to the housekeeper's reprimands, found herself sinking a little in her chair. "Young people have no respect, and not a lick of sense either. And with help so hard to find nowadays, there's little to be done about it." The rest of the servants around the table looked up at those words, dumbfounded to hear Mrs. Sanders admit such a thing. She scowled at her mistake. "Don't any of you go thinking you can pull the wool over my eyes, because you can't. I was not put on this earth to suffer the impudence of fools."

"No, ma'am," came from several of them.

Eva finished her breakfast and hurried upstairs. Lady Phoebe tended to be an early riser and Eva believed that would be the case today, since they were planning to return to St. George's to continue sorting the donations. Eva had more to tell Lady Phoebe about Mr. Peele's sudden retirement and Stephen Ripley's less than amiable character—things Lady Phoebe might certainly wish to tell her grandfather. The earl was not a man to countenance the ill treatment of his employees.

Later that morning, Lady Julia accompanied Eva and Phoebe back to St. George's. Or *Lady Annondale*, as Eva should think of Julia Renshaw now. Last April, she had married Gilbert Townsend, Viscount Annondale, only to become a widow less than twenty-four hours later. Though she had every right to take up residence at the Annondale estate, she had chosen to remain at Foxwood Hall among her own family—where she felt safe and cared for, she had confided to Eva.

Lady Annondale's maid, Hetta, had joined them as well, and the four of them set to work sorting the donations and readying them for delivery. Eva found herself watching Lady Annondale as a hen watches over her chicks. Were her shoes comfortable enough? Had she gotten enough sleep the night before? Had she eaten sufficient breakfast? She seemed fit, and moved about easily in a creation of her favorite designer, Coco Chanel, whose soft fabrics and draping designs helped conceal the contour of a growing belly.

Poor Lady Julia, and the poor child, destined to enter the world without a father.

Lady Annondale noticed Eva's scrutiny. "Please stop your worrying, Eva. Grams says I'm like a peasant of olden times, and she's right. Except for a few bouts of mild nausea early on, I haven't had so much as a twinge of discomfort in the past five months. Grams thinks it's quite inelegant of me to be so hale and hearty while I'm expecting."

"Ya, Madame is well." Hetta Brauer, the Swiss woman hired a year ago to be Lady Annondale's new maid, looked better suited to be a dairy farmer's wife with her blond braids wrapped around her head, stout figure, and muscular arms, but her skills in looking after her mistress's clothing, jewelry, and hair were unassailable. Her eyes, as bright as an alpine sky, beamed with affection at Lady Annondale. "Hetta makes sure she is well fed and well rested every day."

There were times Eva felt twinges of resentment toward Hetta, through no fault of the Swiss woman's own. But Eva had served all three Renshaw sisters, Phoebe, Julia, and the youngest, Amelia, for years before it had been decided that Julia, as the eldest, should have a maid devoted entirely to her. The addition to the household had lightened Eva's burdens, true, but she missed the intimacy with the eldest Renshaw sister as a mother misses the daughter who leaves home for the first time.

Shouts from outside, drifting through the open windows high along the basement's walls, startled them all and halted the progress of their work. Lady Phoebe moved closer to one of those windows and tilted her ear toward it. "What in heaven's name is that?"

Men's voices rose, fell, and rose again. Sharp tones ground like stones one against the other, the words indecipherable but the anger clear. Eva grew alarmed. Typically the only shouts to be heard in their sleepy village were ones of celebration, such as during the upcoming harvest festival, when there would be games and music and competitions that drew crowds from all around Little Barlow. Today was no such day, however, and with the children having returned to school and most people at work on their farms or going about their shopping, what reason could there be for shouting?

"Someone is awfully put out about something," Lady Annondale commented with a shrug, and continued sorting tinned goods into various boxes. After a brief lull, the voices built to a crescendo that threatened violence.

"I'm going to see what it is." Lady Phoebe headed up the steps.

"My lady . . ." Eva scrambled after her, holding her calf-length skirt as she climbed the basement stairs. Outside, Lady Phoebe shaded her eyes with her hand as she gazed beyond the immediacy of the churchyard in search of the kerfuffle. Eva searched, too, and thrust out a finger.

"There, my lady." She went to the churchyard gate and leaned out to see down the row of shops that lined High Road. Pedestrians strolled along the pavement outside the post office, haberdashery, and the other shops, and Eva saw that most of them were craning their necks to see across the road. Outside Little Barlow's tiny branch of the Bank of England, a small crowd had gathered. At the center of it, two men faced each other—or faced each other *down*, Eva amended. They were both glaring with the effrontery of rutting bulls, ready for a fight. One wore a derby and trench coat open over a dark business suit; the other, the flannel and corduroy of a farmer. A third man, gray haired and slightly stooped, came out of the bank and joined them. Eva recognized him as the bank manager, Mr. Evers. He held out his hands as if to soothe the other two. "Why, that's Keenan Ripley and Mr. Evers. I can't make out who the other fellow is."

"Is it his brother?" Lady Phoebe came to stand beside her at the gate. "Can you hear what they're saying?"

"No. But the fact that they're arguing outside the bank worries me. I do hope . . ." Without completing the thought, she opened the gate and headed toward the fracas. Thus far, no fists had flown, thank goodness. But it appeared they might, and soon. Keenan raised a closed hand. "I will never sell my half. Never."

"Mr. Ripley, see reason." Mr. Evers put a hand on Keenan's shoulder. Keenan angrily shook it off. The gathering around them took a collective step back.

"You're in league with him." Keenan rounded on the bank manager. "You're to blame for this. If you hadn't gone blathering about my personal finances to this complete stranger—"

"I most certainly did not, Mr. Ripley." The manager pulled up to his full height. "I would never do such a thing."

"He's right," said the third man. He was of late middle years, his eyes small and crinkled, not from laughter, Eva judged, but from squinting, from narrowing his gaze on whatever target drew his interest. Funny she should think of it that way, but that was how he struck her. His nose was wide, bullish, his chin uncommonly large. He was no one she recognized, certainly no one from Little Barlow. "He didn't tell me a thing. Your brother did."

Keenan went utterly still but for his mouth, which fell

open. He stared, unblinking, at the stranger. By now Eva and Lady Phoebe stood at the fringe of the onlookers. More villagers had crossed the street to gawk. The scene had taken on the atmosphere of a cockfight. Eva only hoped wagers weren't being laid.

The stranger lifted the corners of his wide mouth in a gratified smile. "That's right, Mr. Ripley. Your argument isn't with me, nor with Mr. Evers. It's with your own brother."

Eva realized the man spoke as no one else did from this region, nor any other part of England. He was an American, the first she had encountered anywhere but in London.

"We are businessmen, Mr. Evers and I," the stranger continued. His nostrils quivered as though he were scenting his prey. "We are merely doing what we do best, which is buying up properties in arrears and making them profitable."

"I am not in arrears." Keenan's fists clenched so hard his knuckles glowed white.

The bank manager cleared his throat. "The bank records say otherwise, Mr. Ripley."

Keenan swung to face Mr. Evers. One fist came up, prompting the bank manager to recoil. "You know I'll pay my debts in full as soon as the harvest is in. I've got an arrangement with the Samuel Smitters brewery in Gloucester. Give me time to get my pears off the trees and you'll have your money."

"Mr. Ripley . . . Keenan . . . please." Mr. Evers wrinkled his brow in apology and wrung his hands in a gesture of helplessness. "Based on last year's harvest, I simply don't see how you'll be able to make your payments. You're mortgaged twice over."

"What farm isn't nowadays?" Keenan snapped. "Last year's harvest was smaller, I'll grant you that. It's taken this long since the war to bring production back up to what it was. It's not as though I qualified for help from the Land Girls while I was away fighting, not for perry cider. And now, with so many men off to try their luck in the cities, I hadn't enough help last year even if the harvest had been bigger. But I've got three workers lined up. If you'll only trust me and give me the time . . ." He left off, panting and heaving as if he'd run a mile.

Eva's heart went out to him. The unfairness of it stung; her own father had taken loans against the farm during the war. What if the bank suddenly said pay up or get out? She wished to intervene, to back up Keenan's promises of a good harvest, but what did she know of pears? Or brewing? She only knew she didn't want to see yet another farmer in Gloucestershire forced to sell or worse, foreclosed on, as so many had since the war ended.

Before she knew it, Lady Phoebe had disappeared from her side. Panic rippled through Eva as her lady eased her way through the crowd until she stood before the arguing men. Eva hurriedly pushed her way through as well, earning more than one grunt of annoyance from onlookers.

"Mr. Ripley, Mr. Evers, perhaps my grandfather can be of assistance. I know for a fact he would not like to see any of Little Barlow's citizens put out of business."

Before either man could reply, the American spoke up, conveying not the slightest hint of deference. "What can your grandfather do about the situation, miss? Mr. Ripley's brother wants to sell his portion of the land, and I intend to buy it. As half owner, I've got the right to put pressure on *this* Mr. Ripley to pay his bills or sell his half to me."

Lady Phoebe shook her head and scowled. "What do you want an orchard for? You don't strike me as the farming type."

"Farming? Bah. With the stream and the pond, and the

views of your quaint countryside hereabouts, it'll make a grand spot for a resort. Hunting, fishing, golf . . . You can be assured I'll fill that resort with money-spending Americans." He addressed his next comment to the gaping villagers, as if to appeal to their better sense. "Business will boom. This lonely little do-nothing backwater will be the better for it, you'll see."

Phoebe had never felt so tempted to shake another individual as she did this impertinent American businessman. How dare he invade Little Barlow with his vulgar plans and ill-gotten gains—or so she assumed they were—and claim he could improve life for any of them? What could he possibly know about their lives? Or this village? Or the fact that Keenan Ripley's great-grandfather had planted that pear orchard as a legacy to the generations that would follow him, as a way to ensure their livelihood and their independence?

And when she thought of Stephen Ripley skulking back to Little Barlow after so many years away, not caring a whit about the village or his brother, returning only in the hopes of profiting at his brother's expense . . . why, what wouldn't she like to say to him? She was quite certain that when she informed Grampapa of this development, he would seek a new head gardener immediately.

Unflinching, she stared straight into the American's shrewd little eyes with their nondistinct, muddy color. "Perhaps we don't wish Little Barlow to be any better than it is right now. Perhaps we like it the way it is."

"Spoken like a sentimental woman with little business sense."

Eva leapt forward, half in front of Phoebe, so that Phoebe had to take a half step back. "You will not speak to the Earl of Wroxly's granddaughter that way."

From the corner of her eye, Phoebe saw more than a few villagers nodding in agreement. The American had the audacity to laugh.

"Yes, yes, very well. If you'll excuse me." He started to go, but Phoebe sidestepped to block his way.

"We already have a hotel here," she persisted. "We don't need another."

"The Calcott Inn?" The developer laughed. "That stodgy old pile of stones? I'm staying there, and let me tell you, you most certainly do need another hotel. A real one, not a convalescent home for widows and little old men."

"Oh!" Phoebe had more to say, but a village man stepped up beside her and bellowed at the American.

"I've been listening to all of this, and there's one thing I'd like to know." Joe Murdock, the proprietor of the Houndstooth Inn, had been serving Little Barlow's male population their ale, cider, and whiskey for nearly his entire life, as had his father, and his grandfather before that.

The American eyed Mr. Murdock up and down, taking in his rolled-up shirtsleeves, his plaid waistcoat, and his comfortably worn-out boots. "And what might that be?"

"If you close down Keenan's orchards and his brewery, where am I supposed to get my perry?"

The crowd's agreement came verbally, rising swiftly in volume. A new tension gripped the villagers as the full implications of this potential land sale hit them. Perry was a favored drink here in Little Barlow, as it was everywhere in Gloucestershire.

The American gave Mr. Murdock a blank stare. "What the devil is perry?"

"It's a kind of cider, and it's what's made from my pears." Keenan Ripley spoke as if to an idiot. "We send a portion of the harvest to a brewery in Gloucester, but the rest I bottle here and sell to the village."

"Is that all?" The American shrugged and addressed the crowd. "I'll make sure we find the best . . . what was it? Ah, yes. Perry. We'll find the best perry in England for your little hamlet. I'll even cover the difference in cost, if there is any."

"Keenan's perry *is* the best in England," someone called out. Several others voiced their emphatic agreement. That tension Phoebe had noticed in the villagers thickened considerably, and she began to fear its results. She nudged Eva, who looked as worried as Phoebe herself felt.

"Let's move away," Eva said before Phoebe had the chance to suggest the very same thing. Other women, too, began crossing to the opposite side of High Road. Several called after their men, but to no avail, for not one of them budged from the line of defense they had formed. The American no longer looked at all sure of himself.

He attempted a nonchalant smile. "If you'll all step aside please, I'll be on my way." No one moved. Two men, fellow farmers, flanked Mr. Ripley, their arms crossed, their feet spread wide in a show of solidarity.

Phoebe nudged Eva again. "Perhaps you should alert Miles."

Eva took a step and stopped, then pointed down the pavement. "I don't have to. Here he is."

Police Constable Miles Brannock strode toward them, coming from Little Barlow's tiny, two-man police station, which was part of the Greater Gloucestershire Constabulary. Phoebe was relieved Isaac Perkins hadn't felt it necessary to accompany him, for the often whiskey-tippling chief inspector tended to make matters worse, rather than better. Constable Brannock reached them and paused, his gaze fixed on the unrest across High Road.

"Lady Phoebe, Eva. What's this about?" He spoke with the lightest of brogues, revealing his Irish origins.

It was Eva who replied, for she and the constable had an easygoing rapport; had, in fact, been stepping out together this past year and a half. "Keenan Ripley's brother and some American businessman are trying to force Keenan to sell out."

"What?" Constable Brannock's powerful reply echoed the indignation of the villagers. "Who is this tosser, and what's he want the orchard for?"

Phoebe winced slightly at the epithet Constable Brannock used to describe the American, but she couldn't argue with his assessment. "He wants to build a resort here. For Americans. Rich ones, apparently."

Eva nodded her consensus as the constable's expression darkened to clash with his auburn hair—or, what could be seen of it beneath his high-domed helmet. "We'll see about that, won't we?" He started off across the road, but Eva stopped him.

"What are you going to do?"

He removed his nightstick from his belt and used it to gesture at the crowd. "First, I'm going to break this up before someone gets hurt, and before I have to arrest anyone. Then I'm going to try to persuade this gannet to take his greedy ambitions somewhere else."

Renewed shouting prompted the constable to a run. He arrived a moment too late. Keenan Ripley surged forward, drew back his fist, and drove it into the American's jaw. The resulting crack made Phoebe wince. With a cry, the American fell over backward, landing on the pavement on his backside. Phoebe gasped, and Eva started forward, instinct propelling her, no doubt, to assist her beau. Phoebe grasped her wrist just before Eva moved out of reach.

"Don't," she warned, "or you could make matters worse. The constable can handle it."

Eva nodded and a portion of the urgency drained from

her posture. "You're right, my lady. And it looks like it's over, for now."

Indeed, as one villager helped the American to his feet, two more gripped Keenan's arms to prevent him from attacking again. Constable Brannock positioned himself between them, his arms outstretched as if to mark off two distinct territories. The hand holding the nightstick extended toward Mr. Ripley.

"That will be quite enough, Keenan. As for the rest of you, I'd advise you to disperse and get on with your business. There's nothing more to be seen here."

"Judging by how hesitant everyone is to move, I'd say they're hoping for more to see," Phoebe whispered to Eva. Yet gradually, the villagers eased away.

The constable slowly lowered his arms. "Keenan Ripley, you know better than this."

"He's—" Mr. Ripley began, but the constable cut him off.

"I heard. That doesn't give you the right to take a swing at him."

"Officer, I'm pressing charges." Despite his commanding tone, the American took a backward step away from Mr. Ripley. "That man assaulted me and I want him arrested."

"You oily wanker—"

"Keenan, that's enough." Constable Brannock's sigh carried across the road almost as clearly as the angry shouts had done. "I don't like to do it, but I've got to arrest you."

"Oh, dear," Eva murmured. "I was afraid of that. But what choice does Miles have?"

"Don't worry. I'll ask Grampapa to pay Mr. Ripley's bond. He won't have to spend a night in that jail cell." Phoebe linked her arm through Eva's. "Come, let's finish up for now at the church, collect Julia and Hetta, and go home. I intend to speak to my grandfather about our new head gardener."

On the way back to the church, Eva mused, "I'd like to know what Stephen has to say about all of this."

"Surely none of it will be to our liking. But I'll tell you this: the consequences of his actions won't be to his liking, either. Not once I've spoken to Grampapa."

Phoebe broached the subject with her grandfather that evening. Early the next morning, they made their way, arm in arm, across the tiered gardens, bright with late season mums and roses and flame-like celosia, and through the gate in the privet hedge that separated the formal gardens from the service grounds. An autumn sharpness tinged the air and a bright golden hue tipped the ends of the leaves overhead. Soon, green and gold would turn to fiery reds and russets, and fall would burst forth in earnest. Phoebe was grateful for the sun's lingering warmth.

Their destination lay beyond the hothouses with their bright white framework that stood rather like rib cages against the sky. There, another hedge, this one of yew, once again shielded the pleasure gardens from the working areas. Phoebe kept having to slow her pace to avoid over-taxing Grampapa. Ever the gentleman, he had gallantly offered his arm to her, yet it was she who steadied them over the graveled path.

"Thank you for posting Keenan Ripley's bail last night, Grampapa. But was I right to bring the matter to you?" She had fretted over the decision and wondered if she should leave the Ripley brothers to solve their own dilemma. Goodness knew, plenty of families bickered over land and inheritances. Julia had inadvertently entered just such a feud last spring, one that had yet to be resolved. Members of Julia's deceased husband's family, the Townsends, continued to squabble over the terms of his will, while Julia's pregnancy left much in question. A lot depended on whether she gave birth to a boy or a girl.

Phoebe had been forced to become involved in that dispute, but she had lain awake last night wondering if she was overstepping her bounds by intervening this time. The Ripleys were not her family. She barely knew either man, really.

But of course, matters were more far reaching than that. The servants were hurt and confused by Mr. Peele's sudden departure, and the change in circumstances had left dear Mr. Giles more disoriented than usual. That certainly *was* her business. As was Stephen Ripley depriving William of his proper breakfast before starting work. Grampapa hadn't approved of that one bit.

"We'll talk to the man and hear his side of things," her grandfather replied. "There is always more than one side to everything."

They arrived at the yew hedge, gracefully carved into vertical, undulating waves of green, to find it deserted, at least the side on which they stood. Though growth since the last trimming was minimal, the smooth, rounded contours of the nearly solid wall of foliage were marred by errant leaves that dared to poke beyond the rest as if stretching forward to catch the attention of passersby. This didn't surprise her, however. It would certainly take more than a day, or even two, to complete such a task.

"They must be working on the other side. Let's walk around," Grampapa suggested. Phoebe pricked her ears to listen for the telltale *snip-snip* of the clippers, as well as bits of conversation between Mr. Ripley and William. She heard only the morning song of birds and the rustling of the breeze. They reached the end of the hedge and walked around.

"Where are they?" Phoebe peered along the hedge, some two dozen yards long, cast into deep emerald by the angle of the sun. The gardener's cart, hitched to its pony, stood about halfway down, partly filled with foliage cuttings. The long handle of a rake also stuck out of the cart's barrow. The blond-maned pony stood placidly in his harness enjoying whatever treats Mr. Ripley had stuffed into its feed bag. Phoebe could see where a long section at the farther end of the hedge had already been trimmed back into a perfectly even, gently waving plane, but she detected no sign of Mr. Ripley or William.

Then, in the deep green shadow of the lawn, a darker shadow stood out. . . .

"Is that his ladder lying on the ground?" Grampapa frowned into the distance. As Phoebe's eyes adjusted, she indeed made out the lines of a stepladder. Grampapa started forward. "Come, my dear. I fear Mr. Ripley has had an accident."

They hurried along. The closer they got, the clearer it became that Mr. Ripley's ladder wasn't the only object lying on the ground. A few feet from it, right where he would have landed had the ladder fallen and tossed him from its rungs, lay a figure clad in work denims and a flannel shirt. A pair of spectacles glinted up at her from beyond the tip of a nose, as if trying to crawl back up where they belonged. A brown tweed flat cap lay upside down inches from a wheat-blond head.

"It's Stephen Ripley." Alarm sent Phoebe hurrying ahead of her grandfather. "Mr. Ripley, are you all right?" She wondered where William was, and then answered her own question. Gone for help, of course. But then, why hadn't they passed him on their way here from the house?

The pony snorted and continued munching. Behind Phoebe, Grampapa's lumbering footsteps thudded through the grass. "Is he terribly hurt?"

Mr. Ripley lay unmoving, but, oddly, holding his hedge clippers.

"I don't know. Mr. Ripley! Mr. Ripley?" Phoebe started to crouch beside him, but something held her upright. She was about to call out his name again, until she realized he wasn't holding the clippers at all. The clippers were turned the wrong way around, the handles facing out and the sharp ends sunk—

Her hand went to her mouth. The clippers had been plunged into his torso. A pool of blood seeped out from under him to weave lurid, spidery patterns in the grass. A frigid numbness swept through Phoebe, and the world around her darkened and blurred.

CHAPTER 3

"Drink this, my lady." In the drawing room, Eva crouched at Lady Phoebe's feet and pressed a cordial glass to her lips. Once again, she berated herself for not accompanying Lady Phoebe and her grandfather on their errand to speak with Stephen Ripley.

Poor Stephen Ripley. Only an hour ago Eva would not have believed she would attach that term to a man she so disliked. But she certainly hadn't wished ill on him—at least not such a permanent sort of ill. She had only wished fairness to prevail, for Keenan to be allowed to keep his orchard and William to eat his breakfast.

But this—*this*—wasn't fair. Death never was.

Lady Phoebe took the leaded crystal glass from Eva and obediently sipped her sherry. She regarded Eva with solemn eyes. "Do you think it could have been an accident, Eva? Could he have fallen in such a way that the clippers . . ." She trailed off with a shake of her head. "How *could* they have flipped around and, and done *that*?"

"That's for the authorities to decide, my lady." By *authorities*, she meant Miles Brannock. Chief Inspector Perkins would make his observations, take his notes, but in the end he would most likely reach the wrong conclusion. He always did. And Miles always corrected that conclusion—with Eva's and Lady Phoebe's help.

"Does Julia know yet?"

Eva shook her head. "I don't believe so."

Across the room, closer to the cheerful fire lapping away in the hearth, the Earl and Countess of Wroxly were speaking in hushed tones. The countess had taken the news with the same stoicism with which she endured all ill tidings.

"Let's not tell her until it's necessary. There's no point in upsetting her." Lady Phoebe shuddered. "It wouldn't be good for the baby."

"No, indeed, my lady. But your grandparents have telephoned the chief inspector, and once he arrives there will be no keeping anything from anyone. Here." Eva gestured toward the glass of sherry. "Keep sipping. It'll warm you."

"I never thought I could be so cold, especially on such a pleasant day. I've seen death before—we both have—but not like this. This was so unbearably . . . violent. Even if it *was* an accident." Eva was nodding at the sentiment when Lady Phoebe added in an undertone, "Which I'm quite sure it wasn't."

Eva stood as the countess approached. Her black silk skirts swept against her ankles, for no matter what the Paris fashion houses dictated, the countess would raise her hems no higher than that. Nor would she put off the mourning she had donned the day her only living son had died, more than four years ago now, during the war. Maude Renshaw, Countess of Wroxly, bore her grief as she bore all of life's adversities, with a steady gaze, a sure stride, and her slender frame pulled up to its full height of nearly six feet.

With a glance over her shoulder at her husband, who

was speaking quietly now to Vernon, she bent lower to address her granddaughter. "How are you feeling, child?"

Lady Phoebe showed her a feeble smile. "Better now. I was just so taken aback."

"Of course you were." The countess sat beside her granddaughter on the settee and Eva moved aside to allow them a modicum of privacy while remaining readily on hand. "I'm only glad you weren't alone, that your grandfather was with you."

"I'm not, Grams. I wish he hadn't seen. The shock of it can't have been good for him."

Lady Wroxly patted her hand. "He's all right. He's stronger than you think."

But Eva detected the worry behind the countess's assurance. So did Lady Phoebe, for she said, "I never should have spoken to him about Stephen Ripley."

The countess looked puzzled. "What do you mean?"

With a sigh, Lady Phoebe explained everything they had learned about the head gardener in the past two days.

"And when were you going to tell me any of this?" Lady Wroxly demanded, though not unkindly.

"Grams, don't you have enough to do worrying about Julia?"

The countess couldn't deny it. "Well, I'd like you to keep out of it. You and Eva both." She glanced up at Eva with a knowing glint. "You both know what I mean."

Eva nodded and cast her eyes at the floor, but Lady Phoebe said, "If we had kept out of it last spring, where would Julia be now?"

Lady Wroxly compressed her lips and swallowed whatever emotion threatened her stoic poise. "That was different. Julia is family."

"And so is Keenan Ripley." Lady Phoebe's retort drew a nod from Eva and a frown from her grandmother. Lady Phoebe hurried on. "The Ripley family has lived in Little

Barlow for . . . well, forever. Some of his ancestors served in this very house. He and his brother fought in the war. Doesn't all that make them family as well? Don't we at Foxwood Hall have an obligation to ensure the well-being of the local population—those less well off than we are? I know Grampapa believes so."

Lady Wroxly held up a pale, blue-veined hand. "Yes, yes. What you're saying is true. But that doesn't mean you should go putting yourself in danger. I can assure you your grandfather doesn't believe that's what you should do. Leave everything to the police, Phoebe. Please."

That final plea, a simple word voiced in a calm manner, held a world of urgency that gripped Eva's conscience. Already she could feel sharp tugs in opposite directions. Whatever Lady Phoebe asked of her, she would do without hesitation. Yet she understood the countess's fears, her desperation to keep her granddaughter safe. Eva had the same obligation. She had been hired to attend the wardrobe and personal effects of the Renshaw sisters, but she was also expected to watch over them, advise them, and gently guide them out of harm's way. So far, especially in regard to Lady Phoebe, she had made a poor job of it.

She looked on as Lady Phoebe pinched her lips together and nodded. "All right, Grams."

Eva knew a fib when she heard one. But apparently the countess did not, for her countenance cleared and she embraced her granddaughter before rising to rejoin her husband.

The earl, too, had got to his feet. "Vernon tells me William hasn't turned up."

Lady Phoebe accepted Eva's help to stand. "His bed has been checked?"

"That's the first place we looked," Vernon replied. "No one saw him at breakfast this morning. We all assumed he grabbed some food and went out to work."

"Thank you, Vernon, that will be all for now." Once the footman left the room, the earl said, "William must have seen something—perhaps how Mr. Ripley died—and ran off, terrified. Perhaps he fears he'll be blamed."

Eva traded a look with Lady Phoebe. "Vernon's right," said Eva. "William was nowhere to be seen this morning. Like the others, I assumed he started work early to avoid another unpleasant scene with his new superior."

Lady Phoebe appeared to consider this, then turned back to her grandparents. "If it's all right with you, I'd like to go upstairs and lie down."

"That sounds like an excellent idea, my dear. I'm sure the chief inspector will wish to speak with you when he arrives, but for now, do rest." The earl held out his hand to her. Lady Phoebe went to him and took it. He kissed her cheeks, then drew her into an embrace. Over her shoulder he met Eva's gaze. "Take care of her."

"I will, my lord." But as Eva crossed the room to leave with her lady, the countess conveyed, with a lift of her eyebrow, both a warning and a sense of resignation. She knew her granddaughter would not sit idly by in her room when there might be something she could do to help.

Phoebe did indeed stretch out on her bed after Eva removed the satin throw pillows and turned down the coverlet. But while Phoebe leaned back against the headboard, she didn't crawl under the covers. She was too jittery to sleep, and too eager to find out what happened to Stephen Ripley. And to William, too.

She didn't like voicing the thought foremost on her mind, but she found no way to avoid it, not if she wished to be realistic. "This won't look good for Keenan Ripley, you know. I'm sorry to say it, but his behavior in town yesterday is going to reflect poorly on his character. And it being his brother who died . . . Well."

Eva perched at the edge of the mattress and squared her shoulders. "I hate to believe it, but you're right. Keenan struck another man and expressed his anger toward his brother in front of witnesses. I don't think that makes him guilty—in fact, I'm sure he's not—but I'm afraid others will be quick to condemn him."

By *others*, Phoebe knew she primarily meant the chief inspector. "If Keenan has a good alibi for this morning, he can't be held to blame."

"But what if he doesn't?" Eva looked glum. She was silent a moment, then asked, "What exactly did you see when you found Stephen?"

"His ladder had been pushed over and he lay on the grass. And the clippers . . ." She shivered.

"Was there a lot of blood?"

"Of course there was a lot of blood. What do you think happens when a man is stabbed in the gut?" Taut silence stretched between them before Phoebe reached out. "I'm sorry. I didn't mean to snap at you."

Eva took her hand. "It's perfectly understandable. But what I meant was—and I should have asked more clearly— was the blood still coming out of him when you arrived? Because that can help determine how long he'd been deceased before you found him. And how long it took for him to die," she added in a lower voice.

"Of course." Phoebe sat up straighter, putting space between her spine and the pillows behind her. She tried to think back. If only she could envision the scene without the horror of it. That wasn't possible, but she must try to focus on the basic facts. "It was like latticework in the grass beside him. A pattern. Yes, there was a good deal of blood. Which means he didn't die immediately."

Eva nodded her agreement. "How awful to have lain there knowing the end was coming, and perhaps hoping against hope someone would happen by and help him."

"I don't expect anyone could have helped him. Those clippers—they were in too deep." Phoebe shut her eyes against the memory.

A knock sounded at the door. Eva rose to answer it, revealing one of the chambermaids, Connie, on the other side. "My lady, the chief inspector and the constable are here. I was asked to fetch you."

Phoebe found the chief inspector in Grampapa's study, sitting at the heavy desk. Constable Brannock sat off to one side, notebook and pencil in hand. Though Grampapa's physician had forbidden him to smoke his pipe in recent years, the rich, woodsy aroma lingered among the books and furnishings, and the familiar sensation wrapped Phoebe in comfort. Constable Brannock offered her a nod as she came into the room. Chief Inspector Isaac Perkins tersely motioned for her to take the chair across the desk from his own.

He sniffed and took her measure as if he considered her a suspect. Phoebe stared back, taking in the broken blood vessels in his cheeks and nose, and the sunspots that made patterns on his balding pate.

"Tell me what you saw," he said in way of a greeting.

Phoebe told him everything: the ladder, the spectacles, the flat cap, the hedge clippers. And she described the pattern of the blood oozing into the blades of grass. Here, he cut her off.

"It's for the police surgeon to examine the blood and determine what it means."

She said nothing and awaited his next question.

"What did you witness between Keenan Ripley and Horace Walker yesterday? And don't go trying to hide any facts, Lady Phoebe. I've got plenty of other witnesses to the scene."

"Keenan Ripley and whom?" she asked in all earnestness.

The inspector's thin lips pulled down in a grimace. "Really, Lady Phoebe? Are we going to play that game?"

"What game?"

"Lady Phoebe, I warn you—"

"*Eh-hem*, sir?" Constable Brannock leaned forward in his chair. "If I may, Lady Phoebe, Horace Walker is the American who wishes to purchase the Ripley orchard."

"Oh, *that* man." *Or fiend*, she thought. She turned back to the inspector. "They argued over whether or not Mr. Ripley would sell. He doesn't wish to."

"But his brother, Stephen, did," the inspector remarked.

Phoebe nodded. She waited. Chief Inspector Perkins waited. He lifted an expectant eyebrow, and then he scowled. "Blast it, Lady Phoebe, what did you witness?"

She glanced over at Miles Brannock again. He shrugged once and gave her another nod. She sighed. "I heard their voices raised in anger, and at one point, Mr. Ripley struck the other man. This Mr. Walker. But I don't know what Mr. Walker might have said to provoke Mr. Ripley's temper in such a way, because I'd moved to the other side of the road by then. Mr. Ripley has always seemed to be an amiable, reasonable man. As you should well know, Chief Inspector."

"Humph. Constable, did you get all that?"

"I did, sir."

"All right, Lady Phoebe, you can go. But I may need to speak with you again."

Without another glance, he summarily dismissed her. With a sinking feeling about what was going to happen once the chief inspector finished questioning the staff, Phoebe went to find Eva.

As Lady Phoebe brought the Vauxhall to a stop, Eva gratefully unclenched her fingers from the edges of the seat.

She kept telling herself that eventually she would grow used to traveling by motorcar, but so far it hadn't happened.

She got out and took a moment to straighten her sun hat, unpinning it, smoothing her hair, and then pinning it back in place. She looked about her. Though not unkempt, Keenan Ripley's front garden lacked the care that lent her parents' farmhouse its welcoming charm. A few half-hearted chrysanthemums occupied the window boxes on either side of the front door, while scraggly wildflowers circled each gate post. On the other hand, the cottage, out-buildings, and brew house all appeared in good repair. What was lacking was the touch of a woman—a mother or a wife—who would have taken pride in a colorful flower bed and brimming window boxes.

"Do you think he's at home?" Lady Phoebe took a few strides along the garden path toward the front door. "It's frightfully quiet."

Despite several windows being open, no sound came from inside the cottage, and to Eva the place felt deserted. "I suspect he'll be out in the orchard this time of day, my lady." At least, she hoped he would be. Unless, of course, the chief inspector was right in his suspicions and Keenan Ripley had already put miles between himself and Little Barlow to escape arrest. The thought that Keenan could have murdered his own brother made the hair on Eva's forearms spike.

"My lady," she said in little more than a whisper, "perhaps this isn't a good idea. What if Keenan did murder Stephen? We could be putting ourselves in danger by being here."

"Do you really believe that?"

"Well, no, but . . ."

"Neither do I. To the orchard then. Good thing we wore comfortable shoes." Lady Phoebe led the way past the cottage, but suddenly stopped as if changing her mind. A ridge formed above her nose. "On second thought, let's just . . ."

"Just what, my lady?" Eva hurried to follow her mistress around to the front door. "But, my lady, didn't we just agree Keenan would be out in the orchard this time of day?"

"We did." Lady Phoebe knocked twice, waited, and tried the door latch. It yielded to the pressure of her hand. It was, after all, a rare villager who locked his doors by day or by night.

The door opened silently on well-oiled hinges, and they stepped into a front room furnished in serviceable pine and durable, dark fabrics. Exactly what Eva would expect in a man's home. A sitting area occupied one side of the rectangular room, and on the other, a dining table that looked little used, judging by the papers, books, and other odds and ends piled on its surface. Again, not surprising in a home inhabited solely by a man. In the corner beyond the table, a staircase climbed several steps before turning and continuing up to the first floor.

"My lady, we came to deliver the unhappy news about Keenan's brother and warn him the chief inspector will be coming. But now we're trespassing."

"Just give me a moment." Lady Phoebe moved into the sitting area. On a low table before a faded, floral settee sat two cups and saucers. A few dregs of tea gleamed up from the bottom of each. A single large plate lay between them, bearing crumbs and a few stray dots of preserves. As Eva watched, Lady Phoebe lifted the plate to inspect the crumbs more closely. "He had company this morning. A woman, I'd say."

"Why a woman?"

"These crumbs. Scones, yes?"

Eva took a closer look at the plate. "Hmm, I believe you're right."

"What working man eats scones for breakfast unless a woman makes them for him?"

"A good point, my lady." Eva felt a sudden apprehension when she remembered how friendly and familiar Alice and Keenan had become at the church. Would her sister, a married woman, have come for breakfast, alone, at a single man's home?

Then again, if Keenan had had company, it might provide an alibi for the time of his brother's murder.

She only hoped it hadn't been Alice.

"Let's take a quick peek in the kitchen."

Eva knew better than to argue and followed at Lady Phoebe's heels. In the large country kitchen, very much like her parents', the remnants of a much more sensible breakfast of porridge cluttered the sink. Eva felt half inclined to grab a dishrag and begin washing. Instead, she did as Lady Phoebe was doing, scanning the room and searching for anything unusual. The gleam of glass sent her to the mantel of the wide stone hearth. There, she picked up a bottle and an earthenware cup. One sniff told her all she needed to know. The sweetly potent vapors made her cringe.

"It appears Keenan's been drinking. Probably late into last night, judging by the traces of whiskey left in this cup."

Lady Phoebe came to her side and took the bottle from Eva. She glanced at the label. "Probably attempting to drink away his anger at his brother. That's not a good sign."

"No," Eva agreed, "but if he had breakfast with someone today, he can't have been at Foxwood Hall at the time his brother died."

"Let's hope not." Lady Phoebe regarded the bottle again, then the cup in Eva's hand. "Would it be terribly wrong if we . . ." She didn't finish the thought, but Eva easily guessed. Before she could shake her head and advise against rinsing out the cup, Lady Phoebe replaced it on the mantel. "No, I don't suppose we should tamper with what might be evidence. Come, let's try to find Mr. Ripley before the chief inspector arrives."

At the sound of a motorcar pulling onto the property, they both froze. "Perhaps it's too late, my lady." Eva scurried into the front room to glance out the window. It wasn't a black police sedan that rolled to a stop, it was a farm lorry much like her father's. "It's Keenan, my lady. He's home."

She hurried back into the kitchen intending to guide Lady Phoebe out the garden door, but Lady Phoebe stood her ground. "The door was unlocked, after all. And we have good reason for being here."

Eva didn't share Lady Phoebe's rationale, but it was too late to argue. The front door opened and heavy boots thudded on the wide-board flooring in the front room. The footsteps went abruptly silent. "Is someone here?"

CHAPTER 4

Eva's heart pounded. Would Keenan take issue with finding uninvited guests in his home? She believed in his innocence, but based on what? An old friendship, and not a very close one at that. What if she were wrong, and she and Lady Phoebe were standing in a murderer's kitchen?

Apparently, Lady Phoebe entertained few such qualms. Very casually, she strolled into the parlor doorway. "Yes, Mr. Ripley. I'm sorry we barged in as we did, but we have some news. Sad news, I'm afraid."

Keenan's expression went from guarded to astonished as his eyes opened wide and his eyebrows surged upward. Eva couldn't help but notice the circles of fatigue beneath them or that he bore a pallor this morning. A result of his late night of drinking?

A muscle flexed in Keenan's jaw, a sure sign of his continuing perplexity at finding his home occupied. "Lady Phoebe, er, good morning. Is . . . is there something I can do for you? Is everything all right up at the Hall? Er . . . please . . . sit." He gestured to the seating arrangement, then hurriedly went to clear away the teacups and plate.

With a jarring clatter he piled the china on a side table. "Make yourself at home. Can I get you anything?"

Clearly he was unused to visitors of the Renshaws' social standing, so much so that accusing Lady Phoebe of trespassing simply didn't occur to him. As Eva followed her mistress into the parlor, she cast Keenan a sympathetic look, which he returned with a quizzical tilt of his head that conveyed his mystification. This helped strengthen her opinion that he knew nothing yet of his brother's death.

"We have some distressing news," Eva told him gently, believing it would be more easily accepted coming from her. At a nod from Lady Phoebe, who appeared to have read her mind, she gestured for him to take a seat on the settee. She eased herself down beside him. "It's about your brother."

He smirked. "What could be more distressing than Stephen trying to sell the orchard out from under me? Destroying everything our family has worked so hard for these several generations?"

"Keenan, this morning, Lady Phoebe and her grandfather went out to speak with Stephen about a couple of matters and . . ." Eva drew a breath. "Keenan, Stephen is dead."

He frowned as if not comprehending her meaning. He paused for two ticks of the mantel clock. "What?"

"I'm afraid it's true, Mr. Ripley." Lady Phoebe held out her hands as if to offer a physical serving of sympathy. "My grandfather and I found him."

"Found him where?" Keenan raked a hand into his hair and kept it there, fingers tangled in the auburn curls. His eyes took on a glazed look of confusion. "Found him how?"

"Beside his ladder," Lady Phoebe said. "He—"

"He fell?"

"No, Keenan. It appears as if the ladder had been pushed." When Eva hesitated, Keenan turned ruddy with anger.

"Pushed or no, men don't die from such a height unless he was up on a roof and fell onto the pavement." He turned an accusing glare on Lady Phoebe. "Was he on the roof of Foxwood Hall?"

"Keenan, please. We're trying to tell you what happened." Eva placed a hand on his forearm. He jerked it away. "Stephen didn't die from the fall. He was attacked. Pushed over on the ladder, and then stabbed." Her voice became a murmur filled with apology and regret. "With his hedge clippers, I'm very sorry to say."

"His hedge clippers." Both of Keenan's hands slid through his hair now, gripping as if to prevent his skull from shattering. "Who would do such a thing? Although, the why of it . . ." He let go a harsh laugh, stared grimly down at his feet, and shook his head.

"Keenan," Eva said firmly to reclaim his attention, "that isn't all. You need to be ready for when the chief inspector arrives."

He raised his face. "Perkins?"

"Yes," Lady Phoebe said. "He spoke of you this morning, about the argument you had with the American businessman yesterday. How you struck him. And he—"

"Thinks I killed my brother?" Keenan heaved to his feet, his eyes sparking. "And he's coming for me?"

"He's coming to question you," Lady Phoebe replied. "And you must be ready. You know how he tends to jump to conclusions."

"God's teeth." Keenan began to pace, his work boots raising ominous drumbeats.

Eva stood. "Keenan, did you have a visitor this morning? Someone who can verify that you were here at the time of . . . of your brother's death?"

He shot her a wary glance. "No. No one was here."

"But . . ." Eva pointed at the now empty table before the settee. "There were two teacups here."

He glanced over at the china piled on the side table. "They're both mine. One is from last night." He shrugged. "I'm not the best housekeeper."

Eva and Lady Phoebe exchanged a glance, the knowledge that Keenan hadn't been drinking merely tea last night mirrored in their gazes. The traces of whiskey they'd found in the kitchen said otherwise.

"Mr. Ripley, now isn't the time to protect someone's reputation," said Lady Phoebe. "If you had a visitor here this morning, you *must* reveal who it was."

Eva gritted her teeth as fresh worry spread through her. Lady Phoebe had deduced this visitor must have been a woman, and Eva believed she was right. Once more, images of Keenan and Alice in St. George's basement flashed in her mind. Their laughter and Alice's flirting tones echoed in her ears. It had been as if no time had passed since their last meeting: not the war, not Alice's marriage, not her moving away and having children.

No, Eva was overreacting. Surely Alice wouldn't put eight years of marriage and her three young children at risk of such a scandal. Certain matters between men and women had changed since the war, but not everything, and not in small villages like Little Barlow. Breakfasting with a man in his home would set rumors ablaze, and Alice knew that as well as Eva did.

Truly, it could have been anyone here earlier—and that someone could clear Keenan of possible charges. She added her voice to Lady Phoebe's. "Keenan, your life could be at stake."

"I haven't done anything." His profile turned steely. "I've got nothing to hide."

No, nothing except the identity of the person who drank from that second teacup, and who brought Keenan scones and jam this morning. She had a fleeting notion of asking her mother if she had baked scones today. But of course she had. She baked scones almost every morning. So did a lot of other people in this village. It proved nothing either way.

The rumble of a second motorcar forestalled further discussion. Lady Phoebe moved to the window. "It's the chief inspector and Constable Brannock."

Keenan calmly opened the door. Chief Inspector Perkins stopped in midstep on the threshold, peered inside, and pointed an accusing finger at Lady Phoebe. "I'm going to pretend I didn't see you here. But if I encounter you again where you shouldn't be, I'll arrest you for interfering in police business." Lady Phoebe started to protest, but Mr. Perkins made a chopping gesture for silence. "Leave this instant, and take your minion with you."

A spurt of anger sent a reprimand to the tip of Eva's tongue. Not only did she take issue with being called anyone's minion, but she didn't at all like the man's insolent tone as he addressed her lady. But nothing would be gained by aggravating the chief inspector.

A whistled tune carried from outside. Miles came up behind his supervisor and, as if he simply didn't see him, walked into him with a force that sent Chief Inspector Perkins stumbling into the house. He whirled about to hurl a mild oath at his constable.

"Sorry, sir. Didn't see you there." The look on Miles's face assured Eva he had heard Mr. Perkins's comment about Lady Phoebe's *minion.* "I was fishing my tablet and pencil out of my pocket."

The chief inspector blew out a breath, pointed again at Lady Phoebe, and motioned her out the door. Still, Lady Phoebe didn't move.

"We'll go presently, Chief Inspector. But first, may I at least ask if William, our gardener's assistant, has been found?"

"He has not, my lady. Now, if you wouldn't mind." Biting sarcasm accompanied what should have been his polite request. This time Eva and Lady Phoebe didn't hesitate to comply.

Back in the Vauxhall, Phoebe noticed how Eva's hands lay relaxed in her lap rather than clamped on the edges of the seat. Yet her features were tense with concentration. Whatever was on Eva's mind distracted her from even her ever-present fear of riding in motorcars. "You're awfully quiet," Phoebe said. "I hope the inspector's rudeness didn't hurt your feelings."

"No, my lady. Not that I enjoy being called names, but coming from that man, it's no great matter."

"Then what is it?" Phoebe turned the motorcar away from Foxwood Hall and headed to a farm on the very outskirts of the village precincts.

"I was just thinking about who might have been with Keenan this morning."

"Any guesses?"

Eva looked about to speak, but instead she pinched her lips together. Phoebe darted her gaze back and forth between the road and Eva's profile, wondering what was bothering her lady's maid and friend. She gathered breath to ask, but changed her mind. If something was troubling Eva, she would talk about it in her own good time.

They drove out to William's parents' home, hoping for some news of the boy. William's father worked as a laborer on one of Foxwood Hall's tenant farms, and elsewhere when he could find extra work. As Phoebe drove up to the tiny, single-story cottage, her heart went out to the Gaff family. "He has a brother and sister still living at home. Goodness, Eva, this is little more than a shack."

"It's quite small, I'll give you that, my lady. It looks well cared for, though."

That much seemed true. They stepped out of the motorcar, and Phoebe went to knock at the front door. No one answered, but she didn't take the liberty of entering uninvited. Instead, she walked the few short steps to the corner of the cottage and called out if anyone was home.

A moment later two young children came running around from the back garden, followed by a woman with a petite, angular figure. As she approached, she dried chapped hands on her apron and attempted to tuck stray, damp strands of hair beneath a battered sun hat. She was perspiring and a bit out of breath. Phoebe guessed she had been doing the laundry.

"Yes?" She eyed Phoebe's silk shirtwaist, pleated wool skirt, and cashmere cardigan in puzzlement. Then she must have recognized her visitor, for she had a similar reaction to Keenan Ripley's when he discovered the Earl of Wroxly's granddaughter in his house. Mrs. Gaff hastily invited them inside, attempted to further improve her appearance with a pat here, a smoothing of her faded cotton dress there, and nervously offered tea and cake. Phoebe assured her she and Eva would not be staying long. The woman compressed her lips in an attempt to conceal her relief.

Taking in the cramped interior of the house, Phoebe saw that it was well scrubbed and tidy, but lacking in many everyday comforts and conveniences. She made a mental note to include the Gaff family in the charitable deliveries for the RCVF. She knew that Mr. Gaff had, in fact, fought in the war, as had William's older brother, and though they had both escaped serious injury, Phoebe saw no harm in sending a little assistance their way.

"We've only come by to see if your son, William, might be at home," she said to the woman.

"William?" Mrs. Gaff regarded both Phoebe and Eva from beneath her fair eyebrows. "Why, no. It wouldn't be like him to come by other than on Sunday afternoon. His duties at Foxwood Hall keep him much too busy." A wary look claimed her features. "Do you mean to say no one knows where my William is? Has he gone missing?"

Phoebe cast a quick glance at Eva. "No, er, not exactly, Mrs. Gaff."

"Is he in some sort of trouble?" Gone was her accommodating manner, replaced by a simmering anger that sent the two younger children scurrying outside. Phoebe guessed that, innocent or not, William had more to fear from his mother than he ever would from the police.

"Mrs. Gaff, something terrible happened at Foxwood Hall this morning. A man, our new head gardener, has died, and we believe William might have seen what happened. We're afraid he's hiding somewhere out of fear."

The woman seemed to have heard only one detail. "Died how?"

"Intentionally, I'm afraid. Someone took his life. He began as head gardener only yesterday, and today . . ." Phoebe held out her hands. "Are you sure William hasn't been by? He didn't contact you between yesterday and today?"

"Contact me how, my lady?" The woman gestured at the walls of her one-room kitchen and parlor. "We've no telephone, as you can see. He hasn't been by, and since Sunday we've heard nothing of him until just now. But when I do see him, he'll like as not get himself a good cuff on the head for running off and worrying you and me both."

"Please don't do that, Mrs. Gaff. I'm sure there's a good explanation for William not having been found yet. As I said, he was probably frightened by what he witnessed."

The woman sniffed. "Be that as it may."

"Perhaps your husband might know more," Eva suggested.

The woman hesitated, her eyes shifting away momentarily. Then, steadily enough, she said, "If he knew anything about William, he'd have told me. If you wish to come back later tonight and ask him yourself, you're welcome to do that."

Back at home, Phoebe and Eva returned to the yew hedge. At their approach, a brown rabbit hopped out of their path and scrambled for cover. Even from a distance, they could see the body had been removed, and with it all traces of the crime. The cart, pony, and gardening implements were gone, too. Someone had rinsed away the bloodstains, although when Phoebe bent down and looked carefully, she could make out a congealed residue clinging to the roots of the grass. Also bearing witness to Stephen Ripley's death were the indentations in the lawn where he and the ladder had lain.

"I'm very worried about Keenan, my lady," Eva confided. "For all we know, he's already been arrested, for the second time in as many days. What judge or jury will believe in his innocence, especially if he won't help himself?"

Phoebe hesitated before replying. "If we could only find William. He might be able to tell us who did it."

"Are we sure *he* didn't do it, my lady?"

Phoebe walked closer to the incriminating shadows in the grass and leaned down to examine them. "He's so young. Surely Mr. Ripley could have defended himself against a boy."

"He's not that much of a boy, really. Not much younger than you, my lady. And he's no weakling. If he caught Stephen by surprise by pushing over the ladder, he could well have retrieved the clippers and . . . you know the rest."

"But why? Because Mr. Ripley didn't allow him to finish his breakfast yesterday?"

"Perhaps there was more to it. We won't know until we find William."

"*Unless* we find him." At a puzzled glance from Eva, she explained, "I hope nothing has happened to him. I just wish his mother had been more help."

"Should we go back tonight to question his father?"

Phoebe contemplated the possibility, then shook her head. "I think his mother was telling the truth. Or, if she wasn't, then neither she nor her husband will be inclined to enlighten us."

Eva sighed. "From what I understand, Ezra Gaff spends nearly his every waking hour working. I dearly hate to add to his burdens unless we have to." She fell quiet a moment, and then startled Phoebe by blurting, "The Haverleigh path."

"I'm sorry?"

"The path that leads through the woods to the Haverleigh School, my lady. Whoever murdered Stephen might have come and gone by that path without being seen. Remember how your sister's classmate, Jane, used that path to sneak back and forth to the school, with none of us the wiser until I happened to be out by the kitchen garden and saw her."

"Why, you're right." She thought back to the summer before last, when a death at the Haverleigh School had temporarily closed the premises. Several of the students had stayed here at Foxwood Hall, and Jane Timmons used the wooded path to sneak back and forth to visit one of the staff at the school. Phoebe peered into the distance. From here the entrance to the path was invisible, but she knew from experience exactly where it lay. "We like to believe we're secure here, but anyone can enter the grounds from just about any direction. But as you said, the path makes for a discreet entrance and exit."

"Yes, and the Ripley orchard isn't far from the school," Eva murmured. In the next instant she looked as if she'd like to recall the words.

"So are several other farms," Phoebe reminded her. She returned to perusing their surroundings, not quite sure what she was looking for. "When Grampapa and I came out this morning, the cart and pony were here." She indicated the spot by walking several paces from the hedge and holding out her arms to simulate the size of the dray. "Cuttings littered the bottom of the cart, and there were a couple of rakes."

"Nothing unusual so far."

"No." She turned to regard the spot where Stephen Ripley had lain. "His spectacles had slid off his nose, and his flat cap had fallen just there." She pointed at the ground. "A tweed cap, if I remember correctly."

Eva looked sharply at her. "Tweed? What color?"

"A typical brown, I believe. Why?"

Eva's bottom lip slipped between her teeth and her brows gathered. "Stephen wore a plaid flat cap yesterday when he came into the servants' hall looking for William."

"Are you sure?"

"I am. But we could ask the others who were at breakfast yesterday. Vernon might remember. Connie too. She has a sharp eye for details."

"I suppose he could have more than one."

Eva shook her head. "Unlikely, really. Working men, especially single ones, don't accessorize the way women do, nor do they spend their money on unnecessary items. He might own a flat cap, a derby for church, and perhaps a knitted winter hat, but it would be most unusual for a laborer to own more than one of each sort."

Phoebe considered a moment. "There is one way to find out, or at least to narrow down the possibilities."

"Are you suggesting searching the gardener's cottage, my lady?"

Their gazes met, and all Phoebe said was, "Let's get to it."

Eva and Lady Phoebe hesitated outside the gardener's cottage. "You know, Eva, I felt few qualms about entering Keenan Ripley's home, but for some reason now, even though no one is likely to walk in on us, I don't want to go inside."

"Afraid of Stephen Ripley's ghost, my lady?"

"Perhaps. I've got an odd sensation, as if we're about to commit sacrilege. Is that silly of me?"

"I don't think so. It's a little like disturbing a grave, in a way." Eva tightened her cardigan about her. "The cottage is full of the man's possessions, yet he'll never return to claim them."

"Do you think Constable Brannock and the chief inspector already searched here?"

"I'm sure they have, my lady, but I doubt very much they will have thought to look for a second flat cap. Why would they? Everyone would assume the one found by the hedge was Stephen's."

"I certainly thought so. I never would have questioned it if not for you." Lady Phoebe stepped up to the door and tried the latch. Like Keenan's, it moved easily under the pressure of her hand, with only a faint squeak. It would have been unusual to lock a door here, on the estate, or even in the village, a place where nearly everyone knew everyone else.

The main room was draped in shadow, and somewhere, a clock ticked off the seconds. Though the house certainly felt empty, it didn't yet hold the air of abandonment Eva expected, as if any moment Stephen Ripley would come whistling up the path after a day's work, stride in, and make his afternoon tea.

While Lady Phoebe searched the main room, Eva went into the kitchen, such as it was. More of an alcove off the parlor, the room held a small range, an old woodstove, and a table big enough only for two. A work bench sat beside the drain-board sink, and beneath it, a small cupboard held essentials. She found nowhere a hat might be hiding.

"Find anything in here?" she asked Lady Phoebe upon returning to the parlor. Lady Phoebe was bent over a wicker basket that held a few items of clothing—a jumper, a pair of gloves, and yes, a hat, but a knitted sort, not a flat cap.

Lady Phoebe straightened. "We should have a look upstairs."

They crept up the narrow stairwell, both of them instinctively trying to avoid the inevitable creaking step. Two rooms opened onto a small square landing, one barely larger than a linen cupboard, the other containing a dresser, a chest, and an iron bedstead. They didn't need to search at all. A plaid flat cap hung from one of the bedposts. Lady Phoebe retrieved it. "Is this the one?"

She held up the cap, its gray, green, and black pattern bold against the white walls and cream coverlet.

"That's it, my lady. That's the one I saw Stephen with yesterday. Odd he didn't wear it today."

"Perhaps when he saw how shady it is by the hedge in the mornings, he decided he wouldn't need it. The tweed cap could be William's. I don't like to think it, but it might have fallen off during a struggle between the two, and William ran off without it."

Eva tried to remember if she had ever seen William wearing a tweed cap, but flat caps were such a common sight on working men—especially tweed ones. She had only noted Stephen's the other morning because of its unusual plaid pattern. "Or it belongs to someone else entirely—whoever murdered Stephen Ripley."

"I do hope it doesn't belong to Keenan."

Eva couldn't agree more. "We need to get this to Miles. He can compare the sizes of the two caps, and the wear marks. He might even be able to find hairs in the fibers, and determine whether or not the two caps belonged to the same man."

"That's a brilliant idea, Eva."

They went downstairs, Lady Phoebe with the flat cap in hand. At a noise from the kitchen, they both froze. A footstep thudded inside the kitchen doorway, but whoever had made it remained out of sight. Eva's heart pounded against her ribs. Lady Phoebe sucked in a breath. All went silent in the kitchen, as if whoever was in there had heard them, and a kind of standoff ensued between adversaries unable to see one another. Lady Phoebe touched Eva's shoulder.

"There are two of us," she mouthed, "against one."

Eva didn't like even those odds. But dared they waste an opportunity to perhaps discover who had killed Stephen? A coal shovel and an iron poker leaned against the stone surround of the fireplace. After motioning firmly for Lady Phoebe to stay put, Eva tiptoed to the hearth and grasped the shovel. The handle made a slight scraping sound against the stone as she lifted it from its resting place. Did the intruder in the kitchen hear it? Was he, too, finding a weapon? A cast iron frying pan, perhaps? But she had no intention of engaging in violence. She wished only for a glimpse of this individual before she and Lady Phoebe made their escape.

Gripping the shovel in both hands, Eva moved soundlessly across to the kitchen doorway. She saw no one inside. Had she imagined the sounds? But no, Lady Phoebe had obviously heard them as well. She placed a foot over the threshold and raised the shovel, ready to strike.

A solid weight barreled into her, knocking the breath from her lungs and sending her tumbling onto the flagstone floor. Pain splintered through her as Lady Phoebe cried out, "Eva!"

CHAPTER 5

A blur of dark clothing streaked past Phoebe's vision. The figure didn't pause for an instant, not even after running roughshod over Eva and knocking her down. Phoebe ran to her, at the same time attempting to make out who had come charging out of the kitchen. She saw only his back before he disappeared out the front door.

Instinct nearly sent her darting after him, until Eva groaned. Besides, he was moving so fast she doubted she could have caught up to him, especially if he had dodged into the woods behind the cottage.

Crouching, she placed her hands gently beneath Eva's shoulders, supporting her as Eva struggled to sit up. She groaned again, then winced.

"Perhaps you should lie still," Phoebe said. "There's a telephone here. It only connects to the main house, but I can have someone there call for a doctor."

"No . . ." Eva gripped Phoebe's forearm and made another effort to sit up. This time she succeeded, but not without a grimace. "If you help me to my feet, I'm sure I can make it back to the house. But take the shovel, just in case he's still somewhere outside."

"I doubt he's waiting around." Phoebe nonetheless retrieved the shovel, and also found the flat cap that she had dropped in her alarm.

Once Eva gained her feet, Phoebe slipped her free arm around her and encouraged Eva to lean against her side. The first few steps were wobbly, but Eva gained strength and steadiness as they went. Once outside, she straightened and let out a shaky sigh.

"I think I'm all right now. Mostly he knocked the wind out of me. I wish I'd gotten a look at him, but he came at me so fast. Did you see who he was?"

"I'm afraid I saw little more than you did. I know it was a man. A workman, as he wore denims and flannel. But I'm sorry to say I never saw his face. I suppose I should have gone after him."

"No, you should not have done, my lady. You did the right thing. Let's get home so I can telephone Miles."

Soon, the house with its peaks and turrets came into view. Eva said, "You know, my lady, I don't think he meant to hurt me."

"He did a good job of it all the same."

"He seemed more frightened than dangerous. I'm not even sure why I say that, because I saw so little of him, but it's the impression I got. He simply wished to be gone, to get away from us."

"Well, I certainly won't thank him for his lack of malicious intent," Phoebe said wryly. "He might have broken your neck the way he bowled over you." Then she sobered and considered what Eva had said. "Someone who is afraid to be seen. Or afraid to be caught. Are you thinking what I'm thinking?"

"That it was William? I am." As they continued walking, Eva staggered a bit off the path, and the uneven ground sent another grimace to her face.

"I do wish you had let me call for help."

"I'll be fine. As for William, normally he has quarters be-lowstairs at the house. He shares with Josh, the hall boy."

"Do you suppose he's been hiding out at the cottage since Mr. Ripley's death?"

"He might have reasoned that it was the one place no one would think to look, once the police had finished their search of the place. Since Stephen didn't die there, they have little reason to return."

"But is he afraid because he's guilty, or because he's a witness and is terrified of becoming the next victim?" Phoebe swung the shovel head at the grass beside the path. They had reached the tiered gardens and would soon be home.

"His family." Eva came to a sudden halt. "He wants to keep his distance from his family. That's why he hasn't gone home. He doesn't wish to give whoever murdered Stephen any ideas of threatening his family."

"That's quite possible. Maybe he's already turned up." She pointed toward the roofline of Foxwood Hall.

"A hunch tells me he isn't, my lady. I intend to ask around when we get back."

"Not until you're feeling better, please."

Although Eva stubbornly resisted the idea of being seen by a doctor, Phoebe went belowstairs with her to make sure Mrs. Sanders knew of her injury. The woman soon had Eva wrapped in a colorful knitted afghan on the small settee in the housekeeper's parlor, sipping tea, while Mrs. Ellison made up an herbal poultice for her sore ribs. Phoebe also asked Mrs. Sanders to lock the plaid flat cap in her desk drawer, not to be taken out until they could hand it over to Constable Brannock.

"Do you mind if I use your telephone?" Eva asked be-fore Mrs. Sanders left to resume her duties. The house-keeper replied with a nod and a gesture toward the device. Phoebe brought it from the desk to the settee, stretching the wire to its full length. Her cup and saucer set aside, Eva dialed the exchange girl and asked for Miles Brannock at the police station. It took several moments, but Phoebe heard his voice even from where she sat. Eva quickly informed him of everything that had happened since they had seen the constable and the chief inspector at Keenan Ripley's house. She included the discovery of the plaid flat cap and the intruder who knocked her down.

Phoebe leaned forward in her chair and waved a hand to catch Eva's attention. "Ask him if Mr. Ripley has been arrested."

Eva did, nodding as the constable evidently replied. She glanced up at Phoebe. "Not yet. But he thinks it won't be long. Keenan won't offer an alibi and Mr. Perkins can conceive of no other suspects."

That set Phoebe's mind racing. As soon as Eva hung up, Phoebe said, "We need to consider what we know so far." She counted off the facts on her fingers. "Keenan Ripley appears to have the strongest motive for wanting his brother dead because of the potential of losing his orchard and brewery. But Stephen might have been bullying William Gaff, who then killed him in a fit of rebellion. Then there is Joe Murdock of the Houndstooth Inn, who wouldn't have wanted to lose his most popular drink."

"Murder over perry, my lady?"

"No, murder over money. There's no doubt the Ripley perry brings in a tidy sum for Mr. Murdock."

"All right, then. That's Keenan, William, and Mr. Murdock." Eva appeared to mull over these names. Her eyebrows went up. "The Corbyns."

Phoebe recognized the name of one of Little Barlow's sheep farmers. Why, Mrs. Corbyn had helped with the RCVF donations. "What about them?"

"Don't you remember when Keenan and Stephen brought the pears to the church?" In her eagerness, Eva sat up so quickly her blanket slid to the floor. "Keenan offered to drive my sister home, because he had to stop by the Corbyn farm. He said it was time to extend their grazing rights in one of Keenan's pastures."

Phoebe's heart beat faster. "The northeast pasture, he said. And the Corbyns would surely lose those rights if the land sold." She sat back, suddenly deflated. "That doesn't seem to be enough of a reason to kill someone."

"It does if the northeast pasture was the main source of water for the Corbyns' sheep. A stream runs right through that parcel of land, and the Corbyns have built a dew pond that's fed by the stream. As you said, my lady, murder because of money. The sale of Keenan's land would put the Corbyns' livelihood at risk."

Phoebe stood to retrieve the fallen afghan and spread it over Eva's legs. "I hope every one of these people has an alibi. All of them. I want Stephen Ripley's killer to be someone who followed him from Dorset, or someone who met him along the way. He doesn't seem to have been a very likable individual, so I wouldn't be surprised if he'd made enemies everywhere he went."

"That's my hope, too, my lady." Eva pulled the blanket higher, nearly to her chin, and shivered. Phoebe guessed her trembling had nothing to do with being cold. "I need to speak with my sister."

"Mrs. Ward? About this?"

Eva's grim nod spread foreboding through Phoebe. "It might have been Alice at Keenan's this morning."

"What on earth makes you think that?"

Eva let go a breath. "I didn't want to bring attention to it, but I couldn't help noticing how exceedingly friendly they were with each other at the church." She pursed her lips before continuing. "They used to show an interest in each other, before Alice married. And I'm afraid that now . . ."

"But your sister is still very much married."

Eva nodded. "But there's something wrong with Alice's life at home. I know there is. She showed up at my parents' house without her children, saying she left them with their Ward grandparents. She claimed she needed a holiday, but when my mother tried to question her, Alice evaded the subject." She met Phoebe's gaze. "What mother goes away without her children unless she was contemplating making a drastic change to her life? I'm very worried about her. And I'm worried she is the person Keenan wished to protect this morning."

"I'm sure you're wrong, Eva. You'll see. As soon as you're able, I'll drive you out to your parents' farm so you can speak with your sister. Tomorrow, if you're feeling up to it."

Phoebe didn't know whether Eva's bleak look stemmed from her fears concerning her sister, or the prospect of having to ride, once again, in the Vauxhall. Phoebe always hoped Eva would eventually warm toward motorcars in general, and Phoebe's driving in particular. So far, neither had happened.

Eva waited until she heard Lady Phoebe's light footsteps fade away on the service staircase up to the ground floor. Then she threw off Mrs. Sanders's afghan, came to her feet, and stretched her arms high overhead. The resulting twinges brought on a wince or two, but she saw no reason to lie about for the rest of the afternoon. Only Lady Phoebe's concerns had induced her to put her feet up for as long as she had. But now, she had questions to ask of her fellow staff.

The first person she tracked down was Josh, the hall boy, who brought in the coal, swept the storerooms, polished the other servants' boots, and generally performed the tasks no one else wished to do. She found him outside cleaning built-up coal dust from the chutes that brought the coal sliding down to the bins in the furnace room. It was filthy work, and poor Josh, a slight youth in his mid-teens, looked like the kind of graveyard wraith she and her childhood friends would conjure while telling ghost stories to frighten each other.

He nodded in greeting and continued the work of scrubbing the mouth of the chute with a wire brush, reaching in until nearly his entire arm disappeared. "Something you need, Miss Huntford?"

"I wish to ask you something, Josh." His shrug gave her the permission she sought. "You room with William, yes?"

"Sure, Miss Huntford. Everyone knows that. We're the low men on the ladder here, so we share a bunk. It's all right by me. William's a good fellow."

"Last night, did he say anything to you about his new supervisor, Mr. Ripley?"

Josh's expression became shuttered. "Not to me."

"You've heard what happened to Mr. Ripley this morning, didn't you?"

"Heard he fell off his ladder right onto his shears."

His answer surprised Eva. So the police hadn't been forthcoming with the facts when they questioned the servants earlier. "Did William seem to get along with Mr. Ripley?"

Another shrug, this time with a show of disdain, or as much disdain as was possible to display on features that were as obscured as midnight. "It'd only been one day, but no, Will was none too happy about Mr. Ripley taking Mr. Peele's job."

Eva noticed how he phrased that—*taking* Mr. Peele's job, as if Stephen had forced Mr. Peele's retirement. Perhaps that wasn't how the boy meant it, but it might be a notion worth pursuing. "What did William say?"

"He didn't say anything, Miss Huntford. That's just it. When Will came to bed last night, he crawled under the covers and wouldn't talk to me. It was odd because he never comes in that late. I mean, what were they doing, trimming hedges in the dark? Anyways, when I asked him how his day went, he told me to shut up. Just like that. Shut up. Will never said that to me before, not even when I kept him awake 'cause I couldn't sleep and wanted someone to talk to."

"He never said a word about his day?"

"Not a peep. Just told me to shut up and turned his back to the wall." Josh's expression turned sheepish. He glanced about the service courtyard before adding, "I noticed something before he turned. I think—I'm not positive—but I think he had a bruise on his face."

"A bruise?" Poor William. Had Stephen Ripley struck him? If so, that would add weight to the possibility that William retaliated against the man, perhaps killing him unintentionally. "When was the last time you saw him? Maybe very early this morning?"

"He went out before I was awake." The hand holding the brush had gone still these several minutes past, and Josh only now seemed to remember he had a job to do and would receive an earful from Mrs. Sanders if he didn't complete it in good time. He scrubbed the wire brush back and forth again.

"Do you have any idea where he would go if he were particularly troubled by something? Please think hard, Josh. It's important."

The scrubbing once more subsided. "Has Will gone missing?"

"I'm not sure. But I think he might be a bit frightened, considering what happened this morning."

Josh's eyes narrowed. "Miss Huntford, Mr. Ripley's death wasn't really an accident, was it?"

"I . . . I really don't think I should answer that, Josh. We shouldn't be speculating. You know how Mrs. Sanders feels about gossip." Eva felt a twinge of guilt avoiding an honest reply, but she knew Josh couldn't argue with one of Mrs. Sanders's decrees. "I'm just trying to locate William."

"Well, I don't know where he is, but if he shows up, I'll tell him you're looking for him."

"Thank you, Josh." She started to turn away, until she remembered another vital question. "Josh, does William own a brown tweed flat cap?"

"Brown? Not that I've seen. He wears a gray flannel."

The scrubbing resumed, raising a *screech-screech* of metal on metal that raised the hairs on Eva's nape. As she reentered the house, luck brought her directly in George Vernon's path. The head footman was carrying a box of silver—candelabras, decorative platters, things of that sort—into one of the service rooms. After stepping aside to allow him to pass, Eva followed him inside.

"George, when was the last time you saw William?"

George had retrieved a tin of silver polish and a soft flannel rag from a cupboard against the wall. "Not since last night, Miss Huntford." His brows drew together in a show of concern. "Wasn't he here earlier when the police were questioning everyone?"

"No, apparently not." Eva wondered if William had gone without breakfast again this morning out of fear of Stephen Ripley. Or did he even report to work today? Perhaps that bruise Josh spoke of dissuaded William from coming within arm's reach of the new head gardener. "Did you see him last night? I heard he came in later than usual, after dark. I'm wondering what might have kept him working so long."

George dipped his rag in the silver polish and began rubbing in slow, circular motions along the base of a four-branched candelabra. "No, but if he came in late I wouldn't have seen him, would I? These days, without much company upstairs, we footmen go off duty directly after dinner is cleared away. I was probably already up in my room before Will came in."

"And you haven't heard him say anything about how he likes working for Mr. Ripley?"

"There's hardly been time for him to have an opinion, has there?"

Eva didn't know about that. In fact, she believed Stephen had made it easy for William to form an immediate opinion, and a far from favorable one. She thanked George for his time and left him to his polishing. In the corridor, she leaned against the wall, absently holding a sore spot on the side of her ribs as she considered. The hedge ran between the formal gardens and the hothouses, and Stephen and William had begun trimming the far side, out of view of the house. In short, it's quite likely no one saw them while they were working.

Her hand fell to her side. No one might have been able to see them, but someone might have *heard* them. Especially if they had been at odds.

Especially if they had come to blows, or worse.

She mentally ran through the list of everyone who might have gone out to the kitchen gardens and hothouses. Mrs. Ellison, Foxwood Hall's longtime cook, came immediately to mind. She went out daily, sometimes more than once, to choose herbs and vegetables for the meals. The woman took pride in selecting almost every morsel herself, with the strictest standards regarding ripeness and freshness. Dora often accompanied her, and sometimes Mrs. Ellison sent the kitchen maid out alone for more simple selections.

Who else? Eva herself often went out to the hothouses for flowers to arrange in Lady Phoebe's room. Hetta, too, for Lady Julia. And the countess's maid, Miss Shaw, she supposed, also clipped flowers for her mistress's bedroom.

She would begin with Mrs. Ellison.

*   *   *

Phoebe heard her name called from the Rosalind sitting room, named for her great-great-grandmother's love of the rose garden that grew directly below its windows. She passed her bedroom door—her intended destination—and continued toward the summons. She found Grams sitting alone on the dusky mauve velvet settee, a cup of tea on the tray table before her.

"Shut the door, please," Grams said. "And come and sit down."

Curious, vaguely alarmed, Phoebe did as Grams bade her. "How did you know it was me in the hallway when you couldn't see me?"

"I know your tread." Grams took a sip of her tea. "I know the tread of everyone in this family."

Phoebe didn't doubt the claim. Nothing escaped her grandmother's notice, which had always gone a long way toward ensuring that Phoebe and her siblings did as they were told. Their mother had died when Phoebe was young, and their father lost his life on a battlefield in France, leaving Phoebe, her two sisters, and their brother, Fox, in the care of their grandparents. Grams ruled with a silk-clad fist, or so Phoebe liked to think of it. Firm, unbending, yet at the same time kind and generous in her stoic way. Grampapa, too, when it came to Fox, but as far as his granddaughters were concerned, he could just as easily be swayed by a smile as by a tear.

"Is there something wrong, Grams?" Phoebe hoped it wasn't something she had done, and quickly reviewed her actions in the past few days. Had she forgotten an appointment? Was she supposed to have been somewhere when she and Eva went to warn Keenan Ripley of his brother's murder?

"It's your sister," said Grams. "I'm worried about her

again and I'd like you to find out what's troubling her. Besides the obvious, I mean."

The obvious being Julia carrying the child of her dead husband, a man she admittedly married for his money, whom she hadn't loved, but to whom she had promised to be a good wife nonetheless. Now, months after his death, the guilt of her actions continued to plague Julia, though she did her best to put up a good front.

"I'm not sure what you wish me to do," Phoebe said truthfully, and with a measure of regret. "You know Julia doesn't confide in me. Not much, anyway." This despite having undergone some harrowing experiences together, including the death of Julia's husband and her own subsequent kidnapping. During each traumatic experience, Julia would thaw temporarily, making Phoebe believe they'd finally achieved a sisterly closeness or at least a lasting truce. Then the old resentments would creep back in between them like thick, thorny vines. "Have you considered bringing Amelia home from school for a time? She can keep up with her schoolwork, so that wouldn't be a problem." If anyone could coax Julia out of one of her dark moods, it was their youngest sister, Amelia, with her gentle ways and unending stores of patience. That was one quality Phoebe had yet to fully cultivate.

"If I did that," Grams said with a dismissive wave, "Julia would know I was worried, and I'm afraid that would only alienate her further."

"I suppose you're right about that. If there's one thing Julia can't abide, it's being fussed over."

Grams's silver eyebrows rose. "Especially when there *is* something wrong."

Phoebe nodded her agreement.

"Couldn't you make yourself available to her? Hang about her, you know, as you did when you were girls. You were always following after her, and running to her room every morning and crawling into bed with her."

Yes, before Papa died, she and Julia *had* been close, had been like real sisters. How long ago that seemed, how distantly remote. Another life; another Julia. Still, Phoebe scrunched her nose. "Surely you're not suggesting I behave as I did when I was ten?"

"Well, not quite that, but you can certainly make overtures that will invite a certain intimacy, can't you?"

"I suppose . . ."

"Do this for me." Grams's tone brooked no debate. "For Julia. Invite her to go somewhere with you. To Cheltenham, perhaps. Or even Gloucester. For some shopping. Take Eva and Hetta. It'll be fun for all of you."

"And if she won't go?"

"She'll go." Somehow, judging by the look on Grams's face, Phoebe didn't doubt she and her sister would be spending a lot more time together in the near future.

Unless, of course, Julia decided to give her the cold shoulder.

CHAPTER 6

"Dora, you slovenly girl, I specifically asked you to bring me four cups of dates for the spice cakes I'm making for the countess's meeting at the Haverleigh School tomorrow."

Eva stopped outside the kitchen, halted by Mrs. Ellison's biting tone.

"And how many do I find here?" the cook continued. "Not quite two cups, you lazy chit! Where are you, girl?"

Perhaps, Eva thought, now wouldn't be the best time to question Mrs. Ellison and Dora about what they might have heard from the other side of the yew hedge yesterday morning and today. From where she stood in the corridor, Eva couldn't see Mrs. Ellison, but she could certainly hear her mutterings and half-muffled oaths, including what she would do to that undependable Dora when she got her hands on her.

Not that Eva worried over much about the young assistant. Mrs. Ellison's threats, much like the housekeeper's, always sounded much worse than they were in practice. The fact that Dora was in her third year here at Foxwood Hall attested to that.

"What are you going on about, Mrs. Ellison?" that errant young woman said as she apparently shuffled in from one of the pantries off the kitchen. Eva moved closer to the doorway until, by leaning slightly to the left, she could bring the two main kitchen workers into view.

Mrs. Ellison snatched a bowl from the center worktable and shook it in Dora's direction. "The dates, girl. The dates! I sent you to the hothouse to pick a quart of dates, and this is what you bring?"

"What's going on in there?"

The murmur beside Eva's ear made her jump half a foot and nearly cry out, except that she recognized the speaker immediately. Turning, she rammed the flat of her hand into the woolen, black-clad chest of Miles Brannock. "Don't sneak up on me like that."

Having removed his policeman's helmet, he ran his hand over his red, wavy hair and grimaced in apology. "Sorry. Mrs. Sanders let me in, and I noticed you eavesdropping here—"

"I'm doing no such thing."

"Saw you eavesdropping," he continued as if she hadn't interrupted, "and heard the argument coming from inside." He gestured into the kitchen. "Anything serious?"

"No, just the usual war of words." The fright he'd given her forgiven if not quite forgotten, she smiled in lieu of pecking him on the cheek. Such a display wouldn't do here, where one of the other servants might see. Still, his appearance gave that familiar lift to her spirits, as if she'd taken a particularly potent tonic.

"I hadn't expected to find you on your feet." He leaned in closer, his gaze filled with concern. "How are you? Any lingering hurts from your fall earlier?"

"A little sore on my side," she admitted, "but nothing that won't ease on its own. I'm glad you're here. I've realized that while no one saw anything this morning, someone might very well have *heard* something from the other side of the hedge. Did the chief inspector make inquiries of that nature?"

Miles's lips went flat as he shook his head. "No, he didn't, and I had the same thought. And while I'd love to be out searching for whoever plowed into you at the gardener's cottage, I'm glad to have another chance to be here and follow up on matters Perkins left dangling. Where's the cap you found, by the way?"

"Safely locked in Mrs. Sanders's desk. Keenan hasn't been arrested since we spoke, has he?"

"Not yet." He gestured toward the kitchen again, this time with his chin. Eva once more became aware of the arguing inside, which hadn't ceased for a moment. "What are they going on about?"

"A bit of a disagreement over the amount of dates Dora plucked from the hothouse trees."

"That would be the hothouse closest to the yew hedge, wouldn't it?"

"It would. That's the one where the larger fruit-bearing plants and trees are housed." She inwardly acknowledged the providential nature of his timely arrival. While she was more than willing to ask Dora and Mrs. Ellison the necessary questions, those same questions coming from a police constable would be infinitely more difficult to evade. "So yes, Dora would have gone almost right up to the hedge when she went out for the dates this morning. She might have heard something."

Miles held out a hand. "Shall we?"

Eva didn't grasp his hand however much she wished to, but instead preceded him into the expansive kitchen with its range that took up nearly one entire wall, its several sinks, its many cupboards and work counters. Dora and Mrs. Ellison stood framed in a shaft of sunlight pouring in through the ground level window behind them. Mrs. Ellison wielded a wooden spoon. Dora held no such weapon, but stood her ground firmly nonetheless.

"I told you, I brought in a full quart and then some. Don't you think I know a quart when I see it?" She thrust a finger toward the bowl and the dates barely covering the bottom. "That's no quart, and it's not likely I'd think it was, nor would I want to come back with that scrawny lot only to be hollered at like this. For goodness sake, Mrs. E."

"Then where'd they go? Eh?" Mrs. Ellison struck the air with the rounded end of the spoon. "Tell me that."

Dora was shrugging off the question when she suddenly noticed that she and the cook had drawn an audience. "Miss Huntford. Constable Brannock." A ridge grew above her nose. "Is there something you need?"

"Don't stand there gawping, girl, set the kettle to boil." Mrs. Ellison hurried over to the icebox, where she began rummaging through with her head practically submerged in the cold interior. "Have a seat in the hall, Constable, and I'll bring you some refreshment. I've got some Eccles cakes left over from this morning. And there's some lovely, fresh clotted cream. . . ."

"That's not necessary, ma'am," Miles said in his most accommodating voice.

Eva intercepted Mrs. Ellison as she backed away from the icebox holding a bowl. "That's quite all right, Mrs. Ellison. Put the clotted cream back and save it for Mrs. Sanders's and Mr. Giles's tea. The constable only wants to ask you and Dora a few more questions about yesterday and this morning."

The four of them marched single file into the servants' hall and took seats close together at one end of the table. At this time of the day, they weren't likely to be interrupted, although that would only be true for the next twenty minutes or so. Then the others would trickle in for their afternoon tea before the work of preparing for dinner began.

Miles drew out his notebook and pencil. "What I need to know is whether either of you were out in the hothouse area yesterday morning and this morning, and if so, did you hear anything—anything at all—coming from the vicinity of the yew hedge."

"Like what?" Dora's blunt question nearly made Eva sigh with impatience. Hadn't Miles just explained he wished to know if they heard *anything*?

He showed greater patience than she felt. "Voices, for instance."

"I went out there yesterday," Mrs. Ellison said, "and I did hear Mr. Ripley yelling at William, and once or twice William might have mumbled something that more than likely got him cuffed."

"You could hear him mumbling?" Miles held his pencil aloft.

"I could," the woman said with a nod. "Except when I was inside the hothouse. But from the kitchen garden, and on the path, yes, I could hear them speaking."

"By the time *I* went out yesterday," Dora said with a bit of a pout as if she feared being left out of the conversation, "they'd moved from the hedge to somewhere else on the grounds. Mr. Peele used to do that, too. Start in one area, work a while, and move on to something else. I remarked on it once, and he said he moved with the shifting sun, so he'd never be blinded by too much sunlight or too much shade. Said he needed to work in just the right light to keep everything perfect. I expect Mr. Ripley was doing the same."

"Could you see where they went after leaving the hedge?"

Dora shook her head; her pout persisted. "Being stuck in the kitchen and service grounds all the time, I never can see into the formal gardens. Or the front of the house, for that matter."

"Be happy you've got a situation, girl." Mrs. Ellison

reached over and poked Dora in the shoulder with her fore-finger. "There's many who'd happily take over for you."

Dora scowled.

Miles wrote down their observations. "And what about this morning? Were either of you out there early, when Mr. Ripley and William would have been working on the hedge?"

"I was out directly after breakfast. I went to the far hot-house to gather dates for Mrs. Ellison." The kitchen maid tipped her head at the cook with a prickly, I-told-you-so expression, obviously in reference to their earlier argument. "I didn't hear a thing."

"No voices? Mr. Ripley giving William instructions?" Miles frowned, which soon had Eva frowning as well as she followed the gist of his questioning. "The sound of clipping? The rustling of branches?"

Dora and Mrs. Ellison frowned as well. The younger woman said, "All was silent. Why, now that I think about it, even the birds were quiet. That *is* a bit odd, isn't it?"

"Unless there's anything either of you can add, you may go." Miles closed his notebook.

The two women hesitated. The cook said, "What do you think happened?" She lowered her voice. "Did William kill Mr. Ripley?"

"I've implied no such thing," Miles admonished her in his sternest tone. "So don't go spreading rumors."

"Come to think of it, where *is* William?" Dora showed no signs of gaining her feet until she'd satisfied her curiosity. "With Mr. Ripley dead, it's not as if Will should still be busy with the gardening. He should be back here, shouldn't he? I mean, where else would he go?"

"Maybe he went home," the cook suggested. "His family isn't far from here. I'll wager he's there. Needed his mum, like as not."

Eva didn't see any reason to enlighten the women, and

for all she knew, William might actually be home by now. Except then, who had knocked her down at the cottage?

The next morning, Phoebe changed gears to ease the Vauxhall around a bend and then gunned the engine to urge the motorcar up the hill that immediately followed. Beside her, Julia huffed with impatience. "Can't you make this thing go any faster?"

"Not if you wish to arrive in Cheltenham in one piece," she snapped in return. Despite Julia jumping at Phoebe's suggestion of a shopping trip, she'd been rather out of sorts since they set out. "What's your hurry? It's only shopping. Did you see a particular hat in a magazine you can't live another moment without?"

"Hardly." Julia didn't turn away from the windscreen as she spoke. "We're not going shopping. At least, no more than we must in order to convince Grams that's why we went to Cheltenham."

"Grams will already be unhappy that we went without Eva, Hetta, and the chauffeur." Phoebe wasn't looking forward to that confrontation when they got home. Grams had made it clear she wanted Phoebe and Julia to be chaperoned on this trip, yet Julia had been equally adamant they go alone. It was either go alone, Julia had insisted, or not at all.

"Yes," Julia said in a mocking tone, "Eva and Hetta to see we don't get into any trouble, and the chauffeur to report back on everywhere we go."

A lump of apprehension grew in Phoebe's stomach. "If we're not going shopping, what *are* we going to do?"

Julia's smile spoke of forbidden secrets. "You'll see."

Phoebe knew better than to pester her sister for the details. Once Julia shut those lips of hers, she didn't open them again until she was good and ready. When she had knocked on Julia's bedroom door earlier, as per Grams's request, she'd found her sister in another of her morose moods, exhibiting little enthusiasm for doing anything but sitting and staring out her bedroom window. That was until Phoebe suggested getting out and visiting some nearby shops. Suddenly, Julia's entire demeanor had changed, her enthusiasm such that Phoebe hadn't had the heart to deny her a trip to Cheltenham, despite the distance. She knew there were several shops there her sister favored, and although Julia would much prefer shopping in London, Phoebe had been elated to see how the prospect of today's outing lifted her spirits.

More fool she.

She did, however, regret not being able to track down William before they left. According to Eva, William had reported that Foxwood Hall's former head gardener had moved to Cheltenham to live with his sister. If only Phoebe knew where in Cheltenham to find him, she would have made good use of this opportunity to discover exactly why he left Little Barlow in such a hurry.

And whether he'd had reason to resent Stephen Ripley. That, however, would have to wait for another day.

She kept the motorcar heading north, past Gloucester to the west, until Cleeve Hill, the highest point in the Cotswolds, rose up in the distance. Soon they crossed the River Chelt, which flowed into the Severn. As they descended into the valley, Cheltenham sprawled before them, a city whose most prominent architecture dated to the Regency, when, like the town of Bath, the presence of mineral springs helped transform Cheltenham into a popular spa town. And like Bath, elegant terrace homes built of honey-golden Cotswold stone lined the streets.

Did Julia wish to take the waters? Perhaps someone had told her, or she had read somewhere, that it would be beneficial to the baby. Phoebe hoped that wasn't Julia's intention. Her mouth turned down in distaste. After sampling the waters in Bath years ago, she had permanently sworn off the taking of mineral waters.

"Stay to the south," Julia said, startling Phoebe with the sudden instruction. "We're going into Montpellier." Julia opened her handbag and drew out a piece of paper. With a quick glance, Phoebe discerned an address. Julia pointed beyond the windscreen. "Turn onto Suffolk Square, then go to the right."

"Where *are* we going?"

Julia said nothing. Her secretive little smile had vanished. Instead, shadows of apprehension darkened her eyes, and she clutched her hands over her rounded belly. Phoebe began to worry in earnest. Just as she was contemplating pulling over and demanding to know what they were doing in Cheltenham, Julia pointed again.

"There. That's where we're going."

Phoebe glanced along the line of shop fronts, trying to make out the signs. Julia climbed out as soon as the motor came to a stop, and Phoebe hurried to follow her. To her utter surprise, Julia marched into a shop whose front window displayed a vast array of exotic teas, teapots, and cups.

"We came all this way for tea?"

The bell jingled when Julia went inside, then again when Phoebe opened the door to follow her in. Gas jets lit the dusky interior, bathing the shelves and counters in a soothing glow. The mingling aromas of countless packets and sacks of tea encompassed Phoebe in a sense of warmth greatly at odds with her conviction that they shouldn't be there. Tea had, throughout her life, been more than merely a drink one had with afternoon meals. She had always looked to tea to comfort her, steady her, and fill her with fortitude. And it had always served her well. Now she wasn't so certain.

Several customers milled about the interior. A long oaken table held a half dozen cast iron pots, wisps of steam curling from their spouts, surrounded by tiny cups for sampling. Some of the customers were doing so, and quietly discussing their opinions of this flavor or that.

Julia went to the clerk behind the main counter, a woman in a colorful, tapering frock—wide at the hips, narrow at the ankles—and a fox pelt hanging about her shoulders. A wide headband, flowered to match the frock, kept a riot of curls from falling in her aged but not unattractive face. "I called earlier."

"Ah, yes. We've been expecting you, madame." She spoke with the intonations of someone who had lived all her life in the Cotswolds. "One moment, please." The woman slipped away behind a door, leaving it a few inches ajar. Phoebe could hear faint murmurs within.

She went to Julia's side. "Will you please tell me what on earth is going on?"

The woman came back into the shop. "You may go in now, madame."

Julia started to go, but Phoebe placed a hand on her shoulder to stop her. "I want to know what's going on or I'm leaving."

One of Julia's eyebrows went up as she called Phoebe's bluff. "Leave, then."

"You know I won't do that."

"Then come along. I assure you nothing bad is going to happen to us. The person behind that door came highly recommended by . . . Olive Asquith."

Phoebe studied her sister closely. Olive Asquith was a mutual friend, someone they both trusted and respected. Yet Phoebe had noticed Julia's hesitation, as if she had used the time to search for a reply that would mollify Phoebe's qualms and had landed on Olive's name. Phoebe didn't believe for a moment the practical, levelheaded Olive had sent Julia here. But the shop was admittedly full of people. What could happen?

The woman in the colorful organdy frock tapped her foot impatiently. "Madame? You may go through to the door on your right."

Julia strode away purposefully, leaving Phoebe to hurry after her or be left behind. A small corridor led to what appeared to be a storeroom, for more tea if Phoebe's nose was to be trusted. Julia turned into the doorway on her right, and again, Phoebe went in after her. She entered a room lit by two gas jets. There was a table, several chairs, and a bookcase that held volumes, as well as teapots, small statuettes, and other trinkets.

"Welcome, ladies. You must be Lady Annondale. I am Miss Lara Greenwood." The greeting, in a cultured accent, came from another woman of middle age, but whose appearance was markedly different from the shopkeeper's. Everything about her spoke of wealth and sophistication, from her fashionable suit to her sleek chignon, to her tasteful, subdued jewelry. No vibrant organdy, foxtail pelts, or wide headbands for her. She didn't strike Phoebe at all as a purveyor of teas, at least not like the one presiding over the shop, but, rather, as the kind of woman who would sip tea in elegant surroundings, and who might serve on the board of directors of their church, or at the Haverleigh School for Young Ladies.

With a dignified gesture, the woman motioned them to the table around which several chairs were evenly spaced. "Please, sit." She regarded Phoebe. "This must be . . . your sister?"

Julia gave a nod. "Yes, this is Phoebe. She drove me here."

"Ah, good. Please." She gestured again, this time with a hint of impatience, or so Phoebe thought. Once she and

Julia seated themselves, the woman went to the two gas jets on opposite walls and lowered the flames. A dimness settled over the room. Miss Greenwood sat, folded her hands on the table in front of her, and smiled. "If I understood correctly, Lady Annondale, you wish to contact your husband today."

Phoebe gasped and whisked a hand to her mouth. "Julia, what are you thinking? A fortune-teller?" She didn't care if she was being rude. She only wished to collect her sister and escape with their purses intact.

"Don't be foolish, Phoebe." Before Julia could say more, Miss Greenwood spoke.

"I am not a fortune-teller, Lady Phoebe. I am a medium. That means I can connect with the souls of the deceased, and sometimes with the living as well." She winked at Julia, who smiled placidly back.

"And what does that mean?" Phoebe sat stiffly upright, refusing to let her back come in contact with the chair. Refusing to relax and accept this chicanery. "You claim you can speak with the dead?"

The woman looked directly at Julia. "Perhaps your sister should wait outside. Her negativity will interfere with the spiritual channels. I might not be able to make the connection."

Julia leaned closer to Phoebe. "If you don't wish to be part of this, you may leave now. If you wish to stay, you must do so with an open mind and a closed mouth."

"Julia . . ." The adamant expression on Julia's face stifled Phoebe's protest. As much as Julia had just ordered her to keep an open mind, Phoebe could see that Julia's mind was quite closed in terms of being dissuaded of this folly. The best thing for Phoebe to do, then, was to remain where she was and make sure no harm came to her sister. "All right. I'll stay, and I'll be quiet."

"Good. Let us begin." Lara Greenwood unfolded her

manicured hands and, after stretching out her arms, placed them palm down on the table, her fingers spread. Julia did likewise, the ends of her fingers touching Miss Greenwood's. They both looked meaningfully at Phoebe. After a moment, she reluctantly stretched out her arms and touched her fingertips to theirs.

"It helps if everyone closes their eyes," the woman said.

Hardly likely. Julia might go along with this sham, but Phoebe intended keeping an eye on things. Someone had to. She didn't know what to expect next. Perhaps some kind of incantation, or that Miss Greenwood would start swaying and humming. But if she swayed toward Julia's handbag, Phoebe would be there to intercept her.

None of those things happened. Miss Greenwood remained quite immobile, her face a serene blank. Then, her eyebrows began to rise, slowly and steadily. Her lips parted.

"Julia."

Through their joined fingertips, Phoebe felt the jolt that went through her sister. She whispered, "Gil?"

"Yes, Julia," the woman continued in a hushed, sibilant tone, like whispers in a cave. "What is it you wish? Why have you summoned me?"

Oh, how ridiculous. Phoebe bit down on her lips to keep from bringing this foolishness to a halt.

"Gil . . ." Julia drew a shaking breath and compressed her lips. A look of pain came over her features. "Do you blame me? Was it my fault?"

Phoebe wished to cry out that it wasn't. That Julia didn't need a charlatan or even a true presence from beyond the grave to tell her that. A cold-blooded murderer had been responsible for Gilbert Townsend's death last spring.

But then, suddenly, her anger left her. It dawned on her that, if Julia truly needed this sham to convince her of the truth, so be it. Let this woman, this Lara Greenwood—if that was even her name—set Julia's guilt to rest. It would be worth whatever Julia paid her.

"No, my dear," came Miss Greenwood's murmur. "Not your fault."

"But our marriage. You know it wasn't . . ."

"It wasn't any different than many other marriages. You mustn't blame yourself for that. I wished to marry you. And you?"

Julia sat more upright, pulling forward a bit. "I did wish to marry you, Gil. It was my choice. And I wanted to be a good wife to you. But my reasons for marrying you . . ."

"No longer matter, my dear."

"Truly?" The word trembled on Julia's lips. And Phoebe trembled, too—trembled to see her proud, haughty sister brought to such a vulnerable state. It frightened and humbled her to see a side of her sister that had been buried since their father died. Oh, there had been occasional glimpses, but nothing as blatant and powerful as this. Once again she wanted to end this; yet once again she acknowledged that it might help rather than hurt Julia.

"Truly," said the voice that was supposed to be Gil's. Then, abruptly, the voice changed, became Lara Greenwood's again. "Lady Annondale, there was another you wished to know about."

Julia gasped lightly. "Yes, yes that's true. Can you? But *how* can you?"

At the woman's mention of another, Phoebe feared Julia wished to speak with one of their parents, most likely their father. But Julia's question—*how* can you?—left Phoebe mystified, and even more so when the woman spoke again.

"There are no words I can use, Lady Annondale, but I can connect nonetheless." A frown formed between the woman's eyebrows, and her mouth flattened with concentration. Several minutes passed. Phoebe perceived, again through their touching fingertips, Julia's tension and eager anticipation.

Finally, the fingertips to her left, Miss Greenwood's, broke contact, and then Julia's pulled away, too. They opened their eyes, and Miss Greenwood beamed at Julia. "It is," she said.

Phoebe's gaze darted back and forth between them. "What is what?"

Julia came to her feet and opened her handbag. From it she drew several folded bills and placed them in Miss Greenwood's outstretched hand. Neither had stopped smiling. Julia turned to Phoebe. "So then, a little shopping before we go home?"

CHAPTER 7

During their morning apart, Eva continued questioning the servants, within the guise of merely making conversation, about whether any of them had been out by the hothouses yesterday morning. With the exception of Mrs. Ellison and Dora, no one had been in the vicinity. No one had seen William since before the murder occurred. And no one knew anything about a brown tweed flat cap.

While ignoring the soreness in her hip brought on by yesterday's attack, she had gone about her duties, tending to Lady Phoebe's attire and shoes and sorting through Lady Amelia's clothing that had been sent over from the Haverleigh School for washing and mending. Meanwhile, Eva had been on tenterhooks, expecting at any moment to hear from Miles that Keenan Ripley had been arrested. So far no telephone call had come, but Eva fretted all the same. And she continued to wonder about the significance of Dora hearing nothing at all when she went out to pick the dates for Mrs. Ellison's recipe. Had the murder already occurred by then? If so, it might have happened before Keenan's visitor arrived at his cottage. Well before. Which meant he still wouldn't have an alibi.

When Lady Phoebe and Lady Annondale arrived back from their shopping excursion, Eva hurried up to Lady Phoebe's bedroom. She hadn't anything new to share with her, but Lady Phoebe had promised that when she came home, she would drive Eva out to her parents' farm to give Eva a chance to speak with her sister. Eva had said she would walk, but Lady Phoebe wouldn't hear of it, citing Eva's injuries from the day before.

Now, though, seeing Lady Phoebe looking decidedly fatigued, she decided not to bring the matter up. Instead, she helped Lady Phoebe out of her overcoat and shoes and into more comfortable things. Then she attended to the purchases, sitting on the foot of the bed.

Peeking into the shopping bag, she frowned. "All that time and only two small packages?" She lifted them from the bag and peeled away the tissue paper from both. "Stockings and a hat pin? Was there nothing else in all of Cheltenham that struck your fancy, my lady?"

Lady Phoebe sank onto the dressing-table bench, facing Eva. "We didn't go to Cheltenham to shop."

Eva had already surmised that by Lady Phoebe's listlessness. "Then what *did* you go for?"

Eva's eyes widened as Lady Phoebe's story unfolded. At the same time, indignation and anger spread burning embers through her at the notion of Lady Julia being taken advantage of by a brazen fraud.

"She said Julia's baby is a boy," Phoebe concluded.

"She actually claimed to have communicated with the child?" Eva's fury burned hotter still. While her faith was strong and she believed in the possibility of unexplainable occurrences, hokum such as this was for the extremely gullible, or the extremely vulnerable. Lady Julia had never belonged to the former group, but the latter? Oh, yes. More than most people would ever guess. Especially now. "Well," she said with bitter sarcasm, "she's got a fifty percent chance of being right. And if she proves wrong, she'll be long gone before your sister can demand her money back."

"I'm very worried that Julia won't stop here, that she'll continue to seek out one con artist after another." An angry pause permeated the room, before Lady Phoebe said, "The woman wasn't at all what I would have expected. I envision fortune-tellers looking like gypsies—more like the woman who ran the tea shop. But Lara Greenwood spoke and dressed in a cultured manner. We might just as easily have encountered her at a social event."

"Humph. My guess is she dresses to match the occasion. Had someone like my mother hired her services, she probably would have appeared in a homemade cotton housedress and spoken with a Cotswold lilt. It's all part of winning her customer's trust."

"You're likely right about that. A skilled swindler would know how to play her role to perfection." Lady Phoebe's chin went down. She turned toward the dressing table and lifted the silver-backed hairbrush, turning it over, this way and that, while staring down at its etched design. Eva knew she had something specific she wished to say and was searching for the right words. Finally, she looked back up with a fluttering, tenuous smile. "In an odd way, though, I almost feel she did Julia a service. Perhaps a valuable one. Oh, I don't like seeing my sister deceived, but she *did* put Julia's fears to rest, at least temporarily. She told Julia what she needed to hear, and in a way Julia would not have listened to coming from the rest of us."

A retort—not aimed at Lady Phoebe but at the situation—rose to Eva's lips, but she held it back. Could lies, an out-and-out hoax, ever be beneficial? It was true that Lady Julia hadn't listened to anyone who tried to comfort her over the death of her husband and the circumstances that led to her marrying him. Perhaps she'd needed an outsider, someone she could believe held an objective view, even if deep down she hadn't truly believed she had been communicating with her deceased husband. As for the baby . . .

Believing it to be a boy could lead to a vast disappointment in a few months, but perhaps by then it wouldn't matter so much. Lady Julia had made it clear she wished for a boy to carry on her husband's title of Viscount Annondale, and also to secure her own financial stability. The latter would lift a burden from her brother's eventual inheritance, especially since changing times had left the family finances sorely depleted compared to prewar standards. With a baby girl, Julia would inherit a stipend from her husband's estate, and Eva assumed a similar arrangement would be passed on to a daughter. But control of the title and fortune would pass to Gilbert Townsend's cousin and closest male heir, Ernest Shelton, who would have no reason, really, to share his good fortune with either Lady Julia or her child.

Still, Eva firmly believed that once Lady Julia beheld her infant, boy or girl, all other matters would melt away and she would fall deeply and irrevocably in love. Financial issues would settle themselves.

"I'm sorry, Eva." Lady Phoebe hopped up from the bench and retrieved her overcoat from the dressing room. "I said we'd go out to your parents' farm this afternoon. Any word from the constable?"

"It's all right, we needn't go today. You're tired."

"Nonsense. I'm fine. It was just such a shock, discovering the purpose for our ride to Cheltenham. Leave it to Julia to turn Grams's suggestion into something nefarious. But I don't suppose she could have just come out and announced she wished to consult a fortune-teller. Oh, excuse me. Miss Greenwood made it clear she was no such thing. But she could have fooled me. Now, go and get your things, and I'll send for the Vauxhall to be brought back around." She hurried over to the window. "Ah, no need, it hasn't been put away yet. I'll go down now and meet you outside."

"My lady, really—"

"You want to help Mr. Ripley, don't you?"

Eva wasn't so sure. If Alice had been Keenan's morning visitor yesterday, she could provide him with an alibi. But at what cost? Her marriage, her reputation, not to mention causing their parents a good deal of distress.

Eva was up in her room gathering her things when the telephone call came. Connie, the head housemaid, came running up from belowstairs and breathlessly told her Miles had left a brief message. Keenan had been arrested.

She barely noticed the trip to the farm—neither the speed of the Vauxhall nor the ragged condition of the road. When they reached the house, Lady Phoebe didn't climb out of the car. "I'll find an errand or two to do in the village. I could check on the RCVF donations and see if anything else needs sorting. What do you think, will an hour do?"

"That should do fine, my lady. Wish me luck." Although what sort of luck Eva would need, she couldn't have said. And if there had been any form of luck in this business, Stephen Ripley would still be alive, Keenan a free man, and Alice at home with her family.

She found Alice and their mum in the kitchen preparing dinner. Dad, apparently, was still out in the pastures with the cattle, gathering them into the closest pasture for the night. Peeled potatoes sat in a pot of cold water while Alice sliced the skin from a few more, and Mum was cleaning a chicken. They both stopped what they were doing upon Eva's unexpected entrance, washed their hands, cleared space at the table, and set a kettle on to boil.

"What a lovely surprise," Mum exclaimed as she bustled

into the larder for a tin of biscuits. "We didn't expect to see you again until Sunday. Oh, but it's such a treat to have my two girls home together."

"I hope nothing is wrong." Alice brought out the creamer and then went into the pantry for the sugar. "As if our little village didn't have enough upset, what with Stephen Ripley's death. Have they figured out what happened yet? It's not like a gardener to fall off his ladder like that."

So the chief inspector had spread the same story among the villagers as the Foxwood Hall servants. Though Eva was no admirer of the man, she couldn't blame him for his white lie to prevent gossip and panic from spreading, at least initially. Then again, he might merely have wished to put his suspect at ease in the hopes he would grow careless. Did Chief Inspector Perkins possess such cleverness? Up until now, Eva would have said no. Now that an arrest had been made, however, there would be no hiding the facts.

"Stephen didn't fall," she told them.

"What do you mean?" Holding the biscuit tin, Mum went to the table and lowered herself into a chair. She held the tin absently in her lap.

"He was pushed. But not only that. He was stabbed as well. With his own hedge clippers."

"Good heavens." Alice, too, pulled out a chair and sat. "Who on earth would do such a thing?"

"Brace yourselves." Eva sat beside her mother, took the tin out of her hands, and placed it on the table. "Keenan has been arrested."

The color draining from her face, Alice jumped to her feet. "Keenan couldn't have done it. He simply could not have."

Phoebe left the Vauxhall in front of St. George's with every intention of going down to the church basement and taking an inventory of the donations that had been brought in since the last time she'd been there. Instead she found herself drawn to the foot traffic that moved in one distinct direction, like a flotilla caught in a swift channel. If she didn't know better, she'd have estimated half the men of the village to be making their way toward the other end of High Road—to the location of the police station.

There were women present, too, but rather than follow their husbands they stood apart, watching, whispering among themselves, and looking fretful. No one seemed to notice Phoebe's arrival, in itself saying much, for it was a rare day when she or members of her family went unrecognized in the village. People usually went out of their way to bid them good day and express their well wishes with an odd combination of friendliness and formality.

By now they must all know Keenan Ripley had been arrested, then. But why this mass migration to Little Barlow's tiny police station? What could they hope to accomplish? Burning to know, Phoebe decided to approach the nearest farmwife for answers, but just then the rectory door opened and the vicar's wife, Violet Hershel, walked briskly down her garden path. She noticed Phoebe immediately and checked her momentum.

"Lady Phoebe, I see you've noticed . . ." She raised a hand to indicate the flow of male pedestrians.

"I have indeed. What is going on, Mrs. Hershel?"

The woman, some twenty years older than Phoebe, was thin, coifed, and wore a tailored day frock of good, if not the best quality, paisley cotton. She rubbed her palms together before folding her hands at her waist. "Keenan Ripley has been arrested for the murder. Isn't it awful, Lady Phoebe? He always seemed like such a nice young man."

"I heard about it this morning." As soon as Phoebe spoke, she wished she hadn't, for she was fairly certain Constable Brannock had telephoned Eva on the sly earlier.

But Mrs. Hershel was too engrossed in the goings on down the road to bother asking Phoebe where she had heard the news.

"I do hope it's all a mistake," the woman said. "And after Mr. Ripley's very kind donation to your RCVF charity drive—why, how could anyone believe such a man could commit murder? And his own brother, no less."

"I agree, Mrs. Hershel. But do you know why all those men are headed to the police station? That *is* where they're going, isn't it? Or has something else happened?" That thought made her hold her breath in apprehension.

"I wish I could answer that, Lady Phoebe. You see, I was just arranging some flowers in my parlor, and happened to glance out the window. That's when I saw all these people converge on the village. I agree with you; they can only have one destination in mind—Chief Inspector Perkins's office." She glanced at the church behind her. "I do wish Mr. Hershel was back from Gloucester, so I could send him to find out exactly what is going on."

"Why wait?" Phoebe took several steps in the general direction of the police station.

"Lady Phoebe, you mustn't. It wouldn't be proper. Especially for a young lady like yourself. What *would* your grandmother say?"

"Don't worry, Mrs. Hershel, I can handle my grandmother." Phoebe spoke with undue bravado, but she'd worry about Grams later. She had the strangest sensation that something was about to happen that had never happened before in Little Barlow.

She wasn't far wrong. She hurried down the pavement to the police station, which was in fact merely a shop that had been converted into a front office and a single rear "cell," which had once been a storeroom. Little Barlow's constabulary was an outpost of the Greater Gloucestershire

Constabulary, and Phoebe had always wondered what sin, great or small, had landed Chief Inspector Isaac Perkins so far from more illustrious duty.

That gentleman, along with his assistant, Constable Brannock, stood outside the station as a deep chorus of voices bombarded them. In vain the chief inspector held up his hands to forestall the jumble of questions and demands that came flying at him. From her stance across the street, Phoebe could make out words here and there, but nothing that made sense. She crept closer until she stood at the edge of the crowd, just as she had done when Keenan Ripley had his argument with Mr. Evers and that beastly American land developer.

What she now heard shocked her.

And elated her.

"You're wrong about Keenan, Chief Inspector. I was with him that morning. I came by to order my next shipment of perry." The owner of the baritone was Joe Murdock, proprietor of the Houndstooth Inn and Tavern. A white apron stretched across his barrel chest and draped over his long legs to cover his work clothes, as if he had quickly dried his hands and raced out from behind the oak bar in his public room.

"That's right, and after Joe left Keenan, I passed by the orchard and saw Keenan out among the trees. He was harvesting pears like he does every September." The man who spoke warmed to his explanation. "You see, Inspector Perkins, you can't wait until the fruit falls from the tree, because then it's overripe and not good for perry. Keenan knows exactly the right moment to pick them, and that's why his perry is the best."

The chief inspector merely scowled his acknowledgment of this piece of information.

"And before that," another fellow called out, "I delivered mulch for the orchard. Keenan and I spoke. There is no way he'd have had time to go to the Hall for any reason, much less murder."

One after another, the men of the village provided Keenan Ripley with alibis. The chief inspector took it all in with a bemused expression, while Constable Brannock regarded their "witnesses" with no small show of skepticism as he jotted down each word. As much as Phoebe wished to welcome these developments, she, too, had her doubts.

The one person who might legitimately provide Keenan Ripley with an alibi could, at this very moment, be explaining her actions to her own sister, Eva. The fact that Mr. Ripley's friends and neighbors were attempting to extricate him from his jail cell proved that whoever had visited Mr. Ripley that morning had done so in secret. And secrets usually meant nothing good. Worry for Eva, her sister, and their families welled up inside Phoebe and warred with her hopes that Mr. Ripley would be exonerated.

Her gaze landed on a dark-haired man who, like her, stood on the sidelines. He watched the others intently, and once or twice he appeared about to speak, yet held his tongue and pressed his lips together. Phoebe recognized him as Fred Corbyn, who owned the farm neighboring Mr. Ripley's orchard, and who depended on grazing rights to Mr. Ripley's northeast pasture for his sheep.

Alibis continued to be offered at what could be considered a comical rate, but the voices faded from Phoebe's ears as she studied Mr. Corbyn. His expression guarded, he shuffled his feet as if in a hurry to be off, and every now and again he balled his hands into fists. Anxiety? Fear? He had a lot to lose should Keenan Ripley be declared guilty and his orchard go on the auction block. Could Mr. Corbyn afford to purchase the pasture outright? Phoebe didn't think so, especially with a wealthy American developer eager to acquire the land. And that meant he'd had reason to want Stephen Ripley out of the way.

Deciding she could learn little more from her present position, she backed away from the gathering. Many of the men's wives continued watching from a distance, their necks craning and their expressions eager. They too must have wished for Keenan Ripley's release; his perry made for happy menfolk, which in turn made for happy households. Phoebe scanned their faces, her gaze lighting on Fred Corbyn's wife. A sturdy farm woman whose reddish brown curls were pulled back in a loose bun and secured by a kerchief, she lingered in the midst of several other women, yet somehow Phoebe had the impression that Mrs. Corbyn stood apart from the rest. Like her husband, she seemed tense, anxious, and watched her husband fixedly, as if afraid of taking her gaze off him.

But of course, this could mean nothing more than the Corbyns fearing the loss of an essential part of their livelihood. Phoebe backtracked along the road and approached the woman.

"Mrs. Corbyn."

Startled, the farmwife flinched and blinked as she tore her attention away from her husband. "Lady Phoebe. Forgive me, I didn't see you coming."

"I just wished to thank you for your help the other day."

"Help?"

"With the donations."

"Ah, yes. You're welcome."

Phoebe gestured to the gathering at the police station. "It's noble, what they're trying to do here."

Mrs. Corbyn pinched her lips. "Foolishness, if you ask me."

"They're trying to help their friend."

"Excuse me for saying so, Lady Phoebe, but they're trying to save their supply of perry."

"That may be, but if it helps an innocent man, so much the better, no?"

"You're right, of course." Mrs. Corbyn sighed and shook her head. When she spoke again, Phoebe had to strain her ears to hear. "But some fools can't accept change, even when it's for the best." Louder, she said, "If you'll excuse me, Lady Phoebe, it's time to collect my boys from school." With that, Elaina Corbyn turned on her heel.

Phoebe turned back to the commotion in time to see the chief inspector wave his meaty hands to encourage the men to disperse. "All right, that's enough from you lot. We'll take this all into consideration."

He didn't sound very convincing, and murmurs of dissatisfaction accompanied the men as they moved off. One by one the wives reclaimed their husbands, slipping their arms through theirs and hurrying them away. Some climbed into conveyances. Others set off on foot down Little Barlow's narrow side streets and lanes.

Phoebe consulted her locket watch. She had been gone from the Huntfords' farm a little more than half an hour. To pass the remaining time, she doubled back to the church to attend to the errand that had originally brought her into the village.

"Alice, what did you mean?" Eva followed her sister outside and to the edge of the kitchen garden, laid out in its tidy rows that stretched nearly as far as the chicken coop. Alice opened the gate and went through as if on an urgent mission in search of vegetables—if a need for vegetables could *be* urgent. But she made no attempt to stoop and pluck ripened pole beans, radishes, cauliflower, or beetroot. She strode along with her arms crossed in front of her while Eva hurried to catch up.

Then Eva slowed. After all, a sturdy fence lined with chicken wire enclosed the garden, so eventually Alice would be forced to halt her retreat. Behind her, Eva said, "Please explain what you meant when you said Keenan couldn't have murdered Stephen. If you know something about his whereabouts that morning, you must say so."

Alice stopped beside a patch of bushy carrot greens and turned with a defiant expression. "I spoke out of shock, Evie. Of course he couldn't have done it. He's not the murdering type."

"I don't believe Keenan could have committed murder either. But there is more pointing to his innocence than that, although he's staying silent about it, apparently."

"And what is this evidence of yours?" Alice spoke with an edge of disdain. "You've become quite the detective in recent years, haven't you? You and your Lady Phoebe. Honestly, one or two correct hunches has quite gone to your head, hasn't it?"

Eva ignored the jibe. "The morning of the murder, I was in Keenan's cottage. Lady Phoebe and I went to tell Keenan about his brother's death. While we were there it was obvious he'd had company for breakfast."

"And? What of it?"

"We believe it was a woman, Alice."

"All right, then Keenan has a sweetheart. Perhaps she can vouch for his whereabouts that morning."

"Yes, perhaps she can." Eva looked pointedly at her sister and waited.

Alice's expression turned puzzled. Then understanding dawned on her features. "You think it was me?"

"Was it?"

"Certainly not. Why would you think that?"

"Were you home, here, that morning?"

"Of course I was. . . ." Alice trailed off, suddenly looking none too certain.

"Alice? Where were you?"

"Well . . . I went for a walk. Through the pastures."

"Which pastures?"

"Ours. Mum's and Dad's. And to Mrs. Verity's cottage. I wished to visit with her. She was delighted to see me, I'll have you know."

Mrs. Verity was an elderly widow who used to give piano lessons to the local girls along with teaching them useful skills such as sewing and gardening. Things their own mothers were sometimes too busy to show them. She had done so for very little pay, and that mostly in eggs and produce. These days, Eva occasionally stopped in to check on her as well. "Then you didn't wander onto Keenan's land?"

"No. Well, I don't know, I may have done. People do walk, Evie, and there aren't always distinct barriers. I might have crossed a few stone walls, I don't remember."

"Mrs. Verity doesn't live very far from here. Yet you took such a long walk you can't say where you went?"

"I needed to think."

"And did you bring a batch of scones with you?"

Alice once again gaped at Eva in puzzlement. Then anger spread a mottled blush across her face. "As a matter of fact, Evie, I did. Mum and I made scones that morning. Is it a crime to share them with dear old friends?"

"No, it's no crime."

"Then what *are* you going on about?"

"Only that you seemed to have walked farther that morning than Mrs. Verity's house. And someone visited Keenan and brought scones. Again, was it you, Alice?"

"You're out of line and I've had more than enough of this." She pushed past Eva and headed for the gate. There she stopped and whirled about. "I'm a married woman, and I very much resent your accusations." She opened the gate and resumed her course toward the house.

"Alice, wait." Her sister stopped again, but this time did not turn back around. Eva exited the garden after her.

"Why did you come to Little Barlow now? Why not wait for the holidays, when the whole family might have come?"

"I felt like getting away." The answer came from between clenched teeth.

"Yes, but why *now*? Is there . . . is there something wrong at home? Some reason you're not happy there? Troubles with Oliver? Is that the reason for your abrupt visit?"

"Abrupt visit?" Alice turned to face her, her eyebrows rising in scorn. "Am I not allowed to see my parents, my home? Really, Evie, you've taken leave of your senses, imagining all sorts of diabolical things where none exist. Leave it alone. If Keenan is innocent, which I believe he is, he'll come out all right in the end. But I've got nothing to do with it. Go back to Foxwood Hall, where you belong, and take your accusations and your insinuations with you."

Eva watched her stalk away. The encounter left her wretched, yet a little voice inside her continued to whisper that Alice hadn't been entirely truthful, that she had something she was determined to hide. And that made Eva fear for her sister, and for the future.

CHAPTER 8

In the morning, Phoebe once again steered the Vauxhall along the road to Cheltenham. Instead of Julia, it was Eva beside her, making a valiant effort not to appear frightened of the ride. Or perhaps her fears had abated, for Phoebe took special care with this journey, keeping light pressure on the gas pedal and rounding the bends cautiously.

It had been no easy task determining their destination. No one at home knew where Alfred Peele currently resided, except that he had moved in with his sister somewhere on the outskirts of Cheltenham. As they were about to give up on learning anything more, Phoebe remembered that Mr. Giles kept meticulous records on every employee on the estate, including the names and locations of their next of kin. At least, he used to do so, before he'd fallen off his usual routine. She and Eva had had to jog his memory of not only which file cabinet in his pantry held the information, but where he had stashed the key.

Before they could do that, however, Phoebe, with Eva's help, had had to persuade Mr. Giles of the necessity of divulging such personal information about the former head gardener. He might have become forgetful of daily occurrences, but he rigidly adhered to his principles.

On the south edge of the city, where the spires of the Chapel of St. Mary and St. George were silhouetted against a bright autumn sky, Phoebe headed east along the campus of Cheltenham College. She found her way to Sandford Road, and to a large, Victorian house sporting a turret and a wraparound veranda. Phoebe pulled up and cut the engine.

"This is it," she announced, and regarded the blue clapboard façade with its bright gingerbread trim. "Lovely."

Eva let herself out the passenger side and went around to help Phoebe out. "You said she takes in lodgers."

"Mr. Giles indicated she started doing so when her husband died. Mostly she lets to tutors from the school. And her brother now, too, apparently." She craned her neck as if that might help her to see through walls. "I do hope Mr. Peele is in."

They identified themselves to the girl who opened the door simply as Miss Shaw and Miss Huntford, friends of Mr. Peele's from Little Barlow. The girl invited them into a comfortably appointed receiving parlor and disappeared down a hallway. Moments later an elderly woman greeted them. She wore a fashionable if ready-made day dress, low pumps, and a conservative string of pearls around her neck. She was Mr. Peele's sister, Mrs. Riordan, she told them, and offered them tea. They declined, and the woman's countenance turned serious.

"You say you are friends of my brother."

"That's right," Phoebe said. "Is he in?"

The woman's dark, slightly bloodshot eyes regarded her. Her head tilted. "You're Lady Phoebe."

"Oh." The heat of embarrassment flooded Phoebe's

face. "Yes, I am. I'm sorry for not saying so directly, but I didn't wish to upset the household routine. How did you recognize me?"

The woman's lips curled in a shrewd smile. "From your description, of course. My brother has often written about you, all of you, at Foxwood Hall. Now that he's here, you are all he talks about." She held out a hand, gesturing for Phoebe and Eva to sit. She chose a seat for herself in a delicate armchair that faced away from the front windows, throwing her lined face into shadow. Phoebe noticed she moved with confident grace, and she guessed Mr. Peele's sister hadn't always had to take in borders, not until widowhood had forced the issue. She wondered what Mr. Riordan's profession had been. "I believe my brother is sorry he left his position," she said.

The woman's candor encouraged Phoebe to ask, "Did he say *why* he left?"

"Only that it was time he retired. I believe something is troubling him and I've tried to find out what, but he only tells me not to worry." Mrs. Riordan's gaze sharpened. "He's not ill, is he? It would be so like Alfred not to tell anyone if he were seriously ill."

"No," Phoebe hastened to reassure her, then settled back in her chair. "At least, not that I know of. That might explain things. . . ." But on second thought, she shook her head. "No, his leaving Foxwood Hall coincided with the arrival of a former village man who immediately took over the position. It all seemed rather rushed and . . . well . . . odd."

"Odd how, Lady Phoebe?"

Phoebe exchanged a glance with Eva, who nodded her encouragement. "The truth is, Mrs. Riordan, the new head gardener died three days ago. Under suspicious circumstances."

"Good heavens." The woman's hand went to her pearls.

Her initial shock quickly gave way to caution. "I assure you, my brother was already living here at that time. I can vouch for him. So if you're thinking . . ."

"No, we're most certainly not." Phoebe raised the flats of her hands to avert the very notion. "Mr. Peele put in too many years of good service for any of us at Foxwood Hall to suspect him of something as heinous as murder. We are here merely to ask him why he left us so suddenly, and whether anyone, such as the man who died, persuaded him to go."

"And another thing," Eva put in, speaking for the first time. She crossed her ankles and leaned slightly forward in a manner that invited confidence. "There is the matter of his young assistant, William. Perhaps Mr. Peele has mentioned him?" The woman nodded, and Eva continued. "He's been missing since the new head gardener died. He's just a boy, you see. Perhaps your brother might know where we can find him."

One hand still touching her pearls as if they provided comfort, Mrs. Riordan studied Phoebe and Eva silently, her tired eyes running over them repeatedly while she appeared to weigh her options. Finally, she stood. "Follow me, please."

She led them through the house and out to the garden. A table and chairs filled one corner of a flagstone terrace. Two wide steps led down to a gravel path that meandered through manicured shrubbery, various species of rosebushes, and flower beds that encircled shade trees touched with autumn fire. The steady sound of raking drew Phoebe's gaze across the garden, where, beside a freshly painted shed, Mr. Peele toiled to gather up the clippings of a box hedge. He might have retired from his position at Foxwood Hall, but he certainly hadn't lost his love of gardening. Or perhaps after so many years he simply didn't know how else to occupy his time.

His sister called to him, and he looked up to regard Phoebe and Eva with astonishment. "Why, Lady Phoebe. And Miss Huntford. Whatever are you doing here?" He pulled off his work gloves and dropped them to the ground.

When he joined them on the terrace, they took seats around the table. Again, Phoebe and Eva declined Mrs. Riordan's offer of tea. Phoebe folded her hands on the iron tabletop. "Mr. Peele, many of us at Foxwood Hall, both above and below stairs, were dismayed at your leaving. It was all so sudden."

"Yes, I'm terribly sorry about that, my lady. I . . . decided it was simply time to move on."

Phoebe tried to school the doubt from her expression as she once again wondered why a man retired without having secured a home of his own. A lesser servant, perhaps, who hadn't laid enough money by, might retire and move in with relatives. But not a head gardener who had held his position for nearly two decades. When upper servants retired, they tended to have their latter years carefully planned out—home, expenditures, even hobbies, leaving little to chance. A servant who couldn't determine the course of his future simply didn't retire, unless he became so infirm as to be incapable of performing his duties. But that didn't appear to be the case here, for Mr. Peele seemed as fit as he had ever been.

While he continued to explain his actions in the vaguest of terms and apologize for his haste in leaving Little Barlow, Phoebe decided it was time to take a more direct approach. "Mr. Peele, did Stephen Ripley coerce you into leaving Foxwood Hall? Did he threaten you?"

His mouth became a thin line and he dropped his gaze. Phoebe believed she had her answer, or at least part of it, although she could guess at the rest. A glance at Eva suggested she, too, could fill in the blanks.

"Alfred." His sister's voice held a note of alarm. "Is this true? Were you threatened?"

"It was nothing as sinister as all that." He reached over to pat her hand.

"Do not patronize me," she snapped, and slid her hand free with a show of wounded dignity. "Why else would you leave your very good position at Foxwood Hall, a situation you loved, by your own account, to come molder here with me?"

Sunlight gleamed on his silver hair and he looked down at the table in defeat. He let go a sigh. "I merely made room for a younger man."

"Stephen Ripley," Phoebe persisted.

He nodded. "Yes, a well-qualified gardener who needed the position more than I did."

"Is that what he told you?" Eva asked quietly. "Or is that what you told yourself, Mr. Peele, to make leaving more palatable?"

"Please tell us what happened," Phoebe urged him.

With another, heavier sigh, he launched into his story. "Stephen Ripley began by writing to me, telling me urgent family business was bringing him back to Little Barlow, and that when he arrived he wished to speak to me directly. I was puzzled, to say the least. I couldn't for the life of me imagine how I could help him with family business. It's not as though I knew the Ripleys well at all. When he and I met nearly two weeks ago, he told me his brother had made a hash of the orchard and brewery, and that the bank would be foreclosing. While I sympathized, again I didn't see what any of it had to do with me. Then he told me he needed employment to help manage the bills, and that if he had a good position with steady income, the bank would be willing to negotiate with him."

"Didn't it seem strange to you that he didn't go to work

with his brother and try to make their brewing business solvent?" Phoebe asked.

"It did, indeed, Lady Phoebe. And I said as much. And that's when . . ."

"What did he do?" Eva prompted him when he compressed his lips.

"Yes, all right, he made threats. Said he'd find a way to get William fired, and even make trouble for his parents. He said he knew something damaging about William's father, and about other servants at Foxwood Hall. He wouldn't tell me what, but something in his eyes made me believe he'd make good on his threats."

The more Phoebe learned about Stephen Ripley, the more she realized he must have made many enemies, both here in the Cotswolds and at his former home in Dorset. She wondered how two brothers could be so different, and what drove a man like Stephen Ripley to wreak such havoc among well-meaning, law-abiding people. "You should have gone to my grandfather."

The man shook his head. "Forgive me for saying it, but the earl isn't a young man anymore. Neither am I. I thought it best to go rather than bring trouble upon William's family and the others Stephen promised to hurt. He promised me he'd do his best as a gardener, and he did bring a glowing recommendation with him from Dorset. Even your grandfather thought so."

His sister cast a stern look at Phoebe. "I think you should tell him what's happened since."

Mr. Peele looked mystified at that, and Phoebe nodded. "Mr. Peele, Stephen Ripley is dead. He was murdered three days ago."

The former gardener clutched at his chest. "Murdered. Dear Lord. How?"

"With his own clipping shears," Eva told him. "And now we can't find William and we're very worried about him.

Do you know where the boy might go if he were frightened and wished to hide?"

"Do you think William did this?" Mr. Peele spoke with disbelief.

"In all honesty, we don't know." Phoebe tipped her head in apology. "But we—Eva and I—don't believe so, and neither do the police, apparently. They have arrested Keenan Ripley." As Mr. Peele's mouth dropped open, Phoebe hurried on. "We don't think he's guilty either. We don't know who did this. Yet," she added pointedly.

Mr. Peele looked down at his hands, thick, callused, and mottled with old scars. "I feel I made a terrible mistake leaving as I did."

"We understand Stephen wanted your position," Eva said, "but why *such* urgency that you had to leave without bidding everyone good-bye?"

"Stephen made his threats and ordered me gone. I thought, if I had to face all of you belowstairs, someone would see in my expression that I didn't wish to leave. And then they'd start asking questions, and trouble would follow. I thought it best simply to go."

Phoebe leaned back and considered. Then, to Eva, she said, "Stephen Ripley played his hand well, at least that far. He wanted Mr. Peele out of the way quickly and succeeded in that, but why?"

"It must have had something to do with the sale of the orchard," Eva said.

"The sale of the orchard?" Obviously, this additional news took Mr. Peele by surprise. "From what I understand, Keenan Ripley would never sell that land. It's his birthright."

Phoebe took a moment to explain the situation. Then she added, "Stephen needed immediate employment, but why? It wasn't to prevent the orchard from going on the auction block."

Eva frowned in concentration. "Perhaps it wasn't a straightforward sale. Perhaps Stephen wasn't actually relinquishing his share in the orchard, but was going to remain as a stakeholder."

"In that case, the bank might require a source of income on record," Mrs. Riordan suggested, her expression once again shrewd.

Her brother nodded his agreement. "It could well have been an arrangement like that, especially if the orchard was losing money. All interested parties would need to show themselves to be self-sufficient, at least until the business was back on its feet." His fist came down lightly on the table. "That swindler, trying to cheat his brother that way. I wish I *had* gone to your grandfather. And I wish I'd refused to leave my job. I should have stood up to that mongrel."

"And it might have been you lying in the morgue," his sister pointed out matter-of-factly. "The man obviously lacked scruples. I say he got what was coming to him."

"Now, Catherine, you mustn't say things like that," he admonished, but with a gleam in his eye that said otherwise.

"Mr. Peele, now that you know what happened," Phoebe said, "will you consider returning to work at Foxwood Hall?"

"Perhaps, if your grandfather wishes it."

"Oh, he will. I know he will."

"Do something for me, Alfred." His sister took on a look of fierce intensity. "Do not return to Little Barlow until this matter is cleared up. You're involved after all, and . . . have you considered that you, Alfred, might be seen as having had a motive to murder this Ripley fellow?"

"Good heavens, that's very true." Mr. Peele turned back to Phoebe and said quickly, "I was here, of course, by the time he died, but . . ."

"No one thinks you had a hand in his death," she assured him. But privately Phoebe realized that if enough evidence surfaced to exonerate Keenan Ripley, the chief inspector would be forced to seek new suspects. Would he turn his attention to the former head gardener?

His sister looked dubious. "Better to stay here in the meantime, Alfred. As for you, Lady Phoebe, I should think you'll want to speak with the banker and that American." Mrs. Riordan shook her head and scoffed. "Americans. They've no respect for tradition and certainly no sense of fair play."

"I wouldn't go so far as to say that, ma'am." Phoebe suppressed a chuckle. "But yes, you're right about this particular American, *and* Stephen Ripley."

"True, but there's someone lurking in Little Barlow who's even worse than Stephen Ripley." When all gazes converged on Eva, she clarified, "There's still a murderer about, isn't there? We mustn't forget that Stephen Ripley was a victim who paid for his sins with his very life."

On the drive back to Little Barlow, Eva and Lady Phoebe discussed what they had learned from Mr. Peele. Neither had been surprised that Stephen Ripley had used threats, both subtle and overt, to persuade the former gardener to retire.

"One thing I'm not sure I believe, my lady." Eva thought back to exactly what Mr. Peele had said. "This damaging information about William's father. I'm not at all convinced Stephen could have known anything about Ezra Gaff. The man is a farm laborer. He's lived in Little Barlow all his life, while Stephen was gone for many years. What could Stephen possibly have known that the rest of the villagers didn't?"

"It could be something that happened during the war," Lady Phoebe mused.

"I suppose, but I think that when Mr. Peele showed hesitation about retiring, Stephen Ripley thought up a vague lie to increase the pressure. And it certainly worked. He was clever, my lady."

Lady Phoebe smirked. "Not so clever that he avoided being murdered."

Upon returning to Foxwood Hall and slipping belowstairs to prepare tea for herself and Lady Phoebe, Eva waded into chaos. Not a single smile or *good afternoon* greeted her, and, if she weren't mistaken, more than one housemaid and kitchen assistant peered at her through swollen, reddened eyes. Several of the footmen scowled and grumbled beneath their breath as they passed her in the corridor. Raised voices clashed in the kitchen, angry words grating one against another in a bid to be heard.

Eva went into the main kitchen to discover Mrs. Sanders and Mrs. Ellison poised on either side of the center worktable, leaning toward each other in a standoff, with their necks craned and their fists propped on the marble surface.

"Foodstuffs don't simply walk off," Mrs. Sanders pronounced in a voice that declared this a battleground.

"I never said they did." Mrs. Ellison's chubby jowls shook with indignation. "What I said was no one in my kitchen took them, and I won't tolerate your accusations."

"I haven't made any accusations." The housekeeper raised her hands in frustration, and failed to notice the traces of flour that transferred from the marble surface to the sleeves of her black serge dress. "I only said you need to supervise your staff and tighten security."

"Oh, indeed. If that isn't accusing me of running a shoddy kitchen, I don't know what is."

"Can you deny items are missing?"

Mrs. Ellison plunked her hands on her stout hips. "Can you assure me one of the upstairs staff isn't to blame? I can't be here keeping watch all night long, can I?"

In all her years at Foxwood Hall, Eva had never seen a serious incident of theft. Oh, there had been that Christmas when Connie, then new to the staff, had been handing out kitchen scraps to the village's poorest children, but that food would have been scraped into the bins otherwise. Eva wouldn't call that theft. But in some large houses, dishonest servants did steal supplies and sell them on the sly, undercutting market prices by a good margin and pocketing pure profits. She couldn't believe something like that could happen here. Foxwood Hall had always been a fair place to work, where upper and lower servants alike were treated with more regard than they had reason to expect.

Seeing no resolution to this present argument, she went to stand at the end of the worktable—neutral territory between the two women. "Ladies, what is this about? You never have words like this. And why is everyone so upset? Surely you're not accusing all of them of stealing."

Mrs. Sanders straightened. Looking down, she finally noticed the dusting of flour on her sleeves and angrily slapped at the fabric as if at a naughty child. "Everyone is a suspect until we find our culprit."

"I saw that several maids have been crying." Eva shook her head at Mrs. Sanders. "Was that necessary?"

"That's what I'd like to know." Mrs. Ellison, whose apron had slipped askew, tugged it back into place. "We're no closer to revealing our thief, but we now have a houseful of unhappy workers." That last was addressed to Mrs. Sanders. Now she turned to Eva. "You might want to have a talk with Hetta. Try to soothe her. The poor lamb left here positively distraught."

"You accused Hetta?" Eva propped her elbows on the table and dropped her head into her hands. "Mrs. Sanders, what were you thinking? Hetta wouldn't stick a toe out of line. She values her position much too highly."

"She's the newest member of the staff and has the privilege of being able to come and go as she pleases," the woman said defensively. "That gives her plenty of opportunity."

Eva lifted her head. "That privilege, as you call it, is in service to Lady Annondale. If Hetta leaves the property, it's on an errand for her mistress. She certainly wouldn't have time to hunt down black-market buyers, even if she possessed the necessary English to do so." Swiss born Hetta Brauer, while understanding more English than Lady Annondale had believed when she had first hired her, still found conversing fluently in the language an arduous task.

"What sorts of things have gone missing?" Eva asked in an attempt to make sense of the circumstances.

"It began with the dates Dora picked for me the other day," Mrs. Ellison said.

"And it's escalated to cheese—whole rings of it—along with eggs, apples, dried fish, loaves of bread. . . ."

"It sounds like things that don't need much preparation," Eva noted. "And have you tried assigning someone to guard the pantries?"

"We haven't had time," Mrs. Ellison said, once more on the defensive. "This has only just come to light."

"Perhaps if you'd been more aware of who was coming and going in your kitchen and larders, we'd have discovered the situation sooner." Mrs. Sanders gave her steely gray bun a dignified pat.

Realizing she wasn't getting anywhere—indeed, the damage with the staff had already been done—Eva sighed, filled a tea kettle, and set it on the range. Lady Phoebe had sent her down with a request for tea, and she'd already taken far longer than necessary. While the water came to a boil, she went about gathering the necessary items—cups and saucers, cutlery, serviettes. She sliced two pieces of lemon poppy seed cake, set it on a platter, and filled in the remaining space with shortbread biscuits. As she set this on the waiting tray, Dora came into the kitchen.

"Perhaps Eva's our thief," she said bitterly. Eva perceived that Dora's sarcasm wasn't aimed at her and didn't take offense. Adjusting the kerchief that kept her limp hair out of the food preparations, the girl directed a caustic glance at Mrs. Sanders and swept past into the scullery. The clanging of pots and pans voiced Dora's, and probably many of the servants', frustrations at being held in suspicion.

A weighty tray in hand, Eva took the back staircase up to the first floor and pushed her way through the swinging door into the corridor that housed the family's bedrooms. She met Lady Annondale coming out of hers.

"Eva, I'm glad I ran into you. Would you please speak to Hetta for me? You and she are able to communicate. I can't seem to make her believe she's not getting the sack. And I can't for the life of me understand why she's come to such a ridiculous conclusion."

"I'll see to it, my lady. Apparently there's been some thieving down in the pantries, and Mrs. Sanders has taken the approach of everyone being guilty until proven innocent."

"Oh, dear. Perhaps I should speak to my grandmother about this."

Eva judged that to be the last thing anyone belowstairs needed. "I wouldn't, except as a last resort. I'm sure Mrs. Sanders and Mrs. Ellison will have matters in hand before too long."

"I daresay you're right about that. But don't let me keep you. That tray looks heavy." She extended a manicured hand to remove the cover from the platter. "Mmmm . . . I trust you won't mind if I just . . ." With her free hand, she took two of the shortbread biscuits. "I'd take one of those slices of cake, but I fear you'd have to give the other one to

Phoebe and go without yourself. Go on then, Eva, enjoy your tea and whatever schemes you and my sister are currently hatching."

Deciding not to respond to that last comment, Eva moved on to Lady Phoebe's room while Lady Annondale traversed the corridor to the gallery. Eva heard her descending tread on the grand staircase. She chuckled to herself. The typically restrained Julia Renshaw Townsend had not only acquired quite an appetite due to being with child, but had developed an insatiable sweet tooth as well. Luckily for her, her hips had yet to betray the fact.

CHAPTER 9

"Eva, do relax and tell me what's troubling you." Phoebe took another bite of cake and let the moist, lemony flavor melt over her tongue. No one made lemon poppy seed cake like Mrs. Ellison and Phoebe never tired of it.

Across the little table from her, Eva sat as stiffly upright as always, not allowing her spine to touch the petit-point back of the armchair. She raised her teacup to her lips for a small sip and lowered it back to the saucer with the tiniest of clinks. No matter how intimate they had become during their exploits of the past two years, Eva remained careful not to cross the line between mistress and servant and never presumed to be Phoebe's equal. And while Phoebe understood the importance of maintaining employer-employee relationships, in her point of view the difference between her and Eva was just that, while Eva, born in an earlier time, couldn't quite shake old notions of being born to one's station in life.

Phoebe smiled across the space between them. "And I don't mean the unrest belowstairs. It's more than that on your mind. I can tell."

A faint glow came into Eva's cheeks. "You know me too well, my lady."

"Yes, I do. So please stop being so formal, sit back, and talk to me."

Eva glanced wistfully out the wide window beside them, which overlooked the front park, the winding drive, and, more distantly, the Cotswold Hills, each day clad more and more brightly in shades of russet and gold. "It's my sister. I didn't tell you everything after I spoke with her."

"No, I sensed you were holding back. Was it very dreadful?"

"It was, rather. She's frightfully angry with me for making insinuations, yet for all her protests, I don't believe I was far off the mark."

Phoebe studied Eva's countenance as Eva's gaze was once more drawn to the scene outside the window. "If at all."

Eva nodded. "Indeed. And the thought of her being willing to see Keenan condemned for murder in order to protect herself from scandal is"—she sighed—"intolerable."

"She did deny outright being at Mr. Ripley's house that morning. She could be telling the truth. And that would certainly account for her anger with you. From what you told me about what went on belowstairs, plenty of the staff are good and angry about being accused of stealing. It's only natural when one knows one is innocent."

"Yes, all that's true. But Alice didn't or couldn't persuade me of *her* innocence. She couldn't even account for her time that morning. She visited with an elderly neighbor and claims to have gone on a long walk afterward."

"Is that so outlandish?"

"I've never known Alice to be one for long walks. Industry, yes, but not idle walking. She likes to keep busy. And her reasons for coming to Little Barlow so suddenly were equally vague. It leads me to believe there are problems at home."

"Problems she doesn't wish to talk about." Phoebe sipped her tea, a spicy chai blend she had recently discovered to be her favorite. Perhaps she should have purchased some at the tea shop in Cheltenham. Would Julia insist on another visit to see the fortune-teller? "But that, too, is understandable. If she came here to work out those problems, she probably doesn't wish to discuss them just now. And being accused of carrying on with another man would certainly anger her."

"That's why this is troubling me so. Either Alice is . . . well . . . lying, or I've done my sister a great wrong. Either way, there is no good end to this."

"Of course there is. Truth will out, Eva. And if you're wrong, your sister will forgive you."

"Will she, my lady? I have no guarantee that I haven't done irreparable harm to our relationship."

A reassurance was on Phoebe's tongue, but died there. How could she assure Eva of a sister's love when she and her own sister often skirted one another like skittish rabbits? Her younger sister, Amelia, was another story entirely. Phoebe couldn't imagine darling, tenderhearted Amelia ever holding a grudge against anyone, much less a family member, but Phoebe and Julia enjoyed a tenuous camaraderie at best.

"I'll tell you what," she said at length. "Why let things between you and Mrs. Ward fester? Take a couple of hours off this afternoon and visit her. I'll even drive you over."

"Oh, no, I couldn't impose."

"About taking time off or my driving you?"

"Either. Your grandfather doesn't pay me to visit my family during the week. It wouldn't be right."

"Pish posh, as Julia would say. My grandfather is no tyrant. Besides, after last spring you can do no wrong in his eyes."

"I don't like to take advantage of his goodwill. Or yours."

"Again I say pish posh. Let's finish our tea and go."

Eva reached for another shortbread biscuit. "If you don't mind, my lady, I'd prefer to walk. If you can spare me long enough, that is."

"Oh, Eva, does my motoring frighten you that much?"

"Not at all." Phoebe was sure she was lying until Eva continued. "Walking will give me the time to consider what I'd like to say to Alice, and how I might make things right between us."

Phoebe couldn't argue with that.

"But first . . ." Eva set her plate aside. "I need to talk to Hetta and convince her she's not getting the sack."

"Not trouble with Julia, I hope?"

"No, it's the same bee that's under all the servants' bonnets. Apparently Mrs. Sanders questioned Hetta about the missing food items and Hetta's got it into her head she's being blamed."

"Oh, dear. Well, if anyone can set her mind to rest, it's you. Why don't you see to that now and then go on to your parents' farm. Are you sure you don't want me to drive you out?"

Eva thanked her again, declined the offer, and hurriedly left on her errands, once more leaving Phoebe less than confident about Eva's faith in her motoring abilities.

Ah, well. She went to her writing table and began making notations about the RCVF donation dispersal, which would begin soon. As with William Gaff's family, there were others who were not on the main list of recipients, but whom Phoebe wished included. Some of them had written to her with appeals for assistance; others had been recommended by friends and neighbors; still others Phoebe had identified for herself. Without her explicit instructions, however, most of those families would be overlooked, not out of any malice, but in the spirit of caution and not wishing to squander the community's largesse on those who were not deserving. The families Phoebe added to the list were indeed deserving, and once she placed her initials beside their names, no one would think to question the additions.

She was halfway through reviewing the requests and recommendations when someone rapped at her door. An instant later, Julia walked in.

"Are you busy?"

"Yes, actually. I'm going over potential beneficiaries for the RCVF."

"Ah. You can do that later. Come to my room, please."

"Julia, really, I'd like to get this done."

"This has to do with your little hobby, in a way." Julia tapped the toe of her house slipper on the carpet, prompting Phoebe to sigh and set down her pen.

"All right. What's so urgent?"

Julia replied by turning on her heel and exiting the room, apparently expecting Phoebe to follow. With another sigh, she did. On the way down the corridor, she privately berated herself for not standing up to Julia when she did, indeed, have important work to do. But her conversation with Eva remained fresh in her mind, and Phoebe couldn't but admit her compliance now had a lot to do with her ongoing efforts to close the gap between herself and her sister.

The only problem was, jumping to the snapping of Julia's fingers never changed a thing. It might at times melt a bit of the ice between them, but only temporarily. Julia was capable of freezing their détente faster than an icebox could make hoarfrost.

She stopped on the threshold of Julia's bedroom, stunned by the tumbling disarray that greeted her. Garments of all colors and fabrics covered the bed, chaise longue, chairs, and settee, and even hung from the bedposts. "What on earth have you been doing?"

"Do you want any of this? And if not, would any of it be suitable for your charity?"

Flabbergasted, Phoebe ventured into the room. "This is almost the entirety of your wardrobe."

Julia grinned as she gazed around her. "Yes, very nearly. It's all got to go."

"But . . . why?"

"For beginners, none of it fits." Julia placed a hand on her growing belly. "I should think that would be obvious."

"They don't fit *now*, perhaps." Phoebe rather had her doubts about that, for other than her midsection, Julia had so far gained very little weight and most of these fashions featured a drop waist and a loose, flowing fit. But if Julia wasn't comfortable wearing these dresses for the rest of her pregnancy, she should of course set them aside. For now. "They *will* fit again, once the baby is born."

"I doubt that. They say a woman's figure is never the same afterward. And anyway, none of these will be appropriate then."

Baffled, Phoebe went to the bed and lifted a stunning Paul Poiret dinner gown in teal silk faille with a drop waist and a cascading train. "Appropriate for what?" An assortment of crepe de chine, gold and silver lamé, rich-colored velvets, and gossamer lace peered up at Phoebe in supplication, as if to say, *Save us from the trash heap!*

"For the mother of a peer, of course."

Phoebe dropped the gown back on the pile. "Whatever do you mean?"

"I'm not a girl anymore, Phoebe. I have responsibilities now. The mother of the next Viscount Annondale needs a certain dignity and sophistication, and I don't feel any of these dresses meet the challenge." She drifted to the chaise longue and lifted from one of its arms a long-sleeved tunic in a clingy silk knit from the house of Julia's favorite designer, Coco Chanel. She held the frock up in front of her, shook her head, and held it out to Phoebe. "So I repeat my question. Do you want any of this, and what you don't want for yourself, could you use in your charity drive?"

"Does Grams know you're disposing of your wardrobe?"

"What's it got to do with Grams? I'm the one carrying Gil's heir."

"*Maybe* you are." There was every chance the child could be a girl, which would change everything. But Phoebe kept this thought to herself. "Julia, you're rushing things just a bit, don't you think?"

"No, I don't think." Julia issued one of her patented, careless shrugs. "Miss Greenwood is certain I'm having a son. She communicated with him, after all. And it isn't as if Grams and Grampapa will have to finance my new wardrobe. I can buy whatever I want on credit and pay my bills once Gil's heir is born." She turned away, regarding several other frocks and gowns. "I'd ask Amelia next time she's home, but very little of this seems her style."

A gasp drew Phoebe's attention to the doorway, where Hetta stood openmouthed in apparent horror.

"Oh, Hetta, there you are." Julia waved her in. "I take it Eva spoke to you and everything's settled?"

"*Ja*, Miss Eva and I, we speak. I am most happy again. But . . ." Poor Hetta turned florid as she entered the room and saw the full extent of the chaos. "What is Madame doing?"

"We need to get these boxed up—that is, if my sister would kindly answer my questions. Phoebe?"

Sudden insight thrust Phoebe from her haze of bafflement. "Actually, I want it all. What I can't use I'll put away for Amelia—at least the more classic styles that won't go out of fashion while she grows into them—and the rest I'll bring to St. George's for disbursement. Thank you, Julia. This is splendid of you. Why don't you go downstairs now and let Hetta and me work on this."

As soon as Julia left the room, Phoebe turned to Hetta. "Quickly. We'll store this all in the attic until my sister comes to her senses."

In her sturdy walking shoes and only the slightest complaint left in her hip, Eva crossed the village with the best of intentions: try to see matters from Alice's point of view, give her the benefit of the doubt, and apologize to her for the accusations with as much humility as she, Eva, could muster.

If only she could get the possibility of Keenan Ripley swinging from the end of a rope out of her mind. There were times she considered doubling back to Foxwood Hall and leaving this errand for another day. Her conscience kept her plodding onward.

Yet, her feet, as if of their own accord, veered off the path toward home and cut across the fields bordered by stone walls here, hedgerows there, with gates providing access from one to another. Her sister had taken a walk the morning of Stephen's murder. Had that walk brought her to Keenan's house?

Eva rather loathed herself for taking the detour. But if one were to walk past her parents' barns, outbuildings, and closer pastures, one would come upon Keenan's northeast enclosure where Fred Corbyn grazed and watered his sheep. From there, it was only a few minutes due west to the Ripley homestead. Alice would have known that. Unable to resist the tug in that direction, Eva gave in with a little promise to herself that she'd walk twice as quickly to her parents' farm once she was done seeing whatever it was she needed to see.

She skirted the northeast pasture at its southernmost bordering wall. Where the land dipped, the Corbyns' sheep drifted like clouds in a green sky around the artificial dew pond fed by the stream. Minutes later, Eva crossed an expanse of treed acreage—mostly tightly spaced pines and golden-leafed birch that created a windbreak around the orchard. The roof of the two-story brew house came into view—

Eva cleared the trees and halted, arrested by the bustle of activity below her in Keenan's orchard. She knew he had hired workers, and perhaps had given directions to them to continue the harvest while he sat in the village jail—but this!

Just as when they had converged on the police station to provide Keenan with alibis, nearly every man in the village had gathered once again. They filled the orchard like an army, except instead of guns and cannons, they had brought ladders and bushel baskets. They were hard at work harvesting the pears, knowing that to leave them on the branch too long would change the taste of the perry they all relished. Why, there was the broad, lofty figure of Joe Murdock coming down one of the main aisles between the trees, issuing commands in a singsong baritone. Eva guessed he and most of the others had already drunk their fill of perry at Joe's pub before setting to work. Not that they were unsteady on their feet, but the laughter that reached her ears spoke of especially high spirits as they plucked the pears from the trees.

There were women, too, behaving a bit more sedately yet nonetheless cheerful as they carried brimming baskets to the brew house where the fruit would be pressed, strained, and funneled into the vats to begin the fermenting process. As she watched the almost choreographed efforts of Keenan Ripley's neighbors, her heart swelled. Yes, it might only be cider, and in the grand scheme of the world perhaps not worth very much, but it was *their* cider. And Keenan was *their* neighbor and they weren't about to let it all go to the devil.

Whatever Eva had hoped to discover here no longer

seemed important. Somehow, the exuberant goodwill of these villagers had rubbed off on her and she wished only to hurry to her parents' farm and make amends with Alice.

She went on her way, but when she once again reached the northeast pasture, she discovered the Corbyns' sheep no longer alone. Mrs. Corbyn, with the help of her two young stepsons and an energetic, black and white border collie, were rounding up the herd and coaxing them through a gate back onto their own land. Bleating and *baa*-ing, the fluffy animals poured through the opening like a rush of whitewater rapids.

Eva slowed down and returned the wave of one of the children, the older of the pair, judging from his height. They had had a sister born at the start of the war, the natural child of Fred and Elaina Corbyn and the only one, so far, that they had had together. The poor mite had died of the influenza in 1918. The entire village had shared in the Corbyns' grief.

Wearing a straw sun hat tied beneath her chin, Mrs. Corbyn turned toward Eva just as the last of the sheep shuffled through the gate. Brushing her windblown bangs out of her eyes, she waved, and after shooing her children and the dog through as well, she secured the latch and started walking toward Eva. Despite the tufted grass and rocky hillocks, Mrs. Corbyn's strides were long and even beneath a wide skirt that billowed out behind her. A short, belted tweed jacket that looked homemade, yet skillfully so, shielded her upper torso from the draft.

"Hullo, Miss Huntford, what brings you by?"

The question slightly embarrassed Eva, for she had no ready answer that did not include the truth. To stall for time, she smiled and held out her hand to shake Mrs. Corbyn's, then cleared her throat. "I walked over from the Hall to see my parents, and some inclination drew me to the orchard." There, she thought, that was as near the truth as needed to be.

"You were worried about the harvest." Elaina Corbyn dislodged something brown and gooey from the side of her Wellington boot by scraping it against a tuft of grass. She flashed Eva an apologetic look and tucked a strand of red-brown hair behind her ear. Eva pretended not to notice the offending dung, one of the hazards of livestock farming. She'd walked through her father's cow pastures enough times to know that. "It's good of you to care what becomes of Keenan Ripley's business," Mrs. Corbyn went on. "But as I'm sure you saw, he has good friends here."

"It was a heartening sight," Eva replied with enthusiasm. "And I do hope Keenan is released soon. I don't believe he would hurt anyone, much less his own brother."

"Nor do I, Miss Huntford." Mrs. Corbyn paused to watch the progress of children, dog, and sheep as they trekked across the adjoining field. "Of course, they were never close as boys or young men."

"That's true, but that doesn't mean—"

"I only meant it's one more reason for the chief inspector to suspect Keenan. Had the brothers shared a close friendship, it would make it more unlikely in Mr. Perkins's eyes that one would murder the other."

She spoke with a kind of authority, an assertiveness one didn't always hear from the local wives hereabouts. The woman was several years older than Eva, but Eva remembered a more youthful Elaina Tibbetts, as she had been then, a lively, popular girl who had postponed marriage until she'd been good and ready, much to her parents' frustration, at least according to Eva's mother.

"And then, of course," Mrs. Corbyn went on, "there was Stephen's insistence that they sell the orchard. That also appears to give Keenan a reason for wanting his brother out of the way." She held up the flat of her hand when Eva started to protest. "I don't believe it, but the chief inspector likely does."

Eva's good spirits took a downward turn as the realities fell back into place. But Keenan wasn't the only one who would wish to avoid the sale. There was also Joe Murdock, who made a good profit selling the Ripley perry in his tavern. There was also the husband of the woman before her, who needed the land for his sheep. "Speaking of the sale," Eva said, "have you heard anything more about that? Is that developer still hanging about town?"

"According to my husband, he is, and he still wants the land. Maybe *he* killed Stephen."

Eva immediately saw the flawed logic in that. "If the American had wished anyone out of the way, it would have been Keenan, not Stephen." She regarded the rolling pastureland that surrounded them. "What will you and Mr. Corbyn do if the orchard does sell, and this parcel with it? You rather depend on it for the grazing and water rights, don't you?" She hoped her question held the idle curiosity she had attempted to inject into it.

"We do, but perhaps we'd be able to work out a new agreement." The prospect obviously troubled the woman, for she frowned and sighed. "Or perhaps we'll sell out and move up to London. You know, Miss Huntford, the city is full of opportunities, whereas farming is always fraught with uncertainties. Such as now. I tell you, the worries can eat away at a person." The authority and confidence slipped a fraction, until Mrs. Corbyn squared her shoulders and shook away her doubts. "For now we simply have to believe Keenan will be released and all will go on as it has always done. The American can find some other village for his detestable resort."

"It's good to be optimistic," Eva agreed. "But at the same time one must be realistic. Even with Stephen Ripley gone, the bank could still decide to foreclose, and the land will be sold. Perhaps you and your husband could arrange to purchase it outright."

"Perhaps." Her lips thinned and her gaze held no enthusiasm for the prospect. Eva realized she shouldn't have made the suggestion, for it was unlikely the Corbyns had ready cash for anything but essentials. "If you'll excuse me, Miss Huntford. Please give my regards to your parents. Oh, and to your sister. Why, if memory serves, she and Keenan were once rather keen on each other, weren't they?"

Her smile never faltered, yet something in Elaina Corbyn's reminiscence seemed designed to insinuate and accuse. Just as Eva herself had done last time she'd talked with Alice. Did Mrs. Corbyn know something? She had seen Alice and Keenan together at the church before Stephen died. Had she also seen Alice trudging across the fields on the morning of the murder, on her way to Keenan's cottage?

"That was a long time ago," Eva said. "Much has happened since."

"Yes, much has happened to most of us," the woman murmured. A sadness seemed to come over her. Was she thinking about her little daughter? "Well, I must get back to the boys before they burn down the house. Good day to you, Miss Huntford."

As Eva watched her go, she again thought back on a time when they were all younger. Had Alice and Elaina Tibbetts engaged in some sort of feud, one that perhaps continued to fester all these years later? She couldn't remember anything, but that didn't mean there hadn't been ill feelings between the two. Then again, perhaps Eva's mention of this pasture potentially selling had gotten under Mrs. Corbyn's skin.

She headed for her parents' farm, letting the conversation replay in her mind. Mrs. Corbyn had rather facetiously suggested the American developer murdered Stephen. Eva had immediately dismissed the possibility, but now she wondered. She doubted very much Stephen had had a change of heart about the orchard, but what about Horace Walker's intentions? What if Keenan's behavior in town the afternoon before his brother's death had led Mr. Walker to see the benefit of disposing of both brothers— one through death, and the other through incrimination? This would ensure a foreclosure on the property, allowing Mr. Walker to purchase the land cheap and without the inconvenience of retaining Stephen as a shareholder.

Horace Walker, Joe Murdock, Ed Corbyn . . . and even young William Gaff. They were all suspects, or should have been if Chief Inspector Perkins hadn't made up his mind so quickly and arrested Keenan.

Then there was Mr. Peele's claim in his sister's garden that Stephen Ripley had threatened to make trouble for William's family; he had known something damaging about William's father. Did that also make Ezra Gaff a suspect?

Eva shook her head. Speculation achieved little without a scrap of evidence to back it up. There was the tweed cap found near the murder site. It could have belonged to any of them, or at least most of them. She didn't think a wealthy American businessman would own such a cap— unless he'd been trying to disguise himself.

Yet if such had been the case, the American would have been too clever to have made such a mistake in leaving it behind. It also suggested whoever killed Stephen had been in a frightful hurry to get away. Had William come along at that moment, prompting the murderer to flee? Or had William himself pushed Stephen from the ladder, then taken up the clipping shears and . . .

So much depended on finding the boy. But a local youth

who had spent his entire life in Little Barlow would be near to impossible to find unless he wished to be found.

The back of her parents' house came into view. Her mother stood framed in the kitchen window, and as Eva entered the garden, Mum waved and went to open the door.

"Where are you coming from?" she asked with a laugh that revealed both her surprise and her delight to see Eva.

"The Ripley orchard. I walked over from Foxwood Hall." Her mother stood aside to let her enter the house. "Did you know the village men are harvesting the pears?"

Her mother hugged her and pecked her cheek. "Your father heard about the plan last night at the Houndstooth. He might be over there now as well. Did you see him?"

"I didn't get close enough to see everyone who was there. I could make out Joe Murdock and a few others, though."

"Well, if your father isn't there yet, he will be. The men are determined Keenan will have a successful harvest this year."

"So I gathered. I'm glad. How unfair if when he's cleared of the charges against him, he's released to find an orchard gone to rot."

"Indeed. Tea?"

"I'll put the kettle on." Eva went to the range and hefted the iron pot. "I actually came to see Alice. She and I had a word or two . . . and I wish to apologize." After filling the kettle, Eva struck a wooden match to light the burner.

"I'm afraid Alice isn't here, luv. Not just now, anyway."

Eva cast a glance over her shoulder, then turned full around. "Where is she? At Keenan's, helping with the harvest? I did notice there were women helping carry in the pears."

"She might have done by now, but first she went into the village. To the police station to visit Keenan, poor dear."

A hollow sensation formed in Eva's stomach. "Alice went to visit Keenan?"

Her mother smiled sadly and nodded. "Brought him some of my scones and a few other things to make him more comfortable."

"Alice brought Keenan scones?"

"Yes. And a pot of preserves. Is there something wrong with that? She merely wants to see to his comfort, such as it is."

"Alice told me she brought scones to Mrs. Verity the morning Stephen Ripley died."

"She did indeed. What has Stephen Ripley's death got to do with that?"

"Do you suppose she also brought some to Keenan that morning?"

"If she did, she didn't mention it to me. Does it matter?" Mum's eyes narrowed. "Just what are you saying, Evie? Alice is a married woman. She wouldn't simply show up at the home of a bachelor bearing baked goods. Not without very good reason."

"No, I don't suppose she would." Eva went to the pantry to find the tin of tea. When she reentered the kitchen, her mother was setting the cups and saucers on the table. "Mum, were you able to find out why Alice came without the children?"

"Alice explained why." Mum tried to turn away, but Eva placed a hand on her wrist.

"You told Dad you were certain something was wrong and you were going to find out what. Have you?"

"Oh, Evie, can't you leave well enough alone?" With a dismayed look, Mum sank into a chair at the table, and Eva guessed that she, too, had her suspicions about Alice and Keenan but was loath to admit it. Eva pulled a chair closer to her mother's and sat. Betty Huntford lowered her voice, as if they weren't the only two people in the house. "All right, yes. I do think there are problems for Alice at home. But what they are remains a mystery to me, because your sister won't admit to a thing. Tells me all's well and not to worry. *Humph*. That's the same as telling me to mind my own business. I ask you, what devoted mother has ever done that?"

Alice seemed determined to keep her secrets. But Eva was equally determined to find out the truth. She only hoped it didn't destroy what was left of their relationship.

CHAPTER 10

"I don't see why you had to drag me along for this." Julia stood beside the Vauxhall as Phoebe came around the nose of the vehicle and stepped up onto the pavement. The village bank had opened its doors only minutes ago, and several early morning customers filed inside. They were all men, some in workman's clothes, others in merchants' attire, and one in a tailored, dark wool suit. Phoebe knew him from St. Paul's board of directors, a country squire who owned a modest estate a mile outside the village.

"I need you because I couldn't come alone and be taken seriously," Phoebe replied. "Your presence will lend just the right note of authority." Indeed, especially in the new suit Julia wore, with its elongating lines and fur trim on the collar. Phoebe didn't know when Julia had had time to be fitted for the ensemble, but she suspected her sister had decided to update her wardrobe before she made it obvious by emptying her cupboards and dressers.

Julia folded her arms and looked about to dig in her heels. "How so? You've told me precious little about this latest scheme of yours."

"We're going to see Mr. Evers and say we're here on behalf of Grampapa."

Julia narrowed her eyes in suspicion. "Are we?"

"In a way. Depending on what Mr. Evers says on the matter, I'll approach Grampapa about my plan when we get home." With no small amount of apprehension, Phoebe glanced at the plate glass window with the words BANK OF ENGLAND gleaming back at her in gold lettering. "I just hope he'll be amenable."

"Again, to what?" Julia pursed her lips, and Phoebe recognized a distinct possibility that her sister would refuse to cooperate.

"Need I remind you, Julia, that you didn't tell me the first thing about your little plan in Cheltenham before we arrived at the tea shop. And then you went and lied about it with that ridiculous claim that Olive Asquith recommended the place to you."

"That was different. I knew you'd *never* agree to go if you knew my purpose. You'd have got up on your high horse and told me I was wasting my money and my time. And yours, for that matter."

Julia had a point, and besides, Phoebe needed to persuade her sister to play along today if her proposal was to work. "You know Stephen Ripley wanted to sell his family's orchard, yes?"

"Everyone knows that by now." Julia spoke impatiently. "Isn't it a moot point now that he's dead?"

Julia's bluntness drew a grimace from Phoebe, but she quickly gathered herself. "It is not a moot point. The American still intends to purchase the land, right out from under Keenan Ripley."

"As far as I can see, the land won't do Mr. Ripley a bit of good if he's spending the rest of his life in prison, or worse, joining his brother in the hereafter."

Phoebe winced again. "Julia, please. Must you be so insensitive?"

Julia issued her patented one-shoulder shrug. "I've never understood what good it does to mince words. But that's neither here nor there." She made circular motions with her hand, indicating she wished to hear more from Phoebe.

"All right, here it is. I wish to let the bank manager know that Grampapa is also interested in buying the land."

Julia pulled back in surprise. "Is he?"

"Well . . . no. At least not yet. I intend to tell Mr. Evers that he is, that I'm to gather all the pertinent information, and that Grampapa will contact him once he's gone over everything with his solicitor."

"So you're intending to lie."

"Not exactly. I do intend to bring a proposal to Grampapa, and with any luck, he'll see the benefit of buying the land, or half of it actually, to save the orchard. The Ripley perry is, after all, essential to the economic well-being of the village."

"You want him to buy Stephen Ripley's half."

Phoebe grinned at Julia's perception. "Yes, and become a shareholder in the orchard and brewery until Keenan turns enough of a profit to buy back the land. It's perfect, don't you think?"

"And what makes you think Grampapa will go along with something as ridiculously ill-conceived as this? With what funds do you propose he make this purchase? You know now as well as I that our family doesn't have those kinds of disposable assets anymore. Are you really eager to put such a financial strain on our grandfather, not to mention the guilt he'll feel when he's forced to turn down the proposition?"

For several heartbeats, Phoebe wished to melt into the pavement. Julia was right; what *had* she been thinking, coming here to volunteer her grandfather's money—and Fox's inheritance—to alleviate someone else's financial difficulties?

But then she remembered those financial difficulties, and the prospect of Keenan Ripley losing land that had been in his family for generations, didn't only affect Mr. Ripley himself, but the entire village. Eva had told her about the efforts of the villagers to harvest the pears and save next year's perry yield. It had sounded as if nearly the entire adult population of Little Barlow had shown up in support of their neighbor. Shouldn't the Renshaws make the same effort?

And even if Grampapa couldn't purchase Stephen Ripley's half of the orchard outright, he might be able to extend Keenan Ripley enough of a loan to ward off foreclosure. Besides, simply showing an interest in the land could be enough to scare off the American and send him elsewhere to build his resort.

She seized her sister's hand. "I am going inside and you are coming with me. You're going to agree with everything I have to say, and you are going to work your considerable charms on Mr. Evers to persuade him to see things our way. Now, let's get on with it."

An appalled look spread over Julia's features, and Phoebe very much expected her to yank her hand free, climb back into the motorcar, and demand that Phoebe drive her home. Phoebe also braced for a dressing down, certain Julia was gathering breath to deliver one. A cool wind stirred Julia's golden blond curls and sifted through Phoebe's redder locks. Julia's dark blue eyes turned darker still as they held Phoebe, unblinking.

Then her expression cleared and, inexplicably, Julia grinned. "I suppose a bit of subterfuge might be fun. All right then, little sister, let's go talk to Mr. Evers."

*   *   *

After downing her tea quickly, Eva left her mother and retraced her steps, this time taking the turn into the village rather than continuing on to Foxwood Hall. Lady Phoebe and Lady Annondale should be at the bank, as planned; perhaps Eva could squeeze into Lady Phoebe's Vauxhall with them for the ride home.

By now, Alice probably would have concluded her business at the police station. After all, how long did it take to give a man a basket of scones, provided Chief Inspector Perkins had allowed her to visit Keenan at all? More likely, the chief inspector had taken the basket with the excuse of having to carefully examine its contents, pilfered several of the baked treats for himself, and delivered it substantially lighter.

As Eva expected, Alice was not at the police station when she arrived. She would try the shops, and berated herself for not thinking to ask Mum if she had sent Alice into the village with a shopping list. But then, as villages went, Little Barlow wasn't particularly large and there were only so many places Alice could be. A sudden inspiration sent Eva to the post office. Her sister would of course wish to see if any letters had arrived from home.

Eva was reaching for the door handle when someone pushed the door open from inside, forcing her to step out of the way or be struck. The image of a trench coat and black derby filled her vision. Those were common enough garments, but the hastily spoken, "Excuse me, miss," with the flat intonations of an American accent was not.

The land developer. The very sight of him made her temples throb and her throat tighten around words she had been taught never to utter.

His back now to her, he paused on the pavement glancing in the wrong direction in preparation of crossing the road, as Eva had seen Americans do in London because they weren't used to cars driving on the left. Luckily for her, a farm truck lumbered by. It gave her the time to not only make up her mind about what she would do next, but to reach Mr. Walker's side before he set off on his way.

"Excuse me. Sir." She added that last out of habit rather than any respect she felt for him.

He turned to regard her with a bland expression. His eyes were muddy gray, his hair the same, as were the bullish features that sagged with late middle age. Judging by his pallor, she guessed he smoked, a good deal. Eva found nothing pleasing about him, and as their gazes connected she permitted him to glimpse her mounting contempt, which was something she rarely, if ever, allowed to happen.

Their eye contact broke as he swept her with an assessing look. "Is there something I can do for you?"

"There is something you can do for this entire village."

Before she could continue, he had the audacity to snigger. "I didn't realize I held such importance in the lives of the local populace."

"Not importance. Significance, perhaps." She steeled herself with a deep breath in through her nose. "You have the significance to disrupt our lives and destroy the harmony of Little Barlow. You, who can never understand life here or the bonds we share. You'll never contribute anything worthwhile to this village. You may build whatever you wish—perhaps we can't stop you—but you'll never belong here, and because of that your resort will be an empty shell of a building and nothing more. And I see that as a useless waste of money."

"Do you indeed?" Stretching his broad mouth into something resembling a smile, but without the warmth, he looked her over again. "I remember you. You were trailing after the earl's granddaughter the other day. So what are you? Her personal lapdog?"

It was Eva's turn to snigger. "If you mean to insult me, you'll have to try harder, Mr. Walker. I couldn't give the slightest fig what you think of me, as long as you know your project will fail if you build it here in Little Barlow. For one, you won't entice a single villager to work for you." The claim was a bold one, and Eva hoped it would prove true.

"Oh, I think they will, especially when I offer them more money than they could ever make scratching their living from the dirt of their wretched farms."

"Wretched farms? I'll have you know, Mr. Walker, that even as we speak, nearly the entire village has gathered at Keenan Ripley's orchard to harvest the pears. He'll be able to pay his mortgage and then some. That's how much these people care about their farms."

"Are they really?" His eyes gleamed like steel, the first sign of animation Eva had detected. "Well, isn't that lucky for me?"

"Lucky? How so?"

"I'll have *you* know, miss, that the trees will be easier to clear without the fruit clinging to them. Much more convenient this way. So, my thanks to the villagers."

He started to move away, but Eva wasn't about to let an opportunity slip past. "I can think of another convenience. The death of Stephen Ripley."

He once again turned to her, this time with a glare that prompted her to back up half a step. His bulky chin jutted forward. "What do you mean by that?"

"I mean, isn't it so much more convenient to have both Ripley brothers out of the way?" Even as she spoke, Eva marveled at her audacity and wondered where it came from. "Now you may purchase the land in total without having to share your profits."

Hot, fiery color suffused his face. His already wide nostrils widened yet more, and his lips became an inverted crescent, the lower lip protruding beyond the top. "How dare you."

The hissed words sent a chill through Eva, who perhaps should have taken into account the harm he could do her, and the Renshaws, if he chose. Yet she couldn't bring herself to apologize, and what he uttered next made her glad she hadn't. His anger seemed to cool as quickly as it had ignited, and once again he swept her with a leering gaze.

"You can't have much of a future as a lady's maid. I could put you to much more lucrative work in America. Or London. Or Paris, for that matter." He stepped ominously closer. "Yes, I think you'd do very well in the career I have in mind for you, Miss Huntford. Or may I call you Eva?"

Her mouth dropped open, both in outrage at the kind of work he alluded to, and in astonishment that he should know her name. The thought of being on even the barest of familiar terms with this man sent a slithering sensation along her spine. Before she could gather her wits to respond, he gave her a mocking wink, tipped his hat to her, and crossed the street.

Oh, vile, vile man!

Her admonishments had failed miserably, and she was left miserable because of it. Miserable and shaking with anger.

She traced Mr. Walker's progress as he strode along the pavement. He'd just reached the corner in front of the Houndstooth Inn when Joe Murdock, back from pear harvesting, sauntered out of the building and directly into the American's path. Eva strained her ears to hear what passed between them, but they were too far away. Joe held something long and heavy-looking in one hand, while slapping its end against his other palm. Realizing what it was, Eva set off across the street.

"You've no right to speak to me that way," Mr. Walker was saying in a strident tone that resembled the bark of a dog. "Now go about your business or I'll bring a world of trouble down on you."

"That so?" Joe didn't sound impressed. He stood a head taller than the American, and a good deal wider through the shoulders. Eva had no illusions of the kind of damage a man like Joe Murdock could inflict in a fight. In fact, the entire village knew it, which was why altercations rarely if ever broke out at the Houndstooth, no matter how inebriated the patrons. Joe looked up at Eva's approach, his features softening a fraction in greeting. "Miss Huntford, was this man bothering you over by the post office?"

Mr. Walker barely took notice of her over his shoulder. "She approached me, not the other way around. I was minding my own business."

"We'll thank you to mind your business somewhere else," Joe growled to the other man. "Preferably in whatever hole you crawled out of. We don't need your kind here in Little Barlow."

"Come now, I'm growing weary of hearing the same complaints from everyone I meet."

"Then maybe you should heed those complaints and know you'll never be welcome here." Joe slapped the club, which he always kept behind his bar as a precaution against thieves and troublemakers, against his palm again, this time with a resounding *whack*. He stepped closer to the other man, forcing Mr. Walker to raise his chin to look up at him. Fear swam in the whites of his eyes, but he held his ground.

"One more step and I'll have you arrested. Don't think I wouldn't."

"Don't worry. If I take another step, it'll be to throttle

you so soundly you won't be able to make a peep for a week at least."

Fearing violence, Eva thrust herself between them, forcing both men to step back. "Gentlemen, that's enough. Joe, thank you, but whatever Mr. Walker said to me, I'm more than happy to ignore. Please go back inside your pub." To help persuade the large man, she placed a hand on his forearm and gently turned him toward the door of the establishment. Mr. Walker took the opportunity to step around them and continue on his way.

She took another moment, alone on the pavement, to gather her composure. Good heavens, while she knew Joe had only meant to intimidate the American, she wondered if, in other circumstances, he might have been moved to violence and used his club on Horace Walker. She hadn't time to contemplate the possibility for long. A familiar motorcar—a large, black, shiny one—traveled along High Road and stopped outside the bank not far from Lady Phoebe's Vauxhall. Fresh alarm shot through Eva. Lady Phoebe and her sister were still inside, executing a plan that would ultimately involve her grandfather, though he didn't yet know it. But he was about to find out, for his driver was just then holding the door of the Rolls-Royce open for him.

And oh, dear, for his wife, the countess, too.

Phoebe bit the inside of her lip to keep from smiling. Julia had risen to the occasion by utilizing her most charming skills of persuasion with Mr. Evers, who sat listening to her as if transfixed.

"So you see, Mr. Evers, my grandfather considers this a smart investment for himself as well as a contribution to the economic well-being of Little Barlow. Why send his money to work elsewhere, he said just this morning, when he can help the local people, himself, *and* our family by investing in the village itself? After all, what *is* Foxwood Hall without Little Barlow? And what is Little Barlow without its people, its farms, and its businesses?"

"That certainly makes sense, Lady Annondale, and it's most commendable of your grandfather to take such an interest in one small farmer."

"As I said, there is a larger picture, and my grandfather has always been able to see a situation as the sum of its parts. Lose one farmer, and little by little, our village could become a ghost town. You know as well as I do, as does my grandfather, how young people are flocking to the cities these days. We need to give them reasons to stay put."

"Yes, indeed, Lady Annondale." Phoebe heard the relief in Mr. Evers's voice. Apparently, he couldn't have been comfortable with the prospect of foreclosing on the Ripley land and selling it off to a developer, even if the bank stood to profit from the venture. Phoebe didn't doubt he had lost sleep in recent days. "Now, here's what I have in mind for your grandfather. I believe it could work."

"And send that beastly Mr. Walker looking elsewhere for his land?" Julia raised a perfectly delineated and artificially darkened eyebrow.

Phoebe took that as her cue to finally speak up. "I suppose it was Mr. Walker's idea to force Keenan Ripley to sell," she said. "Or *was* it the brother's? Poor Stephen Ripley, gone after only a day working at Foxwood Hall." After shaking her head sadly, she tilted her chin in her most convincing show of idle curiosity. "How *did* all this talk of selling come up? Stephen Ripley hadn't so much as visited Little Barlow since before the war. How did he even know his brother was in arrears?"

"I, er . . ." Mr. Evers patted his graying hair. "I really

shouldn't speak of Keenan Ripley's private affairs, Lady Phoebe."

"Why ever not?" Julia showed her sternest expression, which prompted Mr. Evers to sit up straighter. "We're here to help him, aren't we?"

She had him there. After stuttering a syllable or two, he expelled a breath of capitulation. "Actually, I believe someone in Little Barlow contacted Stephen Ripley and let him know Horace Walker was interested in purchasing land in the area."

"Mr. Walker must have been conducting his search on the sly," Phoebe said. "Or our grandfather would certainly have heard of it."

Julia nodded. "Making quiet inquiries. But who here would have gotten involved, and how did they know the orchard was in financial straits?"

"I honestly don't know," the banker said. "It's possible Keenan confided in some of his friends, and one of them . . . well . . ."

"Betrayed him," Phoebe concluded, and Julia and Mr. Evers nodded. Someone betrayed Keenan by instigating the sale of his land, probably hoping to profit through a commission of sorts if the sale went through. So that person, at least, would not have murdered Stephen and risked preventing the sale.

"But this is all neither here nor there." Mr. Evers rubbed his hands together as if washing them clean of the subject. "Getting back to your grandfather's proposal . . ." He looked past Phoebe's shoulder, his eyebrows arching. "Why, here he is now."

With a gasp she couldn't contain, Phoebe twisted in her seat to see not only Grampapa, but Grams as well, stepping into the lobby. Her eyes opened as wide as they could go, and then connected with Julia's equally round gaze as they turned toward each other. Julia mouthed, "What now?" To which Phoebe only shook her head in bafflement.

Mr. Evers seemed not to have noticed the urgent but silent communication between them. Rather, he came to his feet, straightened his suit coat, and walked around his desk with his hand extended.

"Lord and Lady Wroxly, I didn't expect you yet."

"Yet?" Clearly puzzled, Grampapa shook the man's hand and waited for an explanation. Grams shot a glance at Phoebe and Julia but said nothing.

"Yes, your granddaughters have been apprising me of your wishes concerning the Ripley property, and I've some preliminary ideas for you."

"Do you indeed?" Grampapa frowned as he studied Phoebe and Julia, but again waited for Mr. Evers to lead the conversation. Phoebe stole another glance at Grams, whose expression made her blood rush and her heart pound. She was about to be publicly humiliated and there was nothing she could do about it. Julia would be furious. Judging by the high color in her cheeks, she already was.

"Yes, we're interested to hear what you have to say, Mr. Evers." Grams spoke smoothly, without as much as a ripple in her poise. "We're just surprised you and our granddaughters have come up with a plan so quickly. But we were coming into the village anyway today and decided to stop in."

"Come this way, please." Mr. Evers ushered them to the desk, whereupon both Phoebe and Julia came to their feet and offered their chairs. Mr. Evers made a few quick motions with his hands, and two more chairs were procured, along with tea and a plate of gingersnap biscuits.

After the requisite pleasantries had been exchanged, Mr.

Evers turned his papers around and pushed them across to Grampapa, who set his spectacles on his nose and leaned over to read.

"Now, if it's an investment you're after," the bank manager began, "I can work out a tiered schedule of payments that will accrue interest each year. . . ."

Phoebe once again rose from her seat. "Perhaps Julia and I should go—"

"You sit," Grams commanded with a pointing finger. Then she smiled. "Your grandfather and I might want your highly learned opinion on this matter." She darted a look at Julia and said drily, "Yours too."

Having lingered in the village for nearly an hour, Eva held her breath in anticipation at the sight of the Renshaws' motorcar. Lady Phoebe and her sister certainly hadn't bargained on their grandparents showing up during their initial scheming with the bank manager.

Perhaps *scheming* was too strong a word. Lady Phoebe had only the best intentions, both toward Keenan and her grandfather. She would never recommend the earl invest his money unwisely, and had wished to have a sound plan in place before going to him with her idea. Oh, but how did that kindly gentleman feel about finding his granddaughters at the bank speaking on his behalf without his knowledge? Eva's face burned in sympathy for both Renshaw sisters. But more for Lady Phoebe, who would face her grandparents' censure and her sister's indignation at the same time.

Finally, a doorman opened the street door and out streamed the earl and countess, arm in arm, with their granddaughters following close behind. No one looked particularly upset. But they didn't look particularly happy either.

Without a word Lady Annondale accepted the driver's hand to slide into the backseat of the Rolls-Royce. Eva could see her ladyship's lovely countenance through the window as she stared daggers out at the street. Eva could only imagine those daggers were meant for Lady Phoebe. The earl and countess stopped on the pavement and turned to speak to their younger granddaughter. Was a reprimand coming? Would harsh words drift their way to her ears?

But the earl only laid his hand on Lady Phoebe's shoulder and leaned to kiss her cheek. The countess did likewise, only brisker, the kiss no more than a perfunctory peck before she pivoted and entered the motorcar. Eva didn't know if that meant Lady Wroxly was angry or not, because being demonstrative simply wasn't her way. The earl spoke another few words to Lady Phoebe and followed his wife into the backseat.

Lady Phoebe stood on the curb watching the Rolls-Royce pull away. She looked rather shell-shocked, and Eva hurried across the street to her.

"My lady, what happened? What brought your grandparents to the bank today of all days?"

Lady Phoebe continued to stare after the retreating motorcar until it reached the village's ancient, medieval gates and turned out of sight. "You'll never believe it, Eva."

"Then please tell me. Are they angry? Is your sister furious? Was it very awful?"

Lady Phoebe finally turned to regard her. "Everything is all right." She gave a laugh. "It turns out my darling, dearest grandfather had the exact same thought I had and came today to speak to Mr. Evers about helping Keenan Ripley keep his land. Have you ever in your life heard of anything so perfect?" She laughed again. "Or so coincidental?"

But then she frowned and nibbled her bottom lip. "Of course, neither he nor Grams were pleased that I took it upon myself to look into the matter without discussing it with them first."

"Oh, dear."

"Yes, but I think they've already forgiven me. And good heavens, Eva, you should have seen them. They utterly hid their surprise—their shock, really—at seeing Julia and me at Mr. Evers's desk like a pair of practiced thieves. I saw a moment's bewilderment in their eyes before they very smoothly joined the conversation as if the whole thing had been their idea in the first place."

"Did they really, my lady? How extraordinary."

"I suppose I *should* have gone to Grampapa first."

"I suppose so, my lady."

"I'd just wanted to have a sound plan in place first." She looked regretful for one moment before lifting her eyebrows. "How did your day go? Have you learned anything useful?"

Eva sighed. "I haven't been able to track down my sister. She was out when I reached home, but listen to this, my lady. She'd gone to the police station to bring Keenan Ripley some of my mum's freshly baked scones."

Lady Phoebe's eyebrows rose higher. "Did you say scones?"

"I did, just as someone brought scones to Keenan's house the morning of the murder. Alice and Mum both claimed she brought those scones to the widow Verity's house, but who's to say she didn't save some for Keenan? Anyway, I came looking for her here in the village thinking I'd pass her on the road if she was on her way home, but I never saw a sign of her. It's almost as if she's purposely avoiding me. I did run into someone else though."

Lady Phoebe studied her. "I can see by your scowl it wasn't a pleasant encounter."

"No, indeed. I went to the post office to see if Alice might be checking for letters, and out strides Horace Walker, nearly hitting me with the door. What a cur he is, my lady."

Lady Phoebe stepped closer, her expression gone serious. "What did he say? He didn't accost you, did he?"

"He didn't lay a hand on me, rest assured. First I told him how the villagers had gathered at Keenan's orchard to harvest the pears. You should have seen it—never a more heartening sight. But that awful man had the audacity to say their actions were lucky for him, as it will be easier to clear away the trees without the fruit clinging to them."

"Why, that beastly man."

"Beastly is right, my lady. And then he immediately had a run-in with Joe Murdock."

"It sounds as though Mr. Walker had a busy morning."

Eva nodded. "After he left me, he passed by the Houndstooth, and Joe came striding out holding that club he keeps behind the bar."

"Mr. Murdock keeps a club behind his bar?"

"Well, you know how men can be after a long day's work and several pints." On second thought, Eva realized, Lady Phoebe wouldn't know much about that. Men of her class enjoyed brandy and cigars and quiet conversation after a day of surveying their lands and perusing the account books with their solicitors. "Anyway, Joe was rather threatening. His very bearing, not to mention that wooden club, implied he'd have liked nothing more than to wallop Mr. Walker on the side of the head."

"What did Mr. Walker do?"

"He threatened in the best way a man like that knows how, with legal action against Joe. Finally, I had to step between them, or who knows how it might have ended."

Lady Phoebe looked alarmed. "Eva, you shouldn't have."

"No, it was all right. It helped defuse matters. Both men walked away with their heads and their liberty intact."

"Well, I can't blame Joe Murdock. There are times I'd like to take a club to Mr. Walker's head and knock some sense into him. Do try to steer clear of him from now on, though."

"You can bet on that, my lady. I've had quite enough of him, thank you." She decided her mistress didn't need to know the worst of her conversation with Horace Walker.

CHAPTER 11

Upon arriving home, Phoebe fully expected a summons from her grandparents, and feared they would demand a full account of her intentions and motives in going to the bank. Mr. Giles delivered no such summons as he took her overcoat, and she even checked with the head footman, Vernon, just in case the message had slipped Mr. Giles's often-clouded mind.

Off the hook in the meantime, she arranged to have tea served in the Petite Parlor for herself and Eva. Phoebe loved the Petite Parlor; it had always been her favorite room. Semiround, it occupied the ground floor of the turret in the oldest part of the house. From the tranquil pale green of the walls, to the crisp white woodwork and spacious coffered ceiling, to the lovely garden views, the Petite Parlor had always provided a sense of homey comfort lacking in the more formal rooms.

The family sometimes used the room for informal meals, and she and Eva took a seat now at the round table as Vernon and an assistant brought in tea. She didn't miss Eva's look of apology and even embarrassment at the two young men, as if to tell them she knew she didn't belong in this part of the house, but her mistress insisted and what was she to do?

If they saw the look they gave no indication, and neither did Phoebe. It had long been a point of amiable contention between her and her lady's maid on how strictly the boundaries between them should be maintained. In Eva's mind, they should never sit together at the same table—in fact, it made Eva uncomfortable to sit at all in Phoebe's presence. But Eva had been raised with the staunch traditions of the prewar years, while Phoebe had grown up during the war, her formative years spent working side by side with servants and villagers alike to provide supplies for the soldiers on the Continent. Those efforts had taught her that the similarities among people were far greater than the differences.

"I did learn something else that might be significant," Phoebe said as she poured their tea. "It seems Mr. Walker had been quietly making inquiries about available land, and someone in Little Barlow contacted Stephen Ripley to let him know."

Eva dropped a lump of sugar into her cup. "I've wondered how those two men found each other. Does Mr. Evers know who this person is?"

Phoebe shook her head. She poured a trickle of cream into her tea and slowly stirred. "He said he doesn't. Perhaps he merely didn't wish to divulge confidential information. I don't think this person would have murdered Stephen Ripley, but he might be another piece of the puzzle that will lead to the killer. So I've been asking myself, who in this village knew of Keenan Ripley's financial troubles and stood to gain from the land being sold?"

"Keenan's troubles were probably common knowledge, I'm afraid. But I can't imagine who in Little Barlow would benefit from the sale. Not as Stephen Ripley would have benefited."

"Nor can I."

Eva sighed, and Phoebe regarded her quizzically. "Tell me the truth. Am I forcing you to involve yourself in something you'd rather leave alone? I realize this time events are uncommonly personal for you." The name *Alice* hovered unspoken between them.

Eva hesitated a moment, staring down at her hands before meeting Phoebe's gaze. "My lady, it's always been personal for me. What affects you and your family affects me. Yes, this time it's my family involved, or possibly so, but that makes me want to find the truth all the more. My sigh was one of perplexity, not reluctance."

"I'm glad." Phoebe reached over and set a hand on Eva's wrist. "I don't know what I'd do without you."

"That's something you'll never have to find out, my lady."

Phoebe smiled and made no reply. She believed fully that if she asked it of her lady's maid, Eva would forgo marriage, a family, and a home of her own indefinitely. Perhaps forever.

For now, it was true, Phoebe needed her—but as so much more than a maid. Someday, however, Phoebe must learn to get on without her, for she wanted her dear friend to find her own happiness and distinct place in the world. Phoebe could fairly well guess with whom Eva would find that happiness, but she also knew that on a constable's salary, Miles Brannock could not yet afford to marry and provide for a family. Phoebe believed women should have the right to pursue a career and earn their own money, but for most women options were severely limited. There needed to be at least one dependable income, and it was typically the husband's.

Eva broke the silence. "We're always looking for connections, my lady. We need a strong connection between the person who wanted the sale and the person who didn't."

"But that could include countless people here in the village."

"Not everyone in the village is connected, at least not financially. We need to look for individuals who might have been working at cross purposes, if you see what I mean."

"Hmm. I think I do. In other words, one person got involved and contacted Stephen Ripley about a potential land sale, and another found out and decided to put a stop to it, because it might jeopardize their own financial well-being."

"Precisely, my lady. So, for instance, perhaps one of Joe Murdock's workers—his cook or one of his barkeeps—instigated the sale of Keenan's land, and Joe Murdock got wind of it, feared the demise of his best-selling product—"

"Perry."

"Yes, and made sure the sale never went through." Eva took on a look of alarm. "Not that I mean to incriminate Joe Murdock, you understand. I only used him as an example. But I believe this is the sort of close connection we must look for. If we find whoever contacted Stephen, we might be able to figure out who the murderer is, or at least narrow down a list of suspects."

"Identifying the owner of the flat cap found near Stephen Ripley's body would help, I should think."

"Then as soon as we're done here, I'll ring Miles and see if he's learned anything." Eva went quiet and fingered the table linen before looking up again. "My lady, I'm afraid I might have bungled a chance to find out anything more from the American."

"Mr. Walker? I can't blame you if you had words with him today."

"I fear I went too far. You see, I insinuated he had reason to want both Ripley brothers out of the way. I shouldn't have said it, but I hoped to raise a response from him." She laughed mirthlessly.

"Was he very angry?"

"That would be putting it mildly." Eva looked about to add more, but compressed her lips instead. Then she brightened. "I've an idea, actually. If you could manage to "run into" him, you might issue an apology on my behalf, get him talking, and win his confidence. You might be able to find out who contacted Stephen Ripley for him. Only, don't do so alone, and make sure you're somewhere public."

"I like this plan." Phoebe considered a moment. "But there's no time to waste before he hears about my grandfather's new interest in the orchard. I'm not sure whom to bring with me, though. Not Julia. After the near fiasco at the bank, she's not likely to accompany me anywhere in the near future. Amelia is at school. . . . No, wait. Amelia would be perfect. I could take her out to lunch, couldn't I? I remember Mr. Walker saying he was staying at the Calcott Inn. We'll have lunch in the dining room."

"Your sister is awfully young to be involved."

"She's growing up fast and is much stronger than we give her credit for. Besides, if anyone can make an encounter with Horace Walker appear innocent, Amelia can. And it's not as if I'll be putting her in danger. We're merely going to make conversation with him and apologize for our headstrong lady's maid." She grinned and winked. "You ring the constable to see if he's learned anything, and I'll put a call in to the school and see if I can speak with Amelia."

Eva finished the last of her tea. "And while you and Amelia attempt to engage Mr. Walker, I'll see if I can find out from Joe Murdock who might have contacted Stephen Ripley about his brother's financial problems. After all, the local publican typically knows everything about the villagers he serves. And then I'll continue to look for my sister," she added in a murmur.

When Eva went belowstairs to telephone Miles, she was surprised to discover him in the servants' hall with Mrs. Sanders, Mrs. Ellison, and Mr. Giles.

They sat at the long dining table, Miles taking notes, Mrs. Sanders doing much of the talking, and Mr. Giles looking confused. It wasn't long before Eva gathered that there had been a continuation of the kitchen thefts.

"I tell you, we need a guard 'round the clock." Mrs. Sanders gathered her cardigan more tightly around her and gave a dignified sniff.

"What has been stolen?" Mr. Giles sounded as though he were awaking from a dream. "The countess's jewelry?"

"Foodstuffs, Mr. Giles." Mrs. Ellison spoke patiently, while Mrs. Sanders rolled her eyes.

Miles continued scribbling down their words. "When did you notice the most recent disappearances?"

"Why, right before I telephoned the station, of course." Mrs. Sanders looked for consensus from Mrs. Ellison, who nodded vigorously. "We thought we could nip this in the bud without outside help, but it appears that's a futile hope. We need this matter taken care of immediately, before . . ." Here she faltered, her eyes darting to the far wall and the old-fashioned board that held the bells for the various rooms in the house. Many houses had upgraded their systems to electric buzzers, but the countess had determined that if the old bells had served their purpose so unfailingly these many years, why change?

Eva guessed the matter that most weighed on Mrs. Sanders's mind was having to inform her employers about the disappearing items. She and Mrs. Ellison would of course fear being blamed, for kitchen security lay within their responsibility.

Miles spotted Eva watching from the doorway and waved her in. Despite Mrs. Sanders's pinch-lipped disapproval, Eva took a seat beside Mr. Giles, and even gave him a reassuring pat on the forearm. It was a gesture she never would have offered in the past, for it would have been considered impertinent and overly familiar, but nowadays it never failed to elicit a grateful smile.

"Can you add anything to the matter, Miss Huntford?" Mrs. Sanders's question fell on Eva's ears like a challenge. "Otherwise there is no reason for you to waste your time here."

"I'll be the judge of that, thank you, Mrs. Sanders." Miles suppressed his impatience and gazed past the older woman. "Mrs. Ellison and Mrs. Sanders are convinced the culprit is a member of the staff. There is no rummaging in evidence, but rather a detailed knowledge of what is kept where. And despite the pantries being kept locked at all times now, except when Mrs. Ellison needs access, items are still going missing. Any thoughts?"

"A member of the staff." Eva sighed and tapped her forefinger against her chin. This did indeed seem to implicate one of the servants, for an outsider wouldn't be familiar with the pantries. Once again, she wondered if someone was stealing items to sell as a way of supplementing their income. Eva loathed to think anyone so dishonest resided under Foxwood Hall's roof.

"But how to get through locked doors?" she mused aloud. "Someone would need a set of keys." A dreadful notion struck her. Mr. Giles still retained the keys to every door and window in the house. It was his job to lock up at night, but the system currently in place had Vernon trailing him from room to room to make certain the butler didn't forget or accidentally go around unlocking what should be locked. She cast the slightest of glances at the man beside her before looking away with a sense of shame.

Mrs. Sanders had apparently been studying her closely, for she said, "Don't be ridiculous, Miss Huntford. Mr. Giles would have no need of extra foodstuffs. He can already have whatever he wants simply by asking. And he's always in the house, so he can't be selling things."

Once again, Mr. Giles reacted as if just waking up. "What's that? What can I have simply by asking?"

"Anything you require, Mr. Giles," Mrs. Sanders said deferentially. When Lord Wroxly had first discovered his butler's deficiencies and asked the staff for their help in keeping him in his position, Mrs. Sanders had been the first to wholeheartedly agree. Which had surprised Eva at the time. The housekeeper was a model of efficiency and industry, and Eva would not have thought her capable of such compassion for someone with a diminished ability to do his job well.

She smiled now at Mrs. Sanders, even as a new idea came to her. Abruptly, she rose to her feet, startling the others. Even Miles looked taken aback, until she communicated a silent message to him. Aloud she said, "I'm afraid Mrs. Sanders is right. I can't shed much light on the matter. But there is something else I wish to mention to you, Constable. If I might have a moment when you're through here."

"Of course, Miss Huntford. Where shall I find you?"

"In the boot room, polishing my lady's shoes."

Their pretense wasn't fooling anyone, except perhaps Mr. Giles. Everyone in the house knew Eva and Miles were stepping out together, and the maids especially enjoyed whispering about it when they thought Eva couldn't hear. She didn't much mind. She had nothing to hide, nothing to be ashamed of. For now, they were enjoying a friendship that one day might lead to more.

Ten minutes later, as Eva bent over the task of buffing one of Lady Phoebe's leather pumps, a touch at the back of her neck startled her, but only for a moment.

"You wished to see me," Miles whispered in her ear, sending a shiver across her shoulders.

She playfully swatted him away, but then craned her neck to gaze up at him. He darted a quick look at the doorway before leaning over her and kissing her lips.

"Miles! Someone will see."

"No one did, so don't be such a ninny." His tender look softened the words. "You wished to see me? You've figured something out, haven't you?"

"I think I have." She set the shoe aside. "Not about who killed Stephen Ripley, but who is stealing food from the pantries. It's Josh. It's got to be. He's taking food for William."

"Has anyone seen William since the murder?"

"No, except perhaps for Josh. I don't understand why you and Chief Inspector Perkins haven't made finding William a priority." She raised her chin at him.

"Now, don't go accusing me. I've been looking, but William hasn't wished to be found. There's infinite places roundabouts a boy like that can hide."

"Yes, but he has to eat, doesn't he? He has to come out to find food."

"I thought the pantries are being kept locked."

"True. But Mrs. Ellison needs access to her supplies.

Which means someone else has had access as well. Someone no one pays any attention to, whom no one even sees most of the time."

"Like a ghost?"

"Not a ghost. As I said, Josh, the hall boy. Lowest in the servant pecking order. A hefty wager says he can lead us to William."

CHAPTER 12

As Phoebe predicted, Amelia was only too happy to join her for lunch the next day. Ever since Phoebe and her grandmother had taken an active interest in the affairs of the Haverleigh School for Young Ladies, Phoebe had gained a measure of authority at the school, enough for her to be able to escort her sister off the grounds. She promised to have Amelia back in time for her afternoon French lesson, which elicited a groan from the seventeen-year-old.

Amelia's spirits soared once they were ensconced in the Vauxhall and rumbling down the drive. "It's so much fun to leave school in the middle of the week. Thank you for coming to my rescue, Phoebe."

"Rescue?" Phoebe laughed and patted the crown of her hat, which had shifted slightly in the wind, then tucked a wayward strand of hair behind her ear. "You've top marks in all your subjects. I can scarcely believe school is at all torturous for you."

The wind played with Amelia's hair, too, yanking on tendrils of gold that had begun, in recent months, to darken to a deeper amber hue. Of the three sisters, Julia alone remained a true blonde, while Phoebe's hair tended more toward a light golden auburn, especially in the sun.

Amelia leaned her head back and propped an elbow on the edge of the door. "I suppose I'm just longing to be finished. Although what I'll do once I've graduated, I don't yet know."

Phoebe heard a wistfulness in her sister's voice. "What do you wish to do?" She turned onto the main road, passing a colorful carpet of zinnias growing along the roadside. Only a few months ago Amelia had declared her desire to be a veterinarian, but seeing how young people can change their minds weekly, Phoebe waited for her sister's reply.

Amelia peeked at her from under her lashes. "You'll laugh at me."

"I never would."

"Yes, you will, especially in light of what I just said about being rescued from school. And anyway, it won't happen because Grams would never allow it."

"You're being very mysterious. What wouldn't Grams allow? What is it you wish to do?" Phoebe couldn't begin to imagine based on the lack of hints so far.

Amelia gathered her breath while toying with the buttons down her uniform jacket. "Teach, Phoebe. I'd like to be a teacher. In the sciences, specifically."

It was on Phoebe's tongue to say of course Grams would allow it, but on second thought she decided to say nothing, at first. She and her sisters all knew what Grams expected of them. A pensive silence settled over them, and from the corner of her eye she could see Amelia continue to worry the buttons on her jacket. Then she raised her face to Phoebe's.

"It's not as if I would never marry. I would, in time. But

why couldn't I do both, teach *and* be a wife? Oh, I know a woman can't work and have children, but . . ."

"Why can't they?" Phoebe blurted.

"Well, how can they?"

Phoebe sighed, not having envisioned such a debate when she collected her sister only minutes ago. "I don't have all the answers and I do realize that, at present, female teachers aren't allowed to be married. But things are slowly changing. You've months yet before you graduate. If by then you are still determined to become a teacher— and I think it's a splendid plan, by the way—then we'll go to Grampapa. He'll help make it happen, I'm sure of it."

Amelia was studying her closely, appearing to hang on every word. But when Phoebe again fell silent, Amelia put her hands on her hips. "What makes you think I won't still wish to teach once I've graduated?"

Phoebe only reached over and patted her sister's knee through her pleated skirt, and tried not to chuckle.

They motored through the village and past it, to where the road steadily rose as it encircled a hillside. Soon, a Georgian mansion constructed of golden Cotswold stone rose up to their right, while fields and meadows and distant, rolling hills spread out on all sides. Phoebe turned in at the drive and brought the Vauxhall to a stop in the car park beside the Calcott Inn.

"For widows and old men, indeed," she murmured, remembering Mr. Walker's derisive comment. She stepped out, her feet crunching on the gravel drive. "There's nothing wrong with our hotel."

"I rather like it," Amelia said cheerfully as she came to stand beside Phoebe. "And I'm famished. Shall we?"

They purposely had arrived a little before the noon hour, and they found the dining room only sparsely populated. Phoebe asked for a table with a good view of the doorway, and the maître d' complied without asking questions. She was tempted to inquire if Mr. Walker had already been to lunch, but instead trusted to luck. She and Amelia ordered the cock-a-leekie soup and tea sandwiches, and settled in to wait.

As time passed, Phoebe began to doubt the success of their plan. Mr. Walker might be anywhere in the village, or he might have left the vicinity for the day. The time for Amelia's French lesson approached.

"Perhaps we should go." Phoebe sighed, unable to mask her disappointment.

"Nonsense. Let's order more tea, and are those Eccles cakes I see being brought to that table over there?"

Phoebe caught the sweet, buttery, right-out-of-the-oven scent and confirmed that yes, those were indeed the puff pastries stuffed with brandied currents and raisins that Amelia loved so well. Amelia signaled for the waiter.

The young man took the order and had just walked away when Phoebe leaned to nudge her sister. "There he is." Amelia started to turn. "Don't be so obvious." Phoebe followed his path as the maître d' led him to a small table not far from the doorway. The maître d' attempted to hand Mr. Walker a menu, but he waved it away and spoke some words. The maître d' nodded and walked away.

Amelia pretended to adjust the collar of her frock while attempting to peek over her shoulder. "What's he doing?"

"It looks as though he just ordered his lunch. I'd say our Mr. Walker is a creature of habit. Probably has the same thing every day. I wish you hadn't ordered those Eccles cakes. I'd like to get this over with now. Besides, we don't know how long it takes him to finish a meal. We don't want him rushing out before we've had a chance to approach him."

"We'll have them wrapped and take them with us."

Phoebe nodded and raised a hand to signal the waiter. She asked him to wrap their dessert and cancel the tea.

"We lost track of time," she explained, "and my sister needs to get back to school for afternoon lessons."

Within a few minutes their parcel arrived, and they began to make their way out of the dining room. Phoebe came to a stop before Mr. Walker's table and assumed her most surprised expression.

"Why, Mr. Walker. How fortunate to run in to you here."

A plate of lamb chops and boiled potatoes swimming in butter sat in front of him. He barely glanced up, lifting only his gaze to meet Phoebe's. With his fork, he scooped up mint jelly, slathered it over a hunk of lamb, and popped it in his mouth. Chewing, he said, "Really? And why is that, Lady Phoebe?"

It was all she could do to remain civil. "I wish to apologize, of course."

He stopped chewing and this time raised his face as he looked up. "Indeed."

"Oh, yes." Phoebe took the liberty of sitting at one of the unoccupied seats at the table and placed the package of Eccles cakes on the cloth before her. Amelia sat as well, never mind that neither of them had been invited. Mr. Walker appeared taken aback at this intrusion, but said nothing as he apparently waited for further explanation. Phoebe was all too happy to oblige. With a long-suffering sigh, she said, "Yes, I understand my maid was rather rude to you yesterday in the village. I noticed she seemed troubled later in the day and pressed her until she confessed what happened."

"It's not like our Eva to be rude, sir." Amelia shook her head sadly. "We do hope you can forgive her. And us."

"Yes, I'm afraid it's my fault." Phoebe lowered her chin humbly. "I expressed disapproval of your resort plans that day outside the bank, and Eva perhaps believed she was defending my position with her comments to you. She should not have presumed."

"No, she shouldn't have." Another chunk of lamb and a forkful of potatoes went into his mouth. "But am I to presume that by this apology of yours, you're not as opposed to my plans as you were?"

"You're right about that, Mr. Walker."

"It's partly my doing," Amelia put in eagerly. Phoebe flashed her a look to silence her. This hadn't been part of the plan, but Amelia went on happily. "When I heard about the kind of resort you're planning to build, I thought how wonderful. Little Barlow can be deadly dull sometimes. We could use a noteworthy destination, something to bring people here. And . . . well . . . I find Americans so very interesting. What part of the States are you from, Mr. Walker?"

"New York." He then dismissed Amelia by turning back to Phoebe. "Then your family won't stand in my way?"

Phoebe hadn't expected such a question; the surprise she showed wasn't feigned. "My family?"

He nodded. "I did a little research, and I know who your grandfather is and the kind of influence he has hereabouts. It's feudal and downright ridiculous, but the old guard can make quite a lot of trouble when they want."

"I see what you mean. I don't think you need to worry about that." Phoebe crossed her fingers beneath the table and avoided looking at Amelia for fear they'd both burst out in triumphant laughter. "I can't help but wonder, Mr. Walker, how you found your way to Little Barlow in the first place. I mean, in all of England, why here?"

"I like the look of the Cotswolds. It's brimming with that English charm, you know. The rolling hills, the quaint villages, the sheep dotting the fields. American tourists will eat it up. And there's land for sale here." Having consumed the first lamb chop, he cut into the second. "The orchard and the countryside around it are perfect."

"But how did you know?"

"I'd put out feelers all over the Cotswolds. Had an agent looking into available real estate." His tone became boastful, a man explaining business matters to two young, flighty-minded females. But he wasn't answering the question in a way that satisfied Phoebe.

"I suppose someone at the bank contacted your agent," she suggested, hoping to prompt him into an admission.

The man replied while chewing a mouthful of potatoes. "Nope. That man Evers is as tight as a corked bottle when it comes to his customers' business. No, I can thank one of your local people for the tip."

"Who?" Phoebe and Amelia said as one, and perhaps a shade too eagerly.

Mr. Walker stopped chewing and put down his fork. He studied them, and Phoebe resisted the urge to shrink in her chair. They had been too obvious, and Mr. Walker was on to them. A thin-lipped smile dawned, and he shook his head. "I don't know what you two hope to gain from this line of questioning, but I think I'm going to adopt Mr. Evers's policy and seal my lips." He glanced down at his plate and chuckled. "Except to finish this excellent lunch. Good day to you both."

Before Eva and Miles could seek out Josh the previous day, Miles had been called away on police business. Something about a dispute between two farmers over a ewe and her lamb. Ordinarily Eva might have questioned Josh on her own, but under the circumstances she recognized the wisdom of waiting for Miles to return to Foxwood Hall. The authority of a police constable would surely put fear into the boy's heart, making him more compliant and less likely to avoid telling the truth.

Miles arrived after the servants had their lunch. He and Eva found Josh sweeping the rear corridor, which led out to the servants' courtyard. This time of year especially, it was at least a thrice-daily task to keep the floors free of old, dried leaves tracked in by all the comings and goings of the servants and delivery men.

Eva had already obtained permission from both Mrs. Sanders and Mr. Giles to interrupt Josh's work and question him in Mrs. Sanders's parlor. The housekeeper had looked eager to sit in on the interrogation, and didn't understand why she should be excluded but Eva included. Miles merely thanked her for the use of her parlor and quietly closed the door behind her—and her scowls.

Eva told Josh to take a seat and make himself comfortable; he complied with the former but apparently found the latter impossible. With a wary gaze, he sat at the edge of the wooden settle and twiddled his fingers between his knees. The hobnailed heel of his boot tapped incessantly against the floor. "Did I do anything wrong?" he asked when the silence became too much for him.

Eva took a seat at the other end of the settle and offered him a reassuring smile. But as she and Miles had previously agreed, for now she said nothing.

Miles had taken his time closing the door and choosing a place to sit. He finally eased into Mrs. Sanders's favorite overstuffed chair, after he'd dragged it closer to the settle. With a kind of meticulous deliberation that had even Eva holding her breath, he took his pad and pencil from an inner coat pocket, tested the pencil point on a fresh page, compressed his lips, and finally, at long last, made eye contact with Josh.

"Where is William?"

Poor Josh went as white as Mrs. Ellison's freshly whipped cream. His fingers twisted, and the drum beat of his boot heel increased in speed and volume. "I . . . I . . . er . . . What?"

Eva sat forward and turned partly toward him. "It's all right, Josh. Better if you come clean with Constable Brannock."

"I don't know where Will is. Honest, Miss Huntford. Honest, Constable."

Miles regarded him a lengthy moment meant to increase the boy's discomfort. "How long have you worked here?"

The abrupt change in subject seemed to take Josh aback. Then his expression cleared. Here was a question he wasn't afraid to answer. "Since before the war ended. I took over for Arnold when he enlisted."

Miles nodded and made a note on his pad. "And in all that time, have you ever stolen food before?"

"I didn't . . . I . . ." Josh's eyes filled with tears, reminding Eva of another of the servants accused of such thievery nearly two years ago. Now, as then, she suspected Josh had good reason for committing his crime.

She leaned toward him again and patted his shoulder. "Did William ask you to bring him food?"

Josh nodded and hid his face in his hands.

Miles took on a stern tone. "How have you been getting into locked pantries?"

His face still buried in his palms, Josh shrugged. "I don't."

"No more lying, my boy."

Josh peeked out from between his fingers. "I'm not lying, Constable. The pantries were never locked when I went in. No one pays any attention to me. Most times they don't even see me." Here, Eva cast a knowing glance at Miles. Then Josh went on. "I just go in with an empty wash bucket, fill it quick, cover it with some rags, and go about my business. Nobody notices."

Miles narrowed his eyes. "That easy?"

A SILENT STABBING 181

"That easy, sir."

"Josh, has William been threatening you?" Eva asked him. "Is that why you stole food for him?"

Josh blew out a breath. "I wish I could blame it all on him. He did ask me to do it, but no, he ain't threatened me." His head dipped a moment, then came up, his expression defiant. "I couldn't just let him starve, could I?"

"You knew everyone was looking for him. And you know why. A man has been murdered." Miles let that sink in. "You should have said something."

"I don't know where he's been hiding. He won't tell me."

"Are you sure?" Miles persisted.

"I'm sure." Josh wiped his sleeve across his eyes and cheeks. "Besides, he didn't kill the new gardener. Although I wouldn't 'a blamed him if he had."

Eva remembered something Josh had told her. "You said William had a bruise on his face after his first day working with Stephen Ripley."

Josh nodded.

Miles asked, "Do you know if Stephen Ripley gave him that bruise?"

"He wouldn't say. But yeah, who else woulda done it?"

"So it's safe to say Mr. Ripley bullied William?" Eva spoke gently, a softer touch to Miles's harsher manner. Between the two of them, they were getting their answers. All except one.

"You saw how Ripley practically dragged Will out of the servants' hall that morning," Josh said to Eva. "You think a nice bloke does that?"

"No, I don't," Eva admitted.

"But Will didn't kill 'em."

"What makes you so sure?" Miles tapped his pencil against his pad. "Just the fact that William is hiding out makes him appear guilty."

"Look, I know Will. He'd never kill nobody. But that

don't mean he won't get tossed in jail, or worse. We both remember when that happened to Vernon. He barely got off. Will's afraid the same'll happen to him. Even though he's innocent," Josh added emphatically.

"He's your friend," Eva said.

"Yeah."

"And friends stick up for each other." Miles tapped his pencil again, his gaze riveted on Josh.

"Yeah . . . so?" Josh trailed off, suddenly wary again.

Very quietly, Miles asked, "Are you covering for your friend, Josh?"

Josh shook his head vehemently. "No. I wouldn't help him if I thought he killed someone. I swear on all that's holy, I don't know where Will's been hiding, but I know he didn't kill Stephen Ripley."

Miles absorbed this without a change in his expression. "Where do you meet him, when you bring him food?"

With a sigh, Josh slouched against the high wooden back of the settle. "Out beyond the hothouses. At night."

"Near the yew hedge?" Miles asked. Josh nodded.

"You've been sneaking out to meet him." Eva was well aware of the curfew for the lower servants. They were not allowed to leave the house after sundown without permission. "Are you supposed to meet him tonight?"

Will shook his head. "Not tonight. Tomorrow night."

Eva and Miles exchanged a look. Miles said, "That's all for now. You can go. But if you remember anything else or you hear from William, you're to let me or Miss Huntford know straightaway. Understood?"

Josh had already come to his feet. He nodded and wasted no time in vacating the room.

"So all we have to do is wait until tomorrow night, when William comes back for more food," Eva said as soon as the door had closed.

"Something tells me our William is too clever to be

caught that way. He'll sense a trap a mile away. Still, it
may be our only chance to try."

"Do you think William has Josh fooled?"

"I hope not."

"The hothouses are not only near the hedge where
Stephen died, they're also near the path that leads through
the woods to the Haverleigh School." Eva thought a moment, then shook her head. "But no, I don't think William
would be coming from that direction. There would be
nowhere at a girls' school for him to hide."

"Once in the cover of the woods, who knows what direction he takes? But he's probably been staying somewhere on the property. We've been checking the head
gardener's cottage periodically. But if it was William who
knocked you down that day you and Lady Phoebe were
there, it isn't likely he'd risk going back. There are so
many other places on this estate a man could hide, and
nothing says he's been staying in the same location every
night."

Eva gave a little gasp. "Your mention of the gardener's
cottage just reminded me of the flat cap found near
Stephen's body. Have you been able to determine if it belonged to him?"

Miles's lips turned up in a little smile. "It didn't. Not a
blond hair to be found anywhere on it."

"I knew it couldn't have been Stephen's cap. Did you
find any hair on it at all?"

"We did, but it's inconclusive."

"What on earth does that mean? What color is it? Is it
wavy or straight?"

"It's rather a chestnut color. Neither quite red nor brown
but a shade in between."

"Auburn," Eva suggested.

Miles nodded. "With a bit of a wave, but too short to
show if it could be called curly. Whereas the plaid cap you

found at the gardener's cottage clearly belonged to Stephen. Straight blond hairs were found inside and around the sweatband."

"I see. So the only conclusion to be drawn with any accuracy is that the cap found near the hedge didn't belong to Stephen, or any other man with blond hair. Or black or gray hair, for that matter. But it did belong to a man, since the hair is short. I suppose that's something, though not much."

"No, and it's not enough to clear Keenan. And to give the chief inspector his due, he brought Keenan out into the bright light to compare his hair to the one found in the cap. And what he discovered was that Keenan's hair is a close match, but there's room for doubt because no one's hair is completely one color or another, but a subtle variation of shades. And since Keenan lives alone, there is no one to vouch for whether the cap is his or not."

Eva nodded, having made a similar observation years ago when she first began dressing hair as a lady's maid. "Have you had a chance yet to question Joe Murdock? His hair is brown, but probably has some tones of auburn in it as well. Most brown-haired people do. And he stood to gain from Stephen's death, didn't he?"

"I have, as a matter of fact. He says he was at the pub that morning, taking deliveries."

"Are you sure? Have you been able to talk to the deliveryman?"

"No, but there were several other witnesses. Other business owners preparing their shops for morning customers."

"So, other villagers." Eva skewed her lips to one side.

"Yes. So? Why that cynical look?"

"Did I tell you what I saw when I walked by the Ripley orchard the other day? People from all over Little Barlow helping harvest the pears before they overripen."

"Isn't that what neighbors do?"

"Miles, don't you see? These people not only flock to the aid of their own, they also love their perry cider. It's possible they were trying to shield Joe from suspicion."

"Ah, yes. Like when all those men gathered at the police station to offer alibis for Keenan."

"Exactly," Eva said.

"But at some point, even the people of Little Barlow will want to see a murderer caught and punished, perry or no perry."

Eva's thoughts strayed back to the tweed cap, and what Miles had discovered about it so far. "I'd so hoped the cap could be used as evidence to help Keenan."

Miles was quiet a moment, looking as though he had something on his mind he'd rather not reveal. But reveal it he did. "Have you considered the possibility that Keenan *did* murder Stephen? He had the strongest motive of anyone. One almost couldn't blame him if he did it."

"How can you think such a thing?" she snapped, and then realized she knew the answer well enough. Miles hadn't grown up in Little Barlow. He was a relative newcomer, and as such had few sentiments attached to the people who lived here. He could be objective where she could not. "I'm sorry. I do understand why you have to explore every avenue. Nothing but my intuition tells me Keenan is innocent. But, Miles, I'm going to go on believing he's innocent, and that he will be exonerated."

He took her hand in his. "I wish I could reassure you. But I'm afraid it's not looking good for Keenan Ripley."

CHAPTER 13

Phoebe returned home after dropping off Amelia—and the Eccles cakes—back at school. Leaving the Vauxhall out front for one of the footmen to bring to the garage, she relinquished her coat to Mr. Giles and made her way into the library. A low fire burned in the grate, and Phoebe hesitated. A fire meant someone, probably her grandfather, would be using the room soon. She had effectively avoided being alone with her grandparents since yesterday's debacle at the bank. Should she make her escape, run upstairs to her room like a coward?

But no, even if the footsteps in the Great Hall—heavy ones that suggested a man's oxfords—hadn't alerted her to an imminent arrival, she would not have sneaked off. She settled into one of the armchairs that faced her grandfather's favorite wing chair. If he wished to take her to task, better to have it over with sooner rather than later.

The footsteps came closer, were nearly to the doorway. Perhaps she should have slipped a book from one of the shelves and buried her nose in it, pretend to be terribly busy.

"Phoebe. I didn't know you were home." Grampapa

strolled in with a book of his own, a dark, leather-covered tome with gold embossing. He walked to her chair and leaned down to kiss her forehead. "Did you and Amelia enjoy your lunch?"

A fresh wave of guilt washed over her, and she was glad of the dim lighting and the fire glow that hid her flushing cheeks. That was, until Grampapa switched on the electric lamp beside his chair. The leather creaked as he lowered himself onto the cushion. He had no idea of the true purpose of Phoebe's and Amelia's lunch today. Should she tell him? She couldn't imagine that he would approve. But then, Grampapa, and Grams for that matter, had very little idea of the kinds of activities she and Eva had gotten up to these past couple of years.

"Lunch was lovely," she said. "I don't see enough of Amelia during the school term."

He smiled. "It does my heart good to see how well you two get on." His mouth closed with a regretful slant. Phoebe could guess at his thoughts: that he wished she and Julia would get on equally as well. She wished that, too, for his sake as much as any other reason. She waited for him to bring up the bank. He looked down at his book, his thumb running lightly over the gilded edges of the pages. This took her aback. Grampapa might be a soft-spoken gentleman, but only on the rarest of occasions had he ever been at a loss for words. The silence became awkward.

"Grampapa, I—"

"Phoebe, I wish to apologize."

She blinked and pulled back. She had been about to say the same thing. "For what? I can't think of a single transgression you've ever committed."

His smile returned, accompanied by a quiet chuckle. "You think too highly of me, my dear. Not that I'm complaining. No, indeed. But I'm sorry I didn't go to the bank sooner. I'm sorry you felt forced into initiating something I should have looked into the moment we learned Keenan Ripley was being coerced off his land."

She regarded him closely. His once robust frame had diminished over the past year, and his hair, once thick and golden auburn like Phoebe's, had thinned considerably. Unlike Grams, who recovered from physical and emotional setbacks like a seasoned foot soldier, Grampapa bore the brunt of each foray, and there had been some significant ones in recent months. She looked into eyes very much like her own, and like her father's. "Did you know Julia and I had gone to the bank?"

"No, I didn't. I simply came to my senses, and when I mentioned my plan to your grandmother, she agreed wholeheartedly."

That surprised Phoebe, and she couldn't help showing it in her expression. Again, Grampapa chuckled.

"If nothing else, your grandmother is pleased to thwart this developer and his plans to bring his loud, new-moneyed compatriots to our peaceful village."

Phoebe grinned. "We don't know that they'll be loud."

"Your grandmother insists they will be. And so we must do what we can for Little Barlow, but more importantly, for Keenan Ripley." A worried look came over him.

"Do you think he'll be formally charged?" Phoebe asked him.

He shook his head slowly. "I hope not. Like most people here, I don't wish him to be guilty. A horrible thing to contemplate, brother against brother." He set his book aside and linked his fingers over his abdomen. "It's far more comforting to think a stranger did this."

Phoebe sensed more, as if Grampapa had his own ideas about the guilty party but didn't like to say. The only stranger she could think of in Little Barlow currently was the American, Mr. Walker. But he had no reason to have killed Stephen Ripley. True, she and Eva had bandied the

notion that he might have wanted to be rid of both brothers, but too much would have depended on luck for such a
plan to work. And she didn't think Mr. Walker was the
kind of man to leave anything to luck.

A pounding echoed through the Great Hall, startling
them both. Grampapa came to his feet. The pounding continued. "What on earth? Is that the front door?"

Phoebe beat him to the doorway. "It certainly sounds
like it."

She watched Mr. Giles hurry across the hall into the
vestibule. A moment later the pounding stopped, but a
voice carried through the house. An angry one.

"I demand to see Lord Wroxly. This instant." Both the
voice and the accent identified the speaker as Horace
Walker. Phoebe exchanged a look with her grandfather.

"Don't go," she said. "Don't give that rude man the satisfaction."

But Grampapa stepped around her and traversed the
hall to the vestibule. Before he reached it, Horace Walker
came striding into the Great Hall as if he had a right to be
there. "There you are. I presume you're Archibald Renshaw?"

Phoebe gasped at the man's presumption in addressing
her grandfather as though they were equals. Then she
caught herself. She of all people disdained the notion of
class distinctions. But she also disdained this man and his
audacity in barging into her home and speaking to her
grandfather without a hint of respect. She hurried to her
grandfather's side.

"You." Mr. Walker thrust a finger toward her. "Trying
to get information out of me. Butter wouldn't melt in your
mouth, would it?" His attention swerved back to Grampapa. "Did you send this minx and her sister to do your
dirty work?"

"I beg your pardon." Phoebe heard Grampapa's colossal effort to hold his indignation in check. "I haven't the faintest notion what you're talking about. And I'll thank you never to speak of my granddaughter that way again."

Mr. Walker ignored the latter and addressed the former. "I'm talking about this family sneaking down to the bank and trying to muscle in on my purchase of the Ripley land. I'm not going to stand for it. The land is as good as mine."

"From what I understand, no sale can go through until Keenan Ripley's fate is determined. If he's exonerated, which I fully believe he will be, he will not only own his share of the land, but will inherit his brother's as well." Grampapa assumed the expression of someone striving to be helpful. Yet Phoebe heard the condescension in his voice. "That is how inheritance law works when there is no will. And according to Mr. Evers at the bank, Stephen Ripley had no will. Most young men of his age don't, you realize."

"Don't presume to lecture me about the workings of the law."

"But as an American, you might be unaware of how such things work here in England," Phoebe said, slipping her hand into the crook of Grampapa's arm to present a united front. "And no one sent me to speak with you today. It was merely a coincidence that my sister and I chose the Calcott Inn for lunch. Well, they do have the most complete dining menu in the village."

The American ignored her. "You're not going to get away with this, Lord Wroxly."

"I'm merely interested in acquiring the same parcel of land as you. There are no laws against that. It happens all the time." Grampapa extended his hand to the other man. "May the highest bidder win."

Horace Walker stared at the hand but didn't deign to shake it. His gaze flicked back up to Grampapa's face. "I have big plans for that land. Important plans that will help this village and everyone in it. I can't see a man like you going into the resort business. What could you possibly want to do with it?"

"We have no extensive orchards on the estate, and I've always fancied having one." He turned his face to Phoebe and winked. "Isn't that so, my dear?" She grinned and nodded.

Mr. Walker gave a snort. "I know something about your kind. Since the war, none of you is as rich as you once were. My guess is you're unable to buy the land outright. But I can, and I will outbid you, Lord Wroxly." His voice oozed contempt, inflaming Phoebe's dislike of the man even more. But she kept her features placid.

Her grandfather offered an equally placid smile. "Then as I said, may the highest bidder win. But only after Mr. Ripley's fate has been determined. Good day to you, sir."

"Good day." Mr. Walker spoke the pleasantry from between clenched jaws. "You haven't seen the last of me."

Grampapa had already turned away, and Phoebe with him, to retrace their steps to the library. Under his breath, he murmured, "A pity, that."

Phoebe couldn't have agreed more.

Eva spent the rest of that day and the following morning catching up on chores, such as hand washing some of Lady Phoebe's delicate lace collars, gloves, and silk scarves. Some things were not to be trusted to the laundress or to the harsher detergents she used. Eva often considered such tasks labors of love, not only due to her affection for her mistress, but to her admiration of the lovely artistry of the garments.

About midmorning, Hetta found her belowstairs, just as Eva was about to brew a cup of tea. "Fräulein, you can come, *ja*?"

Eva stood at the range, kettle in one hand, a match in

the other, about to light the burner. The question of whether Hetta's request was imperative came to her lips, but one look at the other lady's maid's clear blue eyes supplied the answer. She blew out the match and set the kettle down. "What's wrong? Is it Lady Annondale?"

Hetta nodded, her plain but pleasing features filled with worry. "Madame is crying. She doesn't stop."

Eva hurried to the backstairs and together they began the climb. "When did this start?"

"Since early. I bring her tea to her room, like always. I find her *weinen* . . . weeping."

"That long?" Eva hurried her steps. "Why didn't you come and get me sooner?"

"Madame say not to."

"Well, you were right to disregard that, though you probably should have done so earlier."

At the family's bedroom wing, Eva pushed through the door that separated the servants' landing from the carpeted corridor. Several doors down she stopped and listened, hearing sobs coming from inside. She knocked softly.

"Go away," came a mournful command from inside. "Please."

Holding the knob, Eva pressed her face close to the panels. "My lady, it's Eva. Please, may I come in?"

A long pause ensued. Then, finally, "All right, yes."

Eva opened the door just enough to slip inside, but held it open long enough for Hetta to follow her into the room. Whatever the matter might be, she felt Hetta had a right to be there. Despite a bit of a language barrier, the Swiss woman's fondness for Lady Annondale was genuine and mutual, and it would be to the benefit of both to learn to get along without Eva's intervention. Someday, Lady Annondale would have a home of her own, as would Lady Phoebe. And possibly, someday, Eva as well.

For now, Eva went to the dressing table, where Lady

Annondale sat on the cushioned bench, her elbows propped on the marble surface and her head in her hands. There were several discarded, damp handkerchiefs lying about, a couple more on the floor. Lady Annondale still wore her nightgown and wrapper. Her hair had been put up loosely, but golden tendrils had escaped their pins and clung damply to the sides of her neck. Eva grasped her shoulders and felt their trembling. "My lady, what is it? Please tell us what's wrong."

From within Lady Annondale's fingers came muffled words Eva couldn't make out. Only their sentiments were clear. This poor woman was distraught and, at present, inconsolable.

"Please, my lady, we can't help you unless you let us." She realized she should have had Hetta prepare a fresh tray of tea, and now, over her shoulder, she mouthed the instructions. When the other maid looked puzzled, Eva said with emphasis, "Tea. Strong." Hetta nodded vigorously and set off. Eva couldn't help thinking she looked rather relieved before she turned away.

Moving around to the side of the bench, Eva knelt and tried to coax Lady Annondale's slender hands away from her face. "Whatever it is can't be as bad as all that, my lady. You have your family around you and a houseful of people who care about you."

More mumbling made its way to her ears.

"My lady, I cannot make out a word you're saying."

The hands finally fell away to reveal swollen eyes and a blotchy face, which still, somehow, remained beautiful. "Eva, I've made a horrible hash of things."

Oh, dear. So much for that fortune-teller relieving Lady Annondale of her cares. "Not a bit of it, my lady. I'm sure whatever feels so wrong at the moment will right itself in time. Before you know it."

Lady Annondale shook her head so adamantly, more

strands of hair cascaded from her coif. "I'm going to be a dreadful mother."

"Why on earth would you say such a thing? You'll be a wonderful mother."

"Why, Eva? What about *me*"—she broke off and gestured at herself—"possibly makes you believe I'll know how to raise a child?"

"Why, many things, my lady." Eva paused to stroke Lady Annondale's hair and gently draw it away from her perspiring neck. "To begin with, you're intelligent and strong and confident."

"I'm selfish, you mean."

"Of course I don't mean that. Those are assets, not faults. Also, you're stylish and artistic and creative."

"Shallow and self-absorbed."

"My lady, please. You have many wonderful qualities to pass on to your child. And love, my lady. I know you'll shower this child with love."

Lady Annondale shook her head, her features crumpling. "I'm cold and intolerant and unforgiving. Just ask Phoebe."

"Your sister doesn't think that about you."

"Doesn't she? She should."

"Come, let's sit on the chaise and you can tell me what's really troubling you, yes?" After opening a drawer in the dressing table and taking out a fresh handkerchief, Eva grasped Lady Annondale's shoulders again and nudged her to her feet. To her relief, Lady Annondale didn't resist. Eva moved some pillows aside and they sat side by side on the chaise longue at the foot of the bed. Eva pressed the handkerchief into the younger woman's hand. "Now then, tell me what brought this on. You've seemed happy up until now."

Lady Annondale dabbed the handkerchief at her eyes.

"I woke up today with the realization that I'm not a good person, Eva."

"My lady, those are the old doubts talking. The ones that rose up after your husband died. None of that was your fault, and you mustn't blame yourself."

"I don't blame myself for Gil's death exactly, but there are so many things I should have done differently. *Would* have done, if only I'd stopped to think first. I try to change, Eva, I truly do. I tell myself I will, that I'll be a stronger, better person. But I simply . . . don't change. Something I can't control prevents me from being what I wish to be. And now, of course, it's too late." She shook her head. "Too, too late."

Was she talking about Theo Leighton, the man she would have married were it not for the family's dwindling fortunes? Eva believed so. The pair had begun an attachment nearly two years ago, rather on the sly, but financial pressures and a sense of duty to the family sent Julia Renshaw in another direction entirely. Tragically. And Eva knew Julia's outward persona of haughty, cool disregard was merely a shield protecting a vulnerable core.

But then, what suddenly shattered that shield? Why today? In the years since her father's death in the war, Julia Renshaw had held herself together with meticulous care.

Her gaze fell to the rounded belly beneath the silk wrapper, and she remembered from her own sister's letters during each of her pregnancies that expecting mothers were sometimes prone to doubts, even regrets, and a general malaise of the spirit. Could that be what had shaken Lady Annondale's confidence?

With a little gasp Eva sat up straighter. *Alice.* Why, all this time, her sister hadn't been acting herself, and Eva suddenly realized the most likely reason why. Good heavens!

She turned her attention back to Lady Annondale and

tried to offer what reassurances she could. "It's never too late to make changes, my lady. But just for now, until the child is born, why not simply concentrate on being happy for his sake? You spend far too much time alone in this room, and that's never good for anyone. One begins dwelling on things and imagining all manner of faults in oneself. It isn't healthy. Meanwhile, your grandparents would like to see more of you each day and . . . why, you could get involved at the Haverleigh School, like Lady Phoebe, and occupy your mind with matters you *can* change for the better. Put your talents to work."

Lady Annondale dabbed at her eyes again and gave a delicate sniff. "Phoebe does seem happier since she joined the school administrators, and of course there's her RCVF."

"Exactly. And you were a great help to her in sorting donations the other day. You could become more involved with that, or you could start a project of your own. I think you should speak with your grandmother about it. I'm sure she could help you come up with ideas."

"I'm not exactly the charitable sort," Lady Annondale said ruefully. "But I suppose . . . maybe something to benefit children, since I'm to be a mother. I believe I might like that."

"There you are, then."

A knock at the door signaled Hetta's return. She shouldered her way into the room and set the tea tray down on a nearby table. Julia rose from the chaise, and Eva came to her feet as well.

"Another thing, my lady." She lowered her voice so the other maid wouldn't hear. "Hetta has a heart as big as the Swiss mountains. I believe she'll be your best ally if given the chance. Let her help you. Don't shut her out."

"I won't. Thank you, Eva. I believe I'm feeling better." Lady Annondale put her arms around Eva and held her close a moment before releasing her. The renewed vigor in her expression assured Eva she would be fine, at least until the next bout of nerves took hold. And when that happened, Eva would be there for her.

Upon leaving Lady Annondale's room, she went back downstairs, her revelation about Alice foremost on her mind. If only her parents' cottage had a telephone, Eva would have set a new plan in motion immediately. Instead, she would give Connie a shilling to bring a message to her mother the next time the housemaid went into the village on errands. Eva hoped it would be sometime today.

CHAPTER 14

It wasn't until after dinner that Phoebe had a chance to compare notes with Eva. The pair set out on a walk through the gardens under a dusky sky edged in pink on the western horizon.

"Horace Walker was impertinent and deliberately attempted to intimidate my grandfather," Phoebe said to Eva once they'd cleared the terrace by several yards. The path took them past the flower beds with their abundant autumn flowers, to the sculpted shrubbery that was already beginning to show a want of care. Phoebe noted the blurring of the typically meticulous lines now that there was no head gardener to tend them. Could they convince Mr. Peele to return to Foxwood Hall?

"His impertinence doesn't surprise me, my lady." Eva paused to secure the top button of her coat. "It's in his nature. But intimidation? With your grandfather? Where does the man summon the cheek?"

"It's probably in his nature as well. He shows a distinct lack of breeding." They shared a chuckle, and she linked her arm through Eva's. "Seriously, he didn't exactly frighten me, but he did unsettle me. I wouldn't want to encounter him alone."

"No, my lady, you most assuredly wouldn't. Not to change the subject, but have you spoken with your sister recently?"

"Julia? Not really since she and I went to the bank. She wasn't pleased with the part I coerced her into playing, so I thought it best to keep my distance for a time."

"If you could, seek her out sooner rather than later."

Phoebe stopped walking and turned to study Eva. "Has she gone off the rails again? Like when she ordered her wardrobe be given away? Good heavens, packages are already starting to arrive from London and Paris. She's spending money she doesn't yet have. And may never have."

"No, it's not like that. It's more to do with what she can't give away. Herself."

"I don't follow." Yet on second thought, Phoebe believed she did. "Julia's unhappy. Or more to the point, unhappy with herself."

Eva looked away, hesitated, and then nodded. That, too, Phoebe believed she understood. It took a lot for Eva to betray a confidence. Obviously, she judged whatever was bothering Julia important enough to mention.

"I'd wager the first indication of her unhappiness was a desire to change all the outward signs of the person she is," Phoebe said. "Her attire."

"Yes. But that doesn't work, does it? I can't tell you the specifics, but suffice it to say she's in a vulnerable state. She is not the pillar of strength people often believe her to be."

They resumed walking. Phoebe scrutinized the gravel walkway, not wishing to stumble in the fading light. "I've long known that. But she makes it so difficult to be close to her. If she would only give an inch. . . ."

"It's even worse now. The pregnancy, my lady. It sometimes affects women this way, leaving even the most confident among them at a complete loss. I fear that's happened to Lady Annondale."

"I suppose that's what sent us all the way to the fortune-teller in Cheltenham. Poor Julia. I thought expecting was supposed to be such a happy time. The glowing mother and all that. No one ever talks about the other side of it."

"No, they don't, more's the pity. I'm sure it's taking your sister quite by surprise."

"I'll be patient with her—even more so than usual," Phoebe amended with a grin.

"I suggested she become more involved with the Haverleigh School or the RCVF. I hope it's all right that I did so. But it got her thinking. She might create her own charitable activity."

"What Julia needs—what we both need—is gainful employment. But since that's unlikely at this point, taking up a cause would benefit her immensely."

From behind them came the sound of a terrace door opening and footsteps coming down the path. They turned to see Vernon approaching, a missive in his gloved hand. "A message from the constable, for Miss Huntford," he said formally. He held out the note and, having completed his task, bobbed his head and turned on his heel in that brisk, efficient manner typical of seasoned footmen.

"What does it say?" Phoebe wanted to know.

Eva unfolded the note and bent her head over it. "Miles is coming presently. He wants to see if William shows up to meet Josh tonight." She looked up. "I suppose he intends to send Josh out with a bundle of food, and he'd like me there to help question William if he's caught. If you'll excuse me . . ."

"I'm coming with you."

"My lady, the constable might not wish—"

"I won't get in the way. But I'd like to hear firsthand what that young man has to say for himself. Especially with how he knocked you over that day in the head gardener's cottage."

"We don't know that was William."

"I think we do."

Minutes later, Phoebe waited near the kitchen garden while Eva went inside to greet Constable Brannock and devise their plan with Josh. By waiting outside she wouldn't disrupt the servants' routine, for whenever she appeared belowstairs they always scrambled to make special accommodations for her. Here, she was also shielded from view should William arrive before the others were ready for him. They had learned from Josh that William wouldn't venture farther than the hedge where Stephen Ripley had died. She wondered, did the spot hold a morbid fascination for him?

A brisk nip in the air had her tightening her cardigan around her. She studied the rows of vegetables stretching along the kitchen garden, some of which had been harvested and gone dormant for the winter. The autumn vegetables continued to flourish: cabbage, carrots, onions, and parsnips, to name a few. Some of them she didn't recognize in their natural state, used to seeing them cooked and prepared with sauces and glazes. The amount of work and forethought that went into the care and feeding of her family often astonished her. It made her feel regretful, and sometimes rather ashamed.

And that made her think of Julia, who, for different reasons, also felt regretful and rather ashamed. Eva had pointed to the pregnancy as the root of Julia's melancholia, but Phoebe guessed her loneliness also played a part. Loneliness in a house full of people—Phoebe believed Julia often felt that way, for who else among them could understand the ordeal of being married and widowed in a single

day, and then living with the consequences of that marriage—a child—for the rest of her life, a living reminder of
a decision she regretted?

What would Phoebe regret? Perhaps *not* marrying? That
was something Julia didn't understand. Why *didn't* Phoebe
marry Owen Seabright? Why risk letting him slip away?
She was certainly old enough to marry. She certainly had
deep feelings for Owen. Yes, perhaps even love. And she
trusted him. They'd spent time together last spring and
over the summer, happy, heady, enjoyable time. And yet . . .
she wasn't ready; nor, she believed, was he. He, with his
aristocratic hands deep into the textile industry, much to
the chagrin of his family. Because of his brother's death in
the last year of the war—of the influenza—Owen would
inherit an earldom. One he didn't particularly want. And
Phoebe—her expected place was at the side of a nobleman.
But like Owen, maintaining family expectations wasn't
what she wanted. She wanted . . .

More. She wanted . . . to know herself fully. To embrace
whatever she might be capable of. And marriage, too soon
entered into, even with Owen, might thwart that dream,
that potential. Might snatch the mystery right out from
under her.

She gazed beyond the vegetables to the hothouses, and
then toward the hedge that separated the service grounds
from the ornamental gardens. The concerns of her uncer-
tain future, she realized, paled when compared to the un-
certain fate of Keenan Ripley, and of Little Barlow. A man
like Horace Walker would destroy this village. At least in
those matters, she knew what she wanted, and what her
role must be.

After a quarter hour or so, hushed tones and three sets
of footsteps advanced toward her from the house. A moment later three forms took shape in the lights from the
courtyard behind them. Eva spotted her and waved. Be-

side her, Constable Brannock lighted the way with an electric torch aimed at the ground. She noticed his nightstick swinging from his belt and hoped he wouldn't have to use it. He acknowledged her with a nod, apparently not surprised by her presence.

As planned, Josh carried a bundle wrapped in cloth, its white hue glowing vaguely in the darkness. When he saw Phoebe, he came to an awkward halt on the path. "Lady Phoebe . . . em . . ."

Although Phoebe couldn't make out much beyond the basic shapes of his features, she could well envision the flames in his cheeks. They had never spoken to each other before. Any time she *had* ventured belowstairs, which was rarely, he had ducked his head and scrambled away, usually with a mop or coal shovel or other such tool in hand. "It's all right, Josh. Thank you for helping us with this matter."

He grimaced. "I don't like it." Whatever he said next was lost to a nervous bout of stammering, silenced when Constable Brannock murmured something in his ear.

Phoebe understood Josh's perplexity. "You feel you're betraying your friend. But William isn't helping himself with his actions. He needs to speak with the constable, and we need to hear what he has to say. You're doing him a favor, though it may not feel like it."

"It surely don't," the youth mumbled with his chin tucked low. Eva put a hand on his shoulder.

"So what happens next?" Phoebe asked the constable.

He exchanged a glance with Eva. "I'm going to wait just behind the hedge, out of sight while Josh waits in the usual place for William. If he shows up, I'll apprehend him."

This earned him a scowl from Josh.

"It's merely police talk," Eva said to him. "Constable Brannock only wishes to speak with William."

Josh stared down at the ground. "He won't be in any

trouble? For disappearing and all? And what about me? I stole the food. If Mr. Giles or Mrs. Sanders finds out, I'll get the sack for sure."

It was Phoebe's turn to offer a reassurance. "No one will have to know anything. As far as William is concerned, I'm sure a lot depends on his answers. Isn't that right, Constable?"

"It is. Now then." With an air of authority, he turned to address the hall boy. "Josh, you're to take up your usual place at the hedge to wait. I'll be close by, so if you think to warn William, I'll hear you. Lady Phoebe and Eva, I'd like you both to wait here, out of sight. Please." This last was added with an intensity, almost an urgency, directed toward Eva. "But once we have William, your presence might be helpful. A gentler touch, as it were." He smiled at Eva, who smiled back, a flush evident in her cheeks even in the shadows.

Phoebe and Eva nodded their assent. Falling briskly into his role of policeman, the constable escorted Josh past the hothouses, the beam of his torch bouncing along the shrubbery until it vanished with a click of its switch. All went dark but for the dim gas lighting inside the hothouses.

Eva released an audible breath and bobbed once on her toes, before folding her hands at her waist and affecting a patient air. It didn't fool Phoebe one bit.

"Is there something I should know?" she asked, careful not to speak above the lowest of whispers.

"Only that we're not expecting this to go as smoothly as one might hope." Eva's reply piqued Phoebe's curiosity, but she let it go rather than risk being overheard by William and frightening him off. But Eva's nervous excitement was catching, and let loose a host of butterflies in Phoebe's stomach.

A shout startled them both. A warning in a boy's high-pitched voice. Josh. Then another shout, this one lower, commanding. The constable. Footsteps thumped across the grass, echoing against the glass walls of the hothouses. The constable's torchlight danced wildly against the shrubbery and the undersides of the trees.

Phoebe and Eva each took a step as if to run toward the ruckus, but before Phoebe could start moving, Eva caught her hand. "No, my lady. Let the men handle it."

Another shout broke through the night sounds, a different voice from the first two. William? It sounded too deep to belong to such a young man. But then, who?

"You said 'men,'" Phoebe suddenly realized aloud. "Who else is out there?"

"Miles enlisted Vernon's and Douglas's help. They took up their positions while Miles and I were in the house talking to Josh. Miles expected to have trouble from William. And from Josh, for that matter. And it sounds as if he was right on both counts."

Douglas was another footman, a bit younger than Vernon and below him in the ranking of the servants. "You didn't tell me this."

"I didn't know until I went belowstairs and talked to Miles."

The continued sounds of scuffling, of a chase across the dark grounds, set Phoebe's nerves on edge. By the sounds of it they hadn't gone far, were playing cat and mouse just beyond the hothouses, still out of sight. Phoebe found it maddening, not being able to see what was happening.

"Perhaps we should go inside," Eva suggested.

"No. If they catch William we'll still be able to help. He'll be terrified, as will Josh. You and I can set them at ease. The constable won't be able to do that alone, simply by virtue of his position on the police force."

"That's true." Eva's tone betrayed her qualms, and Phoebe guessed her maid's protective instincts were on high alert. That made her grin, but only briefly.

The next moment brought a sharp change in the direction of the footsteps and voices. Someone crashed through the shrubbery beside the closest hothouse, and then with a clatter barreled through the kitchen garden fencing. A cry of pain escaped the individual as he dragged wooden slats connected by wires tangled around his legs. Dirt and plant matter went flying as he continued plowing through the garden. Behind him, two men sprinted after him, their path made easier by the destruction William had already caused.

Yes, Phoebe recognized the gardener's assistant. She had seen him often enough at Mr. Peele's side, performing their magic among the flower beds and sculpted hedges and the graceful sweep of the flowering trees.

Eva began tugging on her, urgently. "My lady, come. He's heading this way."

They were about to be mowed down where they stood. They scrambled off the path into the low ground cover of fern and ivy, the leaves brushing at their ankles. But as if they attracted him like a magnet, William swerved course and headed directly for them. Eva tried tugging Phoebe farther out of the way, but suddenly he was upon them. He gripped Phoebe's forearm in one hand, and with the other grabbed hold of her cardigan. He hauled her away from Eva, turned Phoebe so that her back was against the front of his torso, and came to a rigid, panting, desperate halt.

Phoebe could smell his despondency, his fear, like that of a wild animal who finds itself cornered. That, and several days of living rough and not washing. There were now three men coming through the garden, with Josh stumbling after them. Phoebe tried to remain calm and still. She detected no sign of a weapon on William, but as Constable Brannock approached them, William's arm slid upward to lodge at Phoebe's throat.

"Don't come any closer."

Eva cried out but stayed rooted to the spot. Constable

Brannock stopped walking and signaled with a hand out-stretched behind him to the other men. They, too, went still. "William, you're only digging yourself in deeper. Let Lady Phoebe go. All I want is to talk with you. There is no need for this."

The forearm at Phoebe's throat tightened. "Is that why you brought Vernon and Douglas?"

The two footmen glanced uneasily at each other. *This must be exceedingly difficult for them,* Phoebe realized, for it would tug their loyalties in opposite directions. As honorable, honest men, they would want to see the law followed and justice done. But as fellow servants, they wished to protect one of their own. Vernon, especially, would sympathize with William, having been accused of a crime he didn't commit two years earlier.

"I brought them because I feared you'd do exactly as you have done," the constable replied. "Come now. You don't want to hurt Lady Phoebe. She's always been kind to you, hasn't she?"

The forearm eased a fraction or two. "I just want to be allowed to leave. Back away and let me go."

"I can't do that, William." Constable Brannock re-moved his policeman's helmet, ran a hand through his thick, red hair, and took a couple of easy steps in William's and Phoebe's direction. "You disappeared immediately following Stephen Ripley's murder. We need to know why. What did you see that day? What did you do?"

"I didn't murder him." Behind her, William began to tremble, his shivers traveling up and down Phoebe's spine. From the corner of her eye, she made out Eva's anguished look, her hands pressed to her mouth.

The constable took a half step forward. "Then why have you been hiding?"

"Because I knew I'd be blamed. And . . ."

"And what, William?" Eva spoke gently, softly. Her

hands at her sides now, she came slowly forward, only a few short steps, and stopped. "What are you afraid of, William?"

"I'm afraid . . ." He swallowed and filled his lungs with air. Phoebe didn't move; she barely breathed.

Eva extended a hand toward him. "Yes, William?"

"I'm afraid the killer will come after me."

"Why would he do that, Will?" the constable asked.

"Because I saw him. He knows I saw him. He looked right at me."

Eva walked Lady Phoebe into Mrs. Sanders's parlor and wrapped her in the afghan the housekeeper kept on hand. Dora came in soon after with the cup of tea Eva had requested, and she carefully pressed it into Lady Phoebe's trembling hands. She took several sips, seeming to rally with each one.

"Thank you." Lady Phoebe leaned back in Mrs. Sanders's favorite easy chair while Eva perched on the footstool in front of her. "That was something, wasn't it?"

Eva felt a sudden, unexpected burning behind her eyes and blinked rapidly to prevent any tears from forming. "It certainly was, my lady. I've never been so frightened."

"I think you probably have been at some time or another in these past couple of years." Lady Phoebe let out a low chuckle and took another sip of tea. "That's good. Bracing. I needed it. Do you know where the constable has taken William?"

"I believe Mr. Giles's office." A knock at the door brought Eva to her feet. Outside stood Vernon and Douglas, peering past her with concern.

The head footman said, "We just wanted to check if Lady Phoebe is all right."

Lady Phoebe waved at them. "I'm fine. Really. Thank

you both for what you did. If not for you, William might have got away."

Neither young man looked particularly happy about the role they had played, but they pasted on smiles and went on with their duties.

"I intend to make sure my grandfather knows of their courage in assisting the constable. Without, of course, his learning of my part in tonight's excitement." Lady Phoebe winked at Eva, finished her tea, and set the cup aside. When she started to come to her feet, Eva hurried to her.

"My lady, don't. Sit a while longer."

"No, I meant it when I said I was fine. William frightened me, but he didn't hurt me. We should go see if the constable needs our help in questioning him."

Eva knew better than to argue; once Lady Phoebe made up her mind there was no changing it. But she kept close watch on her mistress every step of the way to Mr. Giles's office. Miles admitted them with a resigned air as if he, too, knew there would be no use in trying to send them away. He closed the door behind them.

Opposite the office's walk-in silver safe, William sat at Mr. Giles's desk in the rolling wooden office chair. His hands were curled tightly around the arms. Eva was happy to see that Miles hadn't handcuffed or restrained him in any way; not yet, at any rate. William's eyes were large and glistening with fear, his face leeched of color—except for the fading bruise on his cheek that Josh had described to her. Eva's heart went out to him, despite the possibility that he had murdered Stephen Ripley.

Her heart told her he hadn't.

Miles approached them. "Lady Phoebe, are you all right?"

"Quite, thank you. You mustn't worry about me."

Miles gave a nod, then reached out and touched Eva's

hand, just a warm graze of his fingers against hers. A wave of mingled pleasure and embarrassment swept over her, and she darted a look at Lady Phoebe. But she needn't be chagrined about that slight display of affection, as Lady Phoebe had never shown anything but approval toward her growing friendship with Miles.

His expression becoming somber, he perched on a corner of the desk and looked down at William. "Did you murder Stephen Ripley?"

His head snapping up, William lurched back against the chair as if Miles had slapped him across the face. "No!"

"Are you certain about that?" Miles spoke almost entirely without emotion.

"Of course I'm certain. I didn't kill him."

"How did you get that bruise on your face?"

William's lips became a tight, thin line, and, if possible, he turned even whiter.

Eva went closer to him. "William, it's no good to keep silent or to lie. It only makes matters look worse for you. How did you come by that bruise?" She already knew the answer, but she wouldn't put words in his mouth. She hoped he would find them himself.

When the ticking of the clock became loud and jarring, William clenched his jaws and then slowly relaxed them. "Mr. Ripley hit me. That first morning."

"Why?"

"Because I complained I was hungry. Couldn't help it. He didn't let me eat my breakfast. Isn't that right, Miss Huntford?"

She nodded. "It is. He pulled you away from the table before you had a chance to finish."

"How did it make you feel when he hit you?" Miles glanced at his fingernails as he made the query.

"Feel? Mad. A bloke gets smacked in the face, he sees

red, doesn't he?" His mouth snapped closed again as he realized the significance of his words. Eva bit her bottom lip.

"Mad enough to react in violence?" Miles asked.

William shook his head. "No. I never touched him. I swear. You think I wanted to get the sack and go back to my parents, who can't afford to feed the two little ones still at home?" He slumped lower against the vertical slats on the back of the chair. "I'll get the sack now, though."

"We'll see," Lady Phoebe said softly.

"All right." Miles tilted his chin as he scrutinized William's face with a cold expression that would have chilled Eva's blood had he turned that gaze on her. "Tell us exactly what happened that next morning. Where you were, what you saw."

William swallowed. "I ate my breakfast right quick and went out extra early. We were continuing on the hedge, Ripley trimming and me raking up and tossing the cuttings in the cart. But then Ripley, he sent me back to his shed for another pair of shears. The small ones for doin' the fine work."

That raised a frown on Miles's brow. "Are they something a head gardener would have with him whenever he set out to sculpt a hedge?"

"Usually, yeah."

"Then why wouldn't he have brought them when he set out to work that day?"

"Dunno. Forgot, I suppose."

Eva sensed an important fact had just been disclosed and exchanged a glance with Lady Phoebe.

Miles continued. "So when you left to get the shears, everything seemed normal?"

William nodded.

"And when you returned with the shears?"

William fell forward, landing with his elbows on his

knees. For one awful moment, Eva feared he'd be ill. "He was on the ground. There was blood. And someone standing over him."

"Did you see who it was?" Miles leaned down lower to speak in William's ear.

He shook his head. "He wore a cap and had a scarf pulled up over his mouth and nose. But he saw me—"

Miles interrupted him. "Where exactly were you?"

"I'd come around the far end of the hedge, the end farthest from the hothouses." His voice was tight, choked with suppressed tears. "I'd cut across the formal gardens from the shed. Went fast so the family wouldn't come upon me if they were outside."

"So this person had disguised his face," Miles recounted. "And this cap. What did it look like?"

"Typical. Tweed. Brown, I think."

Eva and Lady Phoebe exchanged another glance. As they had suspected, the cap belonged to the murderer. Miles spoke again.

"If you couldn't make out the face, why are you afraid this person will come after you?"

"Because when he saw me, he stared hard and pointed at me. It was a warning. That's when I ran and kept going until I practically got lost in the forest."

"What can you tell me about the individual? Height. Weight. Anything at all."

William gave a halfhearted shrug. "I dunno. Average, I guess."

"On the slim side, or portly?"

"Slim." William frowned in thought, then nodded. "Yeah, slim. Clothes were loose, baggy."

"Describe them, if you can."

Another shrug. "Brown pants, maybe corduroys. Striped shirt. Blue stripes. Maybe green. Sun wasn't really up yet."

"Was he tall? Or medium height? Think about the person in relation to the hedge. Which is about, what?"

"Ten feet," Lady Phoebe supplied, and William nodded.

"So in relation to the hedge," Miles went on, "was this person tall or short, or as you said, average?"

William once more let his head fall into his hands. "I don't know. Please, can't I go?"

"No, William, you can't go." Miles spoke harshly. "You must think."

Shaking his head, William mumbled, "Average. Like me, maybe."

One thing Eva now knew, as did they all: the killer could not have been the barrel-chested, towering Joe Murdock.

Miles eased his tone. "Where have you been hiding?"

When William didn't reply, Eva said, "That was you, wasn't it, that day in the gardener's cottage? We surprised you there, and you ran into me in your haste to flee."

William's head came up, his expression genuinely puzzled. "No. I wouldn't go there. It's the first place anyone would look. I've been mostly at the old gamekeeper's cottage, and in a corner of the stables. Trevor never even knew I was there," he insisted, referring to the head groom who now also tended to Lord Wroxly's Rolls-Royce and Lady Phoebe's Vauxhall.

"Then . . ." Eva trailed off. With a sickening lurch inside her, she acknowledged that the person who ran into her at the gardener's cottage could have been no other than the killer, perhaps there to root out any evidence that might link him to Stephen Ripley.

What if Eva had gone there to collect Stephen's cap alone? What if she or Lady Phoebe had gone in pursuit after the individual knocked her down? Those questions—and the likely answer—sent chills rippling down her spine.

"William, if you feared for your life, why did you run away?" Lady Phoebe asked. "You could have come to us for protection. My grandfather would have seen to your safety."

William turned his face to her. "Could he have protected me from being blamed for Mr. Ripley's death? From being arrested? I was afraid of that, too. Still am."

Miles leaned back and regarded William down the length of his nose. "As it is, you are going to be arrested."

Eva felt a protest rising inside her, but she kept quiet.

Presently, Miles went on. "Keenan Ripley is still the chief constable's main suspect, but I can't let you go, not with so many questions left dangling. The problem is, what to do with you. There's only one cell at the station, and it's occupied." He sighed. "The only alternative is to have you sent to Gloucester."

Fear burgeoned in William's young eyes. This time, Eva couldn't help herself. She knew a youth like William would rarely have strayed beyond Little Barlow's borders in all the years of his life. "Is it really necessary to send him so far away?"

Lady Phoebe spoke up before Miles could reply. "No, it isn't. I've an idea."

CHAPTER 15

"Thank you again, Grampapa. The constable didn't like the prospect of sending someone as young and inexperienced as William to Gloucester to be dealt with by the police there. And thank you, too, Grams."

Earlier, Phoebe had found both her grandparents in the Rosalind sitting room, enjoying a nightcap before bed. She had explained to them this latest development of Constable Brannock having found the gardener's assistant and taken him into custody. She told them of how the constable had enlisted Vernon and Douglas, along with Josh, and together they had set their trap. She had even told them how Josh, fearing for his friend's life after learning of the murderer's warning gesture, had been bringing William food to keep him from starving. She explained it in such a way as to exonerate Josh of all blame and rather make him look the hero. Neither Grampapa nor even the more stoic, often stern Grams could conscience one friend leaving another to brave danger and the elements alone. They had agreed that, at least for now, neither Mr. Giles nor Mrs. Sanders needed to be any the wiser concerning the missing food items. They would be happy enough that no further thefts would occur.

What Phoebe had left out was her and Eva's roles in the trap they had laid, and how William had held her with his forearm against her throat. All participants had agreed this was something no one needed to worry the earl and countess with. Now, after checking with Eva that William had been secured with no further ado, she had returned to the Rosalind sitting room to fill them in on the accommodations made available for William. Ordinarily he shared a room with Josh belowstairs, but not presently.

"He's upstairs, in one of the unused rooms in the male servants' wing. At the very end of the corridor, farthest from the staircase and away from the occupied rooms." Phoebe referred to the servants' quarters on the second floor beneath the attic. In the past, all the servant bedrooms had been occupied by two or sometimes more individuals, but since the war there were far fewer servants at Foxwood Hall.

"Need we post a guard at the door?" Grams's thin silver eyebrows drew inward with concern. "Are we in any danger? Might he escape?"

"The constable doesn't believe so," Phoebe said. "Apparently they had a long talk and William has promised to stay put."

Grams wasn't reassured. "Can he be trusted to keep such a promise?"

"It was never a matter of trust, Grams. He ran and hid because he was frightened." That much was mostly true. William had been frightened for his life, yes, but also that he might be blamed for Stephen Ripley's murder. She decided not to mention that now. "He's safe here, so he has no reason to try to run again."

"But what if it turns out he's the murderer?" Grams had

apparently decided to pursue all possibilities and would not be satisfied until she had explored them all.

"I don't believe the constable would have agreed to keep him here if he thought the boy could be a danger to us," Grampapa calmly observed. "It would seem that unanswered questions prompted him to hold on to William rather than leave him at his liberty, but if Constable Brannock believed William capable of murder he would have sent him to Gloucester. Or he would have set Keenan Ripley free and put William in his place at the police station here."

Grams's spine relaxed a fraction. "I suppose you're right, Archibald. But, Phoebe, I don't want you going anywhere near that bedroom. Not for any reason."

"In the male servants' wing, Grams?" Phoebe gave a light chuckle. "You needn't worry, that's not an area of the house I tend to frequent." Indeed, a door stood between the male and female servants' wings, secured by a sturdy lock, the key to which Mrs. Sanders kept on her person at all times. Not even Mr. Giles possessed a key to that door. And the only other way into the male wing was by a staircase that climbed directly there from a landing right outside Mr. Giles's office, and which bypassed the first floor altogether.

Grams's shrewd gaze proclaimed her full awareness that there was more to the story than Phoebe was telling them, but that she, Grams, would keep quiet for now to prevent Grampapa from worrying.

Phoebe kissed them each good night and made her way along the corridor to her bedroom. Outside her door, she remembered what Eva had said to her earlier, before all the excitement had occurred. That made her glance across to Julia's room. It had grown rather late and with all that had happened, Phoebe's comfortable bed beckoned in a way that was nearly impossible to resist. But Eva had appealed to her to reach out to her sister, and she doubted sleep would come easily if she didn't first make an effort.

Earlier at dinner, Julia had seemed more at ease than usual. She had even taken an interest in discussing with Grams an addition to the curriculum at the Haverleigh School. The new lessons, intended to introduce sixth-form students to the political sciences, had actually been Phoebe's idea, although Julia seemed to have forgotten that detail. No matter. Only last month, the U.S. government had granted all of its female citizens over the age of twenty-one the right to vote, and Phoebe felt it was just a matter of time before England did likewise, rather than the current voting privileges extended only to women over thirty who were married or owned property in their own right.

The subject gave Phoebe the perfect opportunity to knock on Julia's door now and continue the discussion. Julia answered with a distracted-sounding "Come in."

Phoebe found her sister examining her reflection in her full-length mirror. She stood in profile, her hands smoothing the fabric of her nightgown against the roundness of her belly. "Am I fat?" she abruptly asked Phoebe's reflection in the mirror. The question startled Phoebe, but she pretended otherwise.

"You're expecting a child."

"That doesn't answer the question."

"No, you are not fat." Phoebe went to sit in a chair near the fireplace. "You look like a mother-to-be five months gone, which is exactly what you are."

"Most expecting women begin to swell right about now, and keep on swelling through to the end. And I'm not talking about their stomachs." Phoebe heard no plaintiveness in her sister's voice, only curiosity.

"Well, I don't see any evidence of that happening to you. Except for your belly you're still as svelte as a fashion model."

"Do you think something could be wrong, then?"

Phoebe had fallen right into that trap. She sighed. "No, Julia, I don't think anything is wrong, but of course I'm not the correct person to ask. When do you see Dr. Hayward next?"

"Dr. Hayward." Julia waved a hand in dismissal. "What does a man know about how a woman should feel?"

"I should think a physician knows a great deal about that."

"I'd prefer a midwife."

Phoebe blinked in surprise. "You would?"

"Of course. But it would never be allowed. Grams would have the vapors. Not that Grams has ever *had* the vapors, but something like that would send her over the edge. I don't like physicians. I never have."

Phoebe regarded her. Even in her nightgown, her hair down, the little makeup she wore washed away, Julia maintained a sophisticated, aristocratic beauty, in stark contrast to Phoebe's own rather ordinary looks. That was how Phoebe thought of her eldest sibling: a cool, often indifferent society beauty. Not for the first time, she wondered what else simmered beneath Julia's impeccable façade. "I wouldn't have guessed this. I'd have thought you wanted the most modern methods of childbirth. A midwife certainly doesn't fall into that category."

Julia pried herself away from the mirror. She reclined on the chaise longue and put up her satin-clad feet. "Perhaps not, but what does a man know about giving birth? I mean *really* know. *I* know it's going to hurt more than anyone but another mother can imagine."

"Are you . . . are you afraid?"

Julia shrugged a shoulder. "I don't know. I haven't much choice in the matter. And anyway, I'm not the first woman in this condition. I suppose if others can do it, I certainly can."

It made Phoebe smile to see a bit of Julia's stubborn confidence return.

Julia regarded her with a puzzled look. "Did you want something?"

It was on Phoebe's tongue to bring up the political science lessons planned for Haverleigh. But she had only meant to use that as an excuse for knocking on Julia's door. Somehow, they'd fallen into a conversation without help, a rare occurrence for them in recent years. "No, not really. I wasn't sleepy yet." This, of course, was a lie, but Julia didn't need to know that. "So I thought I'd see how you were doing."

"Hmm." Julia looked her up and down. "Did Grams send you?"

"No, Grams did not," Phoebe was able to say truthfully.

"Well . . . I'm glad you came, because there *is* something I'd like to discuss with you."

Yet another surprise. She kept her features even. "Go on."

"It's about the baby. He'll need godparents."

A tide of elation brimmed inside Phoebe. She reached out a hand. "Oh, Julia."

But Julia wasn't looking. She was inspecting her manicured fingernails. "I'm thinking of asking Amelia to be godmother. What do you think? Is she too young? Is it too much to ask of her?"

Phoebe's delight receded like an outgoing wave, the force of it strong enough to whisk her feet out from under her if she hadn't been sitting. Her hand fell to her lap. She forced herself to swallow past the doughy lump that had formed so suddenly in her throat, and to answer Julia in a steady voice that betrayed no other emotion than approval. "I think Amelia will make the perfect godmother for your child. I can't think of one better."

Julia nodded vaguely, her eyebrows knitted. "I can't for

the life of me think of a proper godfather. Certainly not Ernie Shelton." She shuddered, having referred to her late husband's cousin and heir—until, that was, Julia's child entered the world, assuming it would be a boy. Ernie had made no secret of his resentment of Julia's very existence and that he prayed nightly for her to give birth to a girl.

"No, not Ernie," Phoebe agreed, happy to move past the subject of godmother. A name came into her mind. Theo Leighton, the man Julia should have married if only the family hadn't needed Gil's money to help keep Foxwood Hall solvent. Although a marquess, Theo had little fortune of his own, it having been squandered by his elder and now deceased brother. Phoebe often wondered whether, if Julia did produce the Annondale heir and thus acquired greater access to Gil's money, she would marry Theo after all.

"I'll have to give it some thought," Julia said, and for a startled moment Phoebe thought she was talking about marrying Theo. Then she remembered what they'd been discussing. Godparents. For an instant she had believed Julia wished to bestow on her a priceless gift, and with it a new beginning for them as sisters. But Julia was correct in her choice, and Phoebe couldn't deny it. Amelia would make the most loving godmother a child could wish for.

Julia yawned, her eyes closing and her mouth opening wide. Phoebe took that as her cue to leave. Besides, she no longer had the heart for chitchat. She bade her sister good night and received a preoccupied reply.

The next morning, Eva received a reply to the note she had sent her mother the day before. Mum had responded with an invitation to lunch, and Lady Phoebe was only too happy to oblige Eva with a couple of hours off.

Betty Huntford waited at the open front door as Eva walked up the road. She dispensed with the usual greetings. "Your father won't be in for lunch. He's got business a few farms over, so I thought this would be the perfect opportunity."

Eva shrugged out of her coat, passing it off to her mother, who hung it on the coatrack. "Is Alice here?"

"Not at the moment. She's out again on one of her walks." Mum frowned, obviously uneasy. "But she said she'd be home for lunch. Eva, what is this all about? You said you'd figured out what was making Alice act so mysteriously. Can't you tell me what it is?"

"Let's wait for Alice. I could be wrong, and I'm sure there's more to the story that only Alice can tell us."

Mum led the way into the kitchen. "What makes you think she'll be more forthcoming now when she hasn't been all along?"

"Because of what I think I know. I'm wagering I can open the floodgates."

Mum turned around to face her. "Is it very bad, Eva?"

Eva embraced her mother briefly. "No. In fact, if it's what I think, it's good news. But no guessing. Let's wait for Alice. You're sure she's coming home for lunch?"

"That's what she said."

"And she doesn't know I'm here?"

"You said not to tell her, so I didn't."

Eva gave her mother credit for asking no further questions. The kettle began to steam. Mum took it off the burner and set it on the warming plate. From out the back window, Eva spied her sister walking past the toolshed.

Alice entered through the kitchen door and came to a surprised stop. "Eva, I didn't think we'd see you today. Aren't you supposed to be working?"

"Lady Phoebe didn't need me this afternoon."

Alice looked from Eva to their mother, who began bustling back and forth from the cupboard to the table, depositing first a platter of sandwiches, then cutlery, and then, realizing she'd forgotten this or that item, doubling back again—several times.

Alice watched her with a dawning frown. "Is something wrong with Mum?" she whispered to Eva.

"Not that I know of."

"Mum, did you know Eva was coming today?"

Eva clenched her teeth as Mum stopped short, swinging around to regard her older daughter with a startled expression. No words came out of her mouth. But of course they didn't. Eva had forgotten one small detail about Betty Huntford. While thoroughly capable of keeping quiet about something, she was equally incapable of outright lying.

It didn't take Alice long to reach a conclusion. "Why didn't you tell me?"

"I, er . . ." Mum's gaze flicked to Eva.

Eva folded her hands at her waist. "I asked her not to."

Alice's eyes narrowed as she studied Eva. "What's going on?"

"Well, isn't that exactly what we've been asking you since you first arrived?" Mum had recovered her voice, and then some. No, she couldn't lie, but she could certainly demand answers of her children when she wished. "You've been evasive and secretive, and with these long walks of yours to who knows where . . ."

"Across the fields," Alice said defensively. "For exercise. Is there a crime in that?"

"No, of course not." Eva held up her hands to ward off the drawing of battle lines. "Alice, Mum and I have been terribly concerned about you. Even you have to admit, your showing up here without the children is highly unusual, and your mood has been most peculiar since you arrived."

"Forgive me for not being my usual cheerful self." Alice's sarcasm was impossible to miss.

"That's just it. Something is different about you, Alice. Or different from your usual self." Eva gestured to the table. "Please, let's all sit and have a talk, the way we used to when we were younger, before life sent us in separate ways."

Mum hurried over to the table. Alice sat with a good deal more reluctance, but at least she hadn't stormed off to the bedroom she and Eva had once shared. Eva sat between them and clasped her hands on the tabletop.

"Alice, I believe I know why it was important to you to come to Little Barlow alone."

"And why would that be?" Alice's sarcasm persisted. Their mother looked on in apprehension.

Eva reached toward Alice, but stopped just short of touching her. "Are you expecting?"

Mum gasped. A blush suffused Alice's cheeks, the only answer Eva needed, especially when her sister didn't immediately issue a denial. Several seconds passed. Then came a shaky, "How did you know?"

"I probably would have guessed eventually, but with Lady Annondale being in the same condition, the truth dawned on me yesterday."

"Oh, Alice." Mum jumped up from her seat and threw her arms around Alice. Alice accepted the gesture in silence, one hand coming up to pat Mum's back until she pulled away far enough to look down into her daughter's face. "But why didn't you say something? Why keep it a secret? It doesn't make sense."

Eva thought she knew the answer, or at least part of it—trouble at home. But she waited for her sister to enlighten them. As her mother pulled away to resume her own seat, Alice stared down at her hands. "Because I don't know how I feel about it."

"How you feel about it?" Mum looked incredulous.

"How is there to feel but joyful? Another baby—oh! It's wonderful news, Alice. Wonderful."

"Is it?" Alice spoke low, with little emotion. "Not every new baby is a joyful event. Not when . . ."

"Not when what?" Mum again looked mystified.

This time when Eva reached out, she lowered her hand gently on her sister's and gave a reassuring squeeze. But she said nothing, once again waiting for Alice to continue.

"I feel trapped, utterly," she said. "And there is nothing I can do about it. Especially now, with another one coming and barely enough money for the ones I already have."

"Not enough money . . . ?" Mum trailed off. It was as Eva feared. The Ward farm might not be what one would call prosperous, but up until now their barley and wheat had brought in enough to provide for the family and then some.

Alice shook her head. "Oliver made an arrangement to sell nearly our entire barley crop to a new buyer. The sale fell through, and by then it was too late to find new buyers. Ever since, Oliver's become reckless with money. He's even taken to going down to the pub and gambling at night."

"That's why you left," Mum murmured.

"Yes. I brought the children to stay with their other grandparents and I told Oliver if he wants us back, he'll mend his ways and fast. His parents agree with me."

Mum took this in, her mouth hanging open. "But, Alice, what if he doesn't? Issuing an ultimatum can be dangerous."

"It's not an ultimatum," she said, her chin inching higher. "It's a simple fact. At least, it was until I realized . . ." She placed a hand on her stomach and blew out a breath.

"You can all move here." Mum spoke with defiance. "We'll take in the lot of you if need be."

Alice was already shaking her head before Mum had completed the offer. "The four of us? Five, I mean. How could you possibly?"

"We'll figure out a way. If your father and I have to add a room to the house, we will." Mum glanced through the kitchen doorway into the parlor. "But the money, Alice. Is it as bad as all that?"

"The gambling is making it worse, of course. He's always done, you know, but never so that it made a difference to the family. Pennies, mostly. Now that's changed."

Mum craned her neck as she leaned across the table toward Alice. "Is he . . . is he drinking, too?"

Alice shrugged in an almost Lady Annondale-like way. "I suppose. I've yet to see him staggering drunk, but it's not lemonade those men drink when they're sitting round the table tossing their hard-earned money into the pot." She paused and reached for a sandwich on the platter Mum had placed on the table, which they had all but forgotten. "So you see, this is why I didn't wish to tell you anything. I needed time to think. To figure out what to do." She bit into the sandwich and slowly chewed, her expression pensive.

"Well, good heavens, I for one am glad we finally know the truth. I've been so worried about you." Mum came to her feet and went to the stove to retrieve the tea kettle. "We'll take good care of you and you'll see, everything will be fine."

After lunch, Mum shooed Eva and Alice into the parlor while she cleared the table. Eva sat while Alice went to the hearth and fingered the modest knickknacks on the mantel, Mum's collection of porcelain dogs: a spaniel, a greyhound, a bulldog, and two terriers, a Scottie and a Yorkie.

"I'm sorry, Eva," Alice said over her shoulder. "I know you've been worried, too."

"I'm still worried, Alice."

"As Mum said, things will work out."

"Will they?" Eva couldn't help voicing her qualms. "One thing you haven't yet explained. How does Keenan fit in to all of this?"

Alice turned around, the color draining from her face.

Chapter 16

William's disclosures kept Phoebe awake most of the night, and in the morning those same matters cried out for her attention.

First, according to the young assistant, Stephen Ripley hadn't brought his small shears with him that morning, although he knew he'd need them for the fine work of shaping the hedge. What kind of gardener set out without his proper tools? He had supposedly trained for a head gardener's position for years at his former place of employment, so how could he have made such a glaring blunder?

No, she suspected he had forgotten the shears on purpose, specifically so he could send William back for them. And that suggested he'd had private business to conduct, a prearranged meeting there by the hedge. But with whom? Horace Walker? Perhaps the two men needed to consult about their business dealings, and rather than meet in town where they'd be seen and fuel further gossip, they'd chosen a secluded area concealed even from view of the house. But would Horace Walker have murdered the other man? Perhaps, if Mr. Ripley had had second thoughts about the sale.

William's recollection also brought into doubt another assumption that Phoebe, Eva, and Miles Brannock had made concerning the fallen flat cap. They had concluded the murderer lost his cap in his struggle with Stephen Ripley and his haste to be away. But when William returned to the hedge with the shears, Stephen Ripley was already dead on the ground, the murderer standing over him. At that moment, according to William, the individual was still wearing the cap and took the time to issue a silent warning to the youth.

Did the cap fall off the murderer's head? Or did he intentionally leave it behind, knowing it would incriminate someone once the police discovered it didn't belong to Mr. Ripley? Unfortunately, the killer might have gotten the cap anywhere. He might have stolen it from the pub, might have switched his own with someone else's while visiting or at church.

After having lunch with Julia and their grandparents, Phoebe hurried back to her room. She went to her writing table and, on a fresh sheet of paper, sketched out a diagram. The hedge, the spot where Stephen Ripley fell, the positioning of the tweed cap near his body. This she placed near the bottom of the page and studied the placement of each element as she remembered it. Nearer the top of the page, she drew a box to represent the gardener's cottage and added the trees that surrounded it. There were several directions from which someone might approach the cottage without being seen.

The day following the murder, she and Eva had gone to the gardener's cottage to search for Stephen Ripley's plaid flat cap, and there they had encountered the killer, probably looking for evidence that linked him to Mr. Ripley. The police having already gone through the house, the individual wouldn't have expected anyone else to wander in at that time. But she and Eva had surprised him with their arrival. She wondered if he had found what he'd been looking for, or if they had chased him off too soon. He might not have had a second chance to search, as the police had been keeping a closer eye on the property ever since. The evidence might still be there.

The two matters led to a third concern, a claim Mr. Peele made when she and Eva visited him in Cheltenham. He'd said Stephen Ripley threatened to make life difficult for William and his family, that Mr. Ripley knew something . . . What word had he used? Ah, yes, *damaging*, about William's father, Ezra Gaff. At the time it had seemed no more than a ploy to convince an aging man to vacate his position. But there could be more to it. And while William had seemed genuinely frightened—too frightened to lie outright—during the questioning, could he have been protecting someone? His father, perhaps?

She needed to speak to William. Or perhaps . . . she should go directly to Ezra Gaff. But not alone. On second thought, she should go to Miles Brannock, and bring Eva with her. Eva should be on her way back from her parents' farm by now. Phoebe lifted the in-house telephone and asked that her motorcar be brought around. Then she changed into a pair of pumps and collected her coat and handbag.

Alice came away from the fireplace and sat beside Eva on the settee. After a quick glance into the kitchen, she sighed. "Keenan and I stayed friends through the years."

"How so?" Eva almost didn't want to know.

"Mostly through letters. But only occasional ones."

"Oh, Alice, why? Why would you risk your marriage to maintain a correspondence with another man? What if Oliver found out?" In fact, it struck Eva as odd that Alice's husband had never intercepted one of those letters. "How did you ever manage it?"

"As I said, we only wrote occasionally, and . . ." Alice looked down at her hands, clasped in her lap. "Keenan didn't post the letters himself."

"Then who did?"

Alice hesitated a good long moment while a tide of red rose in her face. "Mrs. Verity," she whispered at length.

"Mrs. Verity?" Eva's mouth dropped open. That kind, prudent, very proper woman? "I can't believe it. Why on earth would she?"

"Well . . . don't you remember? She's actually Keenan's great-aunt by marriage. She's always been fond of him, and there's nothing she wouldn't do for him." Alice breathed in deeply. "Even this."

Eva sat back and studied her sister. From the kitchen came the sounds of her mother washing the dishes. She wondered if Mum was deliberately giving Eva and Alice time to talk alone. "I don't understand. You could have been with Keenan if you wished. Yet you chose Oliver." She raised her hands as she grasped for answers.

"I love Oliver, I do. But there's always been a part of me he doesn't understand. Doesn't even know exists. The part of me that's more like you, Eva."

"Like me?" Eva huffed with indignation. "You see me as inconstant, duplicitous—"

"That isn't what I mean. I'm talking about the part of you that's independent and dedicated and able to make your own way in the world. I gave up all of that when I married Oliver, and it doesn't occur to him that I might be capable of more than raising children."

"And it occurs to Keenan?"

Alice nodded. "He's always understood that about me. It's why I chose Oliver instead. You see, Keenan encouraged me to do more than simply marry, but at the time, I believed as most women did that marriage and children were the only goal worth pursuing."

"Then what changed?"

"The war. It changed everything."

Alice seemed about to go on, but Eva was already nodding in comprehension. She had only to look at Lady Phoebe to understand that, because of the war and the way women had been needed in the workforce while the men were away, many of them were no longer content to while away their lives between the nursery and the kitchen. Poor Alice. She had realized too late that there could be more for her.

"Are you willing to leave Oliver over this?"

"No." Alice sounded adamant. Then a look of pain claimed her features. "I wasn't sure when I first arrived here. I was so angry with him and so fed up with feeling helpless. But now . . ." She reached for Eva's hand, enveloping it with her own. "I miss him, Eva."

Eva smiled. "I'm glad to hear that. But before you came to that realization, what happened between you and Keenan? Will you tell me?"

Another hesitation, longer than the first, nearly convinced Eva her sister had finished confiding. Then Alice sighed and said, "After I learned about how much money Oliver lost, I wrote to Keenan and told him I was coming to Little Barlow. That I wished to see him. He wrote back, and we planned a reunion—the very morning his brother was killed."

"You did go to meet him at his cottage." And then lied about it, Eva acknowledged silently.

"I visited Mrs. Verity first, and then I went to Keenan's." Hearing Alice make the admission twisted Eva's stomach and squeezed her heart, but she held her features steady and waited silently for Alice to continue. "He wasn't at the cottage when I arrived. He must have been in the barn or the brewery, or maybe out in the orchard. I don't know. All I do know is I was standing outside his front door and suddenly became paralyzed with the wrongness of what I was doing. Me, a married woman and a mother. A sense of horror filled me. In something like a panic, I grabbed the bundle of scones from my basket, left them by the door, and hurried home." Alice paused to catch her breath as if she'd been running. "I didn't see him until I brought more scones to the jail. I wished to explain why I didn't meet him that morning, but of course that awful chief inspector wouldn't let me talk to him alone."

"Wait a moment," Eva said. "Then you never went inside the cottage?"

"Never."

"And you didn't see anyone else coming to see Keenan that morning?"

"No, no one. Oh, Eva, do you think I'm horrible?"

Eva shook her head and reached her arms around her sister. "Never. I just wished you'd told me all this sooner. But I suppose I understand why you didn't."

"And now I suppose I should let poor Mum in on my secrets. I know she's been worried, too."

"She has. And I think it would be best for the two of you to speak alone."

Alice's eyes went wide with alarm. "Don't leave me."

"Just tell Mum what you told me. And then maybe a trip to the post office to use the telephone might be in order, so you can speak to Oliver."

Eva left shortly after that, feeling a good deal lighter at heart than she had in days. Along the road back toward Foxwood Hall, she met up with Elaina Corbyn and her two stepsons on their way to the village. Mrs. Corbyn said she was walking the boys back to school for their afternoon lessons.

The woman greeted her with a friendly *hullo* and prompted her boys to do the same. They obliged in shy mumbles, which both endeared them to Eva and made her throat tighten. She remembered encouraging her much younger brother, Danny, to return neighbors' greetings rather than hide his face in her skirts as toddlers tended to do. He hadn't been a shy boy for long; at school he'd been a leader among his friends and quick to raise his hand in class. If Eva was grateful for one thing, it was having told Danny how proud she was of him right before he shipped off to the Continent in his ill-fitting soldier's uniform. . . .

"Have you been to see your parents, Miss Huntford?"

Eva blinked away the memories. "I had lunch with my mother and sister. How are things at the Ripley orchard? Do you know?"

"Coming along, one supposes. My husband went to see Keenan in jail for a quick lesson on how to use the pear press. The juices must be extracted before the pears over-ripen."

"It's splendid of your husband to be of so much help. I'm sure Keenan will be forever in your husband's debt."

"Mr. Corbyn doesn't want anyone in his debt." The words themselves were generous ones, yet Eva heard a cynical note in them. Mrs. Corbyn reached down to adjust one of the boys' caps, which had slipped askew. The child eased away with a shake of his shoulder, as little boys will do when they don't want their mother fussing over them. His older brother snickered and increased his pace along the dusty road.

Speaking of dust, a motorcar approaching them from the direction of the village raised a golden haze. Eva and the others moved off onto the weedy verge along the roadside. Her hand went up in greeting when she recognized Lady Phoebe's Vauxhall. The vehicle not only came to a stop beside them, but Lady Phoebe switched off the motor, opened the door, and hopped out.

An odd sensation gripped Phoebe as she came upon Eva and Mrs. Corbyn. The woman's two young sons had been walking ahead in that funny way boys have of half stumbling—because their feet were growing faster than the rest of them—while picking up pebbles and making a game of seeing how far they could toss them into the field beside the road, or running circles around each other until their mother admonished them to stop.

For reasons she could not have explained, Phoebe climbed out of the motorcar, eliciting puzzled looks from Eva and Mrs. Corbyn. "Hello, Eva. Hello, Mrs. Corbyn. How is everything by you?"

"Quite well, Lady Phoebe, thank you."

"I heard how your husband and nearly all the men of Little Barlow are helping bring in the pear harvest."

"Yes, they're glad to do it. I'm sure if we needed help they'd all be out at our place, too."

"I'm sure they would."

"Is anything wrong at home, my lady?" Eva looked worried, and puzzled by Phoebe's unexpected appearance.

"No, no. I have . . . an errand I'd like your help with." Their gazes held for an instant or two, just enough time for Eva's comprehension to flash in her eyes. She asked no further questions, and instead made ready to leave.

"We should be getting to it, then," she said. "Mrs. Corbyn, it was lovely walking with you. Boys, nice to see you again." They again mumbled their polite though incomprehensible responses, and Eva started toward the motorcar.

Phoebe remained where she was, on the edge of the road with Mrs. Corbyn and the boys. What was it that rooted her to the spot, that had compelled her to leave the motorcar at all when all she'd had to do was pull over and allow Eva to climb inside?

The boys, having lost interest in the adults, resumed walking. They chattered in a way that suggested some form of dispute between them. Phoebe heard words such as "am too . . . are not" and "I could do it . . . just try me." The older laughed at this claim, reached down, and flicked his brother's cap down over his eyes.

Mrs. Corbyn sighed. "Boys! Stop it now." Turning back to Phoebe, she said, "If you'll excuse me. If I don't watch them like a hawk and herd them as though they're sheep, they'll never make it back to school for afternoon lessons."

Phoebe hardly heard her. She had realized what had made her get out of the Vauxhall. "That's a very nice jacket you're wearing, Mrs. Corbyn."

The woman blushed slightly. "Thank you. I made it myself."

"And I see your boys are wearing caps from the same fabric." A brown tweed. "Did you make those as well?"

"I did, actually."

"My goodness, you're quite a seamstress, not to mention hat maker."

"Thank you, Lady Phoebe." Mrs. Corbyn's blush increased, and she smiled with pride. "The fabric came at a reasonable price, so I purchased enough to make good use of it for the whole family."

Phoebe sensed rather than saw Eva's growing confusion over why Phoebe would take such an interest in the attire of a local farming family. She said to Mrs. Corbyn, "I suppose you even made a cap for your husband."

"Oh, er . . . I haven't, actually. I haven't had time to

make another. And I'm not sure there's even enough of the fabric left, you see. And anyway, he has a cap he's fond of. You know how men are. They never like change." A fluttering laugh escaped the woman's lips. Perhaps she feared she'd spoken in too familiar a way to Lord Wroxly's granddaughter.

Phoebe decided to put her at ease. "The only reason I ask, Mrs. Corbyn, is because the RCVF could use your skills. We have some donated fabric. Could I possibly persuade you to help fashion some simple garments for our needy families?"

"Oh, yes, Lady Phoebe, I'd be more than happy to help." The woman's relief was palpable. And Phoebe heard a murmured "Oh" from Eva behind her.

"Good. I'll be in touch. You mentioned the boys needing to get back to school. I won't keep you another moment."

After saying their good-byes, Phoebe and Eva got into the Vauxhall. Eva turned to her with a smile. "A splendid idea, asking her to help sew for the RCVF."

Phoebe, on the other hand, frowned. "She seemed ill at ease, didn't she?"

"Well, most people are when they encounter you or another member of the family."

"Yes, but I don't mean that. Eva, her jacket. The boys' caps. It's the same fabric."

"As what?" Eva's mouth dropped open as she realized the answer to her own question. "As the cap left by Stephen's body?"

Phoebe nodded. "I'd almost swear to it. It's a common pattern, so I'll need to see the cap again, but I'm nearly certain it's the same tweed. And when Mrs. Corbyn denied having made a cap for her husband, she sounded terribly nervous to me."

"You think it's Fred Corbyn's cap, and . . ." Eva trailed off, facing front as Phoebe pressed the accelerator. "Do you think she believes her husband murdered Stephen Ripley and is trying to protect him?"

"Either trying to protect him," Phoebe replied grimly, "or she's afraid of him and trying to protect herself and the boys."

"I'd seen her jacket before and didn't think anything of it. I haven't thought of it again since." Eva pressed her palm to her forehead. "How could I have been so dim-witted?"

"You never saw the flat cap on the lawn by Stephen Ripley's body, so you couldn't have known. And it's not as if tweed is an uncommon commodity hereabouts. I'd say everyone owns something in tweed, myself included. In fact, I could be entirely wrong about this, but the only way to know for sure is to go to the police station and ask to see the cap again."

"The Corbyn family's tweed will be fresh in our minds," Eva agreed. "But, my lady, if Elaina sees us pulling up at the police station, she might become suspicious and warn her husband."

"You're right." Rather than turn into the village, Phoebe passed the gates and kept going toward Foxwood Hall. They circled the countryside for a good half hour before doubling back. Phoebe might have gone by the church on pretense of tending to the donations, but she didn't want to risk Elaina Corbyn volunteering to help. She wanted the woman to go home so she wouldn't see them entering the police station.

Phoebe's and Eva's anticipation tightened further when they discovered Chief Inspector Perkins in—his feet up on his deck, a newspaper open in front of him—and Miles Brannock out. "I'll tell him you were looking for him," the man said with a yawn and without gazing up from the newspaper.

Not about to be dismissed so easily, Phoebe stepped up to the desk and forcibly lowered the newspaper to reveal Mr. Perkins's bloodshot eyes and pocked nose. "Chief Inspector, this is very important. Might we see the flat cap found near Stephen Ripley's body?"

"Why ever would you wish to do that?"

"Because we might know whom the cap belongs to. We need to see if we recognize the color and pattern of the tweed."

The man snickered. "It's tweed, Lady Phoebe. Looks like every other bit of tweed in the world."

"Mr. Perkins, please." Phoebe employed her most authoritative tone, honed from years of hearing it in her grandmother. Eva's eyes twinkled in recognition of the fact. "I'm afraid we're not leaving until you oblige us."

"Very well. I suppose it's the only way you'll leave me in peace to read my paper. I'll have you know this isn't idleness on my part. It pays for a chief inspector to be well-informed on events near and far."

Phoebe indulged him by nodding in acquiescence. "I've no doubt of that, Chief Inspector."

With a deep and long-suffering sigh, the man thrust the newspaper to the desk, heaved himself forward in his chair, and unlocked a drawer in front of him. A moment later he handed the cap to Phoebe. She turned to show it to Eva.

"What do you think?"

"The very same, my lady. I'd stake my life on it."

Phoebe turned back to the chief inspector. "We believe this cap belongs to Fred Corbyn. It would behoove you to take a ride out to the Corbyn farm and question him."

The street door swung open and Miles Brannock entered the building. Catching sight of Phoebe and Eva, he stopped short, his surprise evident. "What's going on?"

They explained their findings while the chief inspector

rolled his eyes, made circular motions with his forefinger beside his ear, and smirked in condescension. But then he said, "To humor them, Brannock, why don't you go and ask Fred Corbyn a few more questions. It shan't amount to a thing, except to prove me right. We already have our killer."

CHAPTER 17

"My lady, that's Ezra Gaff." Eva pointed beyond the motorcar window to the man in tattered work clothes lumbering along the side of the road. He was headed in the opposite direction of the Vauxhall. Up ahead, Miles's police vehicle slowed as it approached the Corbyns' farm. He had agreed to let Eva and Lady Phoebe follow him to the house once they had pointed out that they could be useful in keeping Mrs. Corbyn calm should her husband be arrested.

Lady Phoebe craned her neck to see around Eva's shoulder. Like William, the man making his way toward the village was brown-haired, noticeably thin, and walked with stooped shoulders and a shuffling gait. "Is it? I don't know him well."

"No, nor me, either, but I'm certain that's him. That slight limp he has is the result of a fall he had some years back from a hayloft. William has spoken about it. What a strange coincidence to pass him now. I wonder what he's doing out this way."

"I wish I knew." Lady Phoebe refocused her attention

on the black police sedan ahead of them, just now turning in at the Corbyns' farm. While they had driven around earlier, waiting for Elaina Corbyn to leave the village, Lady Phoebe had filled Eva in on her concerns regarding William and his father. What damaging information could Stephen Ripley have had on Mr. Gaff? And could it exonerate both Keenan *and* Fred Corbyn?

"Do you think the constable noticed him?"

"He must have done, my lady. But in light of what we told him, he probably wants to speak with Fred Corbyn before he goes off on another lead."

Lady Phoebe maneuvered the Vauxhall onto the Corbyns' property beside the house and parked next to Miles's vehicle. A third vehicle, a gray sedan, sat parked nearby. Eva had a sneaking suspicion of whose it might be.

Holding the tweed flat cap in one hand, Miles shaded his eyes from the sun and glanced around. Lady Phoebe and Eva did likewise. They saw no one, and while the area seemed uncommonly quiet, it wasn't particularly odd for that time of day. With the boys back at school, Mrs. Corbyn was probably baking or doing household chores, while her husband might be anywhere on the property. But what about the owner of the third motorcar? The threesome headed for the house first.

"Unless I'm mistaken, that's Mr. Walker's motor," she said. "I wonder what on earth he's doing here."

Miles led the way to the door and raised his hand to knock. He hesitated, and Eva perceived him pricking his ears to listen. The utter quiet continued. He knocked loudly and received no response. After several more tries, he simply tried the latch.

Like most other doors in Little Barlow, this one wasn't locked. All three stepped into a parlor. Braided oval and rectangular rugs of various designs lay scattered over a wideboard floor, while matching throw pillows decorated a settee and several overstuffed chairs. Mrs. Corbyn's sewing talents also showed in the neat curtains hanging over the windows and the bright runner gracing the mantel. Miles called out her name. Eva and Lady Phoebe exchanged puzzled glances.

"Perhaps she lingered in the village after all," Eva said.

"Or went visiting," Lady Phoebe suggested. "She might even have gone to the Ripley orchard to help out."

Eva's doubts about that raised a slight frown. "The morning I met Mrs. Corbyn in the sheep pasture, she hadn't seemed inclined to help harvest the pears. But perhaps she'd been too busy attending to their boys and the farm while her husband was at the orchard."

"Would a man who had just committed murder offer his help to his victim's own brother?" Lady Phoebe mused aloud.

"He would if he wanted to make himself look innocent." Miles peeked into each of several rooms that opened onto the parlor and called out Mrs. Corbyn's name again. "Well, it's safe to say she isn't here and neither is that Walker fellow. I'm going to look in the main barn."

"We'll come with you." Lady Phoebe scrambled out the door after him, Eva taking up the rear. "Mrs. Corbyn might be with him."

"Stay behind me," he told them.

The main barn stood some fifty yards behind the house, a stone structure whose honey-golden walls reflected the afternoon sun. Another, smaller barn and a few outbuildings were spread over the property until the land rose and a stone wall marked the first of the enclosures. Sheep meandered over the hillside, some in groups, others singly, still others disappearing over the verdant crest where the land again dipped.

One of the barn's double doors stood a few inches ajar, enough to warrant Miles pushing it wider and stepping inside. Immediately his arm came up, the hand holding the flat cap angling behind him in a warning for Eva and Lady Phoebe to stop where they were. That didn't discourage Eva from rising on her toes to peer over his shoulder. What had prompted the warning?

The brightness of the day rendered the barn's interior too dark to see. Eva blinked away the dazzle, and as Miles moved farther inside, forms began to take shape. The usual tools hung along the walls. Buckets of various sizes and a stack of feed troughs occupied a corner. An old horse-pulled tractor sat near them, rusting, its paint long since peeled away. On the opposite wall were enclosed pens where Eva assumed the shearing was done.

Her gaze swept from the perimeter walls to the center of the space, where Miles headed with a determined stride. For the most part he blocked her view, but she thought she saw someone standing in shadow.

A gasp drew her attention to Lady Phoebe, who had come up beside her. Lady Phoebe pushed the door open wider still, allowing beams of sunlight to pour in and illuminate a dusty rectangle on the hard-packed earth floor. Tiny, dancing motes filtered through the air to gently shroud the interior in swirling, golden light. Miles subtly shifted his course, and the scene before Eva opened to her view. Fred Corbyn stood at the center of the barn. In his right hand he held something long and thin and curved and gleaming. At his feet . . .

"Good Lord," Eva uttered. Feeling the gorge begin to rise in her throat, she swallowed and turned her face aside. Then she felt Lady Phoebe's arm brush hers. "My lady, don't . . ." Lady Phoebe kept going and Eva hurried after her, until they both came to stand beside Miles. A metallic stench reached Eva's nose, warning her to retreat, to seek the fresh air outside. The cleanness of grass. The warmth of the sun.

Shivering, she forced herself to look down, even as her hand reached out to clutch Lady Phoebe's. Her mistress's fingers shook. Side by side, they stared down at what Eva could only call an act of carnage. A man lay sprawled on his back at Fred Corbyn's feet, his coat open, his vest torn aside, his shirt soaked in a luminous pool of scarlet.

"My lady," she whispered again, deep and throaty. She wished to spare her mistress this horrible sight, but she said no more. Lady Phoebe wouldn't leave the barn any more than she herself would.

"Mr. Corbyn," Miles said quietly, and when the sheep farmer didn't respond, Miles spoke again, louder. But Fred Corbyn didn't look up, didn't move, didn't respond. With his head bowed until his chin nearly rested on his chest, he stared down at what none of them wished to see, and which none of them could tear their gazes away from.

"It's Mr. Walker." Lady Phoebe breathed this pronouncement, and Eva, taking in the wide nose and stony chin, could only nod once in agreement.

Miles didn't take his eyes off Fred Corbyn, nor the sickle-shaped scythe the farmer held aloft in his right hand. Only now did Eva see the blood that had dripped from the blade onto its handle, and from there onto Fred's hand and down into his sleeve. Still clutching Lady Phoebe's hand, she backed away from the farmer, this time silently insisting Lady Phoebe move with her.

Miles placed the hand still holding the flat cap on Fred's shoulder and reached to dislodge the scythe from his grip. Fred didn't resist. Once Miles had it firmly in his possession, he quickly walked to the tractor and laid it on the seat. He returned to Fred and grasped his upper arm.

"Come along. To the house," he said. Fred moved as if in a dream, with a shuffling gait, his vision unfocused, the bloodied hand held away from his side. He appeared to be in shock, and it was clear to Eva he had little sense of what was happening.

In the house, Miles walked him through the parlor and into the kitchen, where he sat him down at the table. Miles sat close beside him, keeping the flat cap out of sight on his lap. With a flick of his gaze he indicated the tea kettle to Eva. She nodded and lit a burner on the enameled iron range. Lady Phoebe rummaged through a cupboard until she found a tin of tea. Eva brewed it dark and strong.

Miles made no accusations, but once Fred cradled his earthenware mug in his two hands, Miles said, "Tell me what happened."

Eva wished he had begun by asking where Elaina Corbyn was. Had she returned from the village? Did she know . . . ? Had she been harmed?

"Gaff came by . . ." Fred stopped short, his eyebrows rising. An edge of hysteria creeped into his voice as he continued. "Gaff did it. He must have done."

Miles held his own voice steady. "What do you mean?"

"He was here." Fred's expression implied the answer was obvious. "Came looking for work, but I told him I didn't have any right now. I'm a sheep farmer; I've got nothing to harvest this time of year. I thought he left, but he must not have."

"We saw him walking toward the village minutes ago," Eva quietly reminded Miles.

He gave a faint nod in acknowledgment, his attention never wavering from Fred. "And then? Why were you in the barn with Mr. Walker? Why was he here?"

"I don't know. I haven't the first idea why he was here."

"You've never spoken with him before?"

"No . . . that's not true either. We've spoken about the pasture. He was going to let me keep grazing my sheep there."

Miles compressed his lips a moment in thought. "Why would he do that? Doesn't he want the land for his resort?"

"He said keeping sheep there would be picturesque, and Americans on holiday would like that."

"And you're sure he didn't change his mind?"

"And what? I killed him?" Fred started to come to his feet, but Miles stopped him with a decisive hand on his shoulder. Fred stayed put, but his control seemed more and more tenuous. "For a sheep pasture?"

"You tell me." Miles eyed him steadily, until Fred squirmed. But when the farmer said nothing more, Miles spoke again. "All right. Again, tell me what happened. Everything you remember."

"Like I said, Gaff was here, but I sent him away. Then I walked out to the south enclosure beyond the barns and spread some feed in the troughs. When I came back, I saw that gray motorcar near the house. But there was no one about, leastwise no one that I saw. So I went into the barn and . . ." His breath rushed out of him. He leaned forward, head in his hands. "And I found Walker like . . . like *that*."

"You were standing over him, holding the apparent murder weapon when we found you."

Fred ran both hands through his hair before lifting his head. "Look, I was shocked by what I saw. Who wouldn't be? I wasn't thinking straight. I know I shouldn't have touched anything, but I did. By God . . . I did." His face burrowed into his palms and his shoulders folded inward.

Miles lifted the flat cap from his lap and placed it on the table in front of Fred. "Is this yours?"

Frowning, Fred lifted his head to peer at it. "Where'd you find it?"

"Is it yours?"

"Yeah. But I lost it somewhere. Thought maybe I left it down at the pub, but when I asked Joe he said he hadn't seen it."

"It was found lying beside Stephen Ripley's body. Where were you the morning he was killed?"

Fred leapt to his feet, the backs of his knees sending his ladder-back chair scraping backward. "I was here. Working. Like always."

"Can your wife confirm that?"

"She made my breakfast and saw me off."

"Off to where?"

"To the pastures. To tend the sheep. Where else?"

Miles let a heavy pause fall, then asked, "Were you anywhere in the vicinity of the Haverleigh School?"

The question clearly confused Fred, but Eva understood that Miles referred to the forest path that connected the school property with the grounds of Foxwood Hall. Fred denied being there—*ever* being there—adamantly.

"And where is your wife now?" Miles asked.

"I . . . I don't know. She always walks our boys back to school after lunch. Then she comes home, or does a bit of shopping first. But she should be home by now." He reached out and stroked the herringbone weave of the flat cap with one finger.

"Your wife made that cap for you, didn't she," Eva said rather than asked.

Fred nodded.

"Why would she deny having done so?" At this question, both Fred and Miles looked up at her, clearly surprised. Eva explained, "Lady Phoebe and I noticed the caps your sons were wearing, and Elaina's own jacket, all made of the same tweed. We asked if she made a cap for you, but she said she hadn't had time yet."

When Fred could offer no explanation, a grim silence

fell over the room, broken only when Miles came to his feet. "I'm sorry, Mr. Corbyn. I'm going to have to take you in."

"Eva and I will stay and wait for Mrs. Corbyn," Phoebe said to the constable as she and Eva followed him into the parlor. Upon his pronouncement that he'd be taking Mr. Corbyn into custody, the farmer had gone silent, accepting his fate without protest. Indeed, Constable Brannock didn't need to drag him out of the house. By all appearances, Fred Corbyn went docilely, if not quite willingly.

Did that mean he couldn't deny the charges, that he murdered not only Mr. Walker, but Stephen Ripley, too? Or was he still too much in shock over Mr. Walker's demise that he couldn't work up the fortitude to protest?

Phoebe hoped he was telling the truth when he claimed he didn't know where his wife was. She told him they would wait for her, meaning she and Eva would be on hand to help calm her when she learned of her husband's arrest. But as soon as Constable Brannock drove off with Mr. Corbyn, she turned to Eva.

"We've got to search for her. I don't believe she's been shopping all this time."

"Nor do I, my lady. I've got an awful feeling."

"Let's not expect the worst. Where should we start? We know she's not in the main barn." And thank goodness; Mr. Walker still lay inside, and would until the constable arranged to have his body collected.

Eva frowned in thought. "There's the smaller barn and the sheds. And beyond that, acres of pastureland bordered by small tracts of forest."

Phoebe blew out a breath. "Let's start with the smaller barn."

They trudged out past the kitchen garden and the coop for the egg layers the Corbyns kept. The smaller barn stood halfway between the house and the first enclosed pasture. It looked shut up tight, even its windows shuttered.

Phoebe stood out of the way as Eva tried the door, which resisted her tugs at first but finally gave a sudden judder and swung open. "I didn't think it would be locked," Eva said. "Just swollen from the weather."

"Why two barns?" Phoebe wondered aloud.

"My guess is this one is for the lambing." Eva cautiously stepped inside, going only a few inches over the threshold. "Is anyone in here?"

No one answered. Again, as when they'd entered the large barn earlier, they blinked to become accustomed to the darkness. Phoebe could now make out several pens in a row, each lined with straw, confirming Eva's guess as to the purpose of the building. Above them, a loft yawned into darkness. They both gazed up into it.

"I'll go." Eva went to the ladder and hiked her skirts above her knees.

"Be careful." Phoebe went to the foot of the ladder and watched Eva's progress, ready to break her fall if necessary. Thank goodness it wasn't, and soon Eva came backing down the rungs.

"Empty."

They tried each outbuilding in turn. One turned out to be empty. The others were used for storage. Mrs. Corbyn continued to elude them.

"We can be grateful she wasn't hurt and tied up in one of these sheds," Phoebe said. "She must be in the village after all."

Eva appeared not to be listening. Not ignoring Phoebe exactly, but concentrating on something. Phoebe let her go on contemplating whatever it was, knowing full well Eva would explain the moment she reached a conclusion. Phoebe wasn't wrong.

"There's somewhere else she could be, my lady." Eva pointed into the pasture. "Unless I'm remembering wrong, there's an old enclosed water pump. The kind with a little shed around it. It would have been used for filling the water troughs before the Corbyns gained access to Keenan's stream. I doubt it's even working anymore, and not many people would know it's there."

"But Mrs. Corbyn would. And her husband."

Eva nodded, and they set off through the gate in the low rock wall, into the first of the pastures. They walked up the hill to its crest, where the land sprawled out before them. Phoebe could make out nothing resembling a pump house. They plodded on, up, then down and back up again, scattering sheep as they went. Finally, in what looked to Phoebe to be a very far distance, a weathered gray structure stood stark and plain against the dull brown and green autumn grasses.

She pointed. "Is that it?"

Eva squinted into the distance. "It must be."

They walked for what seemed an eternity, but Phoebe realized this was merely the result of there being so few points of reference in the rolling fields. Still, her knees began to ache and her thighs to burn, and she drew in sharp breaths while her heart pattered from the exertion. She pretended otherwise, keeping up with Eva, who strode on as if this were nothing more than a short walk from one end of Foxwood Hall to the other. But then, Phoebe hadn't grown up on a farm, walking everywhere on a daily basis. She had grown up riding in Grams's carriage or Grampapa's Rolls-Royce, or sitting on horseback. When she and her family did walk, it was mainly on well-tended garden paths and city pavements.

She made a mental note to include rigorous walking as part of her daily routine from now on.

"My lady, are you all right?" Eva slowed the pace. "If you wish, you could wait here while I continue on."

"No, I'm fine." She made another mental note not to breathe so laboriously until they'd completed their trek, which they did a few minutes later. The pump house was clothed in Cotswold stone, its golden hue grayed from years of wind-borne dirt and neglect.

A sound reached their ears at the same time, and their gazes instantly connected. It wasn't the breeze shirring over the grasses, nor birdsong, nor the bleating of sheep.

"Crying," Phoebe said, fighting the urge to bend over to catch her breath. "Weeping. Coming from inside."

Eva nodded and put her hand on the door latch. Phoebe bit down on her bottom lip. What would they discover inside? A beaten and bloodied Mrs. Corbyn?

"Elaina," Eva called out. "It's Eva Huntford. I'm coming in." As the door squeaked open, the weeping increased to sobs and whimpers of fear. "It's all right, you're safe now." Easing into the shadowy interior, Eva crouched near the cistern pump. Mrs. Corbyn knelt on the ground half behind it.

"I'm not safe. You don't understand." The woman pushed her bobbed bangs away from her eyes. Her forehead glistened with perspiration. "How did you find me?"

"We've been searching for you," Eva told her.

"Where is my husband? Oh, Miss Huntford, it was awful."

Phoebe wondered what those two utterances signified. Had Mrs. Corbyn found Mr. Walker in the barn, and feared for her husband's life? Or had she witnessed her husband murdering the American? She yearned to ask outright but held her tongue and let Eva handle matters for now.

"It's all right, Mrs. Corbyn, he's been . . . he's gone to the police station. For questioning," Eva added quickly.

She glanced over her shoulder at Phoebe. "It's quite safe to come out."

Eva coaxed her by grasping the woman's arms.

"My boys . . ." Mrs. Corbyn began to ease out from between the pump and the wall. Tiny threads ripped as her skirt caught on the rough rocks and mortar.

"They're safe at school. You needn't worry. That's right, just a little more and then you can stand. I'll help you."

Phoebe held her breath as Mrs. Corbyn slowly stood up on wobbly legs. She leaned against Eva as she took a step, and then another, until finally coming to the threshold of the pump house. Though shaking, she seemed physically unharmed; at least she bore no bruises that Phoebe could see. Her eyes, large and dark, held Phoebe's a moment, and then she reached out her hand as if seeking Phoebe's assistance. Phoebe took the hand firmly in her own and helped Mrs. Corbyn step out onto the grass, whereupon the woman collapsed in a dead faint.

CHAPTER 18

Of all the times for a well to have gone dry, Eva thought
as she worked the pump handle vigorously up and down
in hopes of being able to wet a handkerchief to help revive
Mrs. Corbyn. Not a drop issued from the spout and only
rusty squeaks rewarded her efforts. Outside, she could
hear the light taps of Lady Phoebe's fingertips against
Elaina Corbyn's cheeks and the backs of her hands. To
Eva's relief, the woman whimpered. Eva hurried back outside.

Mrs. Corbyn was sitting up with Lady Phoebe's help.
Bits of grass clung to her hair and the back of her cardigan. Eva sank to the ground at her other side. "Are you all
right?"

"I don't know." Hatless, the woman shaded her eyes
with the flat of her hand. "What happened?"

"You fainted," Lady Phoebe said.

Mrs. Corbyn gazed all around her. "In this field? How
did I get here?"

"You're at the old pump house," Eva said. "We found
you inside. Do you remember nothing?" She and Lady

Phoebe exchanged alarmed glances around Mrs. Corbyn's shoulders.

"I dropped the boys off at school . . . and then I came home and . . ." Her eyes became as large as goose eggs. "Oh. I'm beginning to remember. . . ."

Eva and Lady Phoebe granted her the time to collect her thoughts. Presently she said, "I was in the house getting ready to do some mending. I had my sewing basket ready, and I happened to glance out the window. That Mr. Walker—the American—drove up in his motorcar."

"What did he want?" Eva asked.

"I don't know. He didn't come to the house. He started to, but then he turned and set out toward the pastures. I assumed he saw Fred . . . er . . . my husband . . . and went to speak with him. I was in one of the front rooms and couldn't see them, but I assumed my husband had just come back from mending one of our stone walls."

"Yes," Lady Phoebe said, "he mentioned that."

Mrs. Corbyn flashed a quizzical look. "Did he? When?" She shook her head. "It doesn't matter. I could hear voices, but not what they were discussing." She paused, crinkling her forehead. "Some time passed. I mended a pair of trousers each for the boys. Goodness, you don't know how quickly boys can wear out their clothes."

Here she paused again, seeming to have lost herself in thoughts that had nothing to do with her husband and Horace Walker. Eva prodded gently. "Did the men return to the house?"

"No, not the house." Mrs. Corbyn patted her skirts into place over her bent legs. "They must have gone into the barn together." Her breathing increased; her forehead knotted tighter. "I could hear yelling coming from inside the barn. Shouting. They sounded frightfully angry. I wanted to go see what the matter was, but I didn't dare. Fred doesn't like me to interfere, you see."

"What happened then?" Lady Phoebe asked. "What made you run away and hide?"

Mrs. Corbyn stared at the ground for a long moment. Her eyes filled, but she held her voice steady. "Finally, it went quiet outside. I thought Mr. Walker must have left, that I hadn't noticed the motorcar leaving. I can be like that sometimes, not noticing things. I was intent on my sewing, after all."

"Yes." Eva patted her shoulder. "Go on."

"I decided to go find my husband and ask him what all the commotion was about. Fred doesn't mind my asking after the fact. Yet when I went outside, I saw that Mr. Walker's motorcar was still by the house. I didn't see anyone outside, so I thought perhaps they were still in the barn. I decided to peek inside . . . and I saw *him*. On the ground. Bleeding . . ."

"Who was it?" They all knew the answer to Lady Phoebe's question, but they needed to hear it from Mrs. Corbyn.

"The American. Mr. Walker. It was dreadful. So dreadful." She shuddered and drew her arms around herself. "So much blood. And then I heard footsteps, and Fred came into the barn. When he saw me he immediately started shouting at me to run . . . to run and hide. And to tell no one what I'd seen. I didn't know what to think. There was no one else there. Did . . . did my husband kill the American?" She ended on a tremulous whisper.

It was a question neither Eva nor Lady Phoebe could answer. While it certainly appeared that way—Mrs. Corbyn said there hadn't been anyone else there—Eva and Lady Phoebe knew there had been. Ezra Gaff had been to the farm. They didn't know when he had arrived, but they had seen him leaving as they arrived in the Vauxhall.

Fred Corbyn had sent Mr. Gaff away before he'd gone into the barn and discovered Horace Walker there. But he had made no mention of having had an argument with the American. Then again, Mrs. Corbyn had never actually seen the men. Could she be certain Mr. Walker had been arguing with her husband? Perhaps Mr. Corbyn never came in from the pastures until *after* Mr. Walker had been killed.

Perhaps the argument had been between Mr. Walker and Ezra Gaff. And perhaps Mr. Corbyn had ordered his wife to run and hide because he feared Gaff might return.

"It's a long walk back to the house," Lady Phoebe said, rising. She and Eva helped Elaina Corbyn to her feet. She swayed a bit. Lady Phoebe regarded her sturdy Wellington boots and asked, "Do you think you can walk?"

Mrs. Corbyn nodded, again sweeping the bangs off her forehead. "I'll be all right. We can't stay here all afternoon, can we?"

"I might be able to drive my motorcar across the fields," Lady Phoebe offered, but Mrs. Corbyn shook her head.

"No, I can make it. I have to get back. There are the boys to think about." The fear crept back into her eyes.

"The boys are safe," Eva reminded her. "They're at school."

"But they'll hear things soon enough. A man killed in their barn, and their father—" She gasped, her hand rising to her mouth. "You said my husband is at the police station. Has he been arrested?"

Eva and Lady Phoebe traded pained looks. Eva shook her head. "I honestly don't know at this point."

Despite Mrs. Corbyn's insistence that she could manage the long walk, Eva and Lady Phoebe took turns supporting her as her emotions got the best of her. Her eyes filled anew on more than one occasion, and this would cause her to weep blindly and lose her footing, or she'd appear faint and her knees would wobble beneath her. For the first time in her adult life, Eva bemoaned her inability to drive a motorcar, for otherwise she'd have run back for the Vauxhall. She didn't suggest Lady Phoebe do so, not after how clearly taxing the walk to the pump house had been for her.

She breathed a silent sigh of relief when the farmhouse came into view. Once inside, Lady Phoebe suggested making tea as they had done earlier for Mr. Corbyn, but Mrs. Corbyn shook her head.

"I need to collect my boys. Will you motor me into the village?"

"Of course," Lady Phoebe was quick to assure her. "We'll go right now."

"Yes, just let me find my handbag and change into a coat. It's grown chillier, I think. I can't seem to stop shivering. And my shoes. I must change them." She glanced down at the pair of Wellies she was wearing, typical farm footwear.

Eva determined it was the shock making the woman shiver and focus on things that didn't matter, such as what shoes she wore. As Mrs. Corbyn left the kitchen in search of her things, Eva noticed an item hanging near the garden door and went to it.

"Mrs. Corbyn's jacket is here," she said to Lady Phoebe, and touched the brown tweed garment that had helped them identify the owner of the flat cap found near Stephen Ripley's body.

A few minutes later, Elaina Corbyn reentered the kitchen. She had changed into sensible walking shoes and wore what appeared to Eva to be a winter coat made of thick wool with a high shawl collar, large outer pockets, and a hemline that reached her ankles. Poor woman, probably whisked it around her without realizing it wasn't the jacket she usually wore this time of year. And she had forgotten her handbag. No matter; she wouldn't be needing it.

Keeping their gazes averted from the barn where Mr. Walker still lay in a pool of his own blood, they squeezed into the Vauxhall, Elaina Corbyn sitting nearest the door. "I'm feeling dreadfully queasy," she told them. "I'll need the air." As Lady Phoebe pulled out onto the village road, Mrs. Corbyn spoke again, her voice small and tight. "Will I be forced to testify against my own husband, do you think?"

"I think that's getting ahead of things," Eva said. "We don't know that he's been charged with anything."

"The man I married couldn't have committed such a vile act."

"No, of course not," Lady Phoebe said soothingly.

"I've never known him to be violent." The woman took on a desperate tone, as if she were trying to convince them. "But maybe Mr. Walker threatened Fred, and Fred acted in self-defense. They don't hang a man for that, do they?"

Wishing she could offer reassurances, but not wanting to fill Mrs. Corbyn with false hopes, Eva grasped her hand. And then she remembered something Fred Corbyn had told them, which could make all the difference. "Mrs. Corbyn, according to your husband, Mr. Walker was going to continue to allow you to use the northeast pasture for your sheep. Is that true?"

The woman stared at her in puzzlement. "I don't know. I haven't heard a word about it."

Eva's hopes for the man, and for this woman and their family, sank.

The road curved and the Vauxhall came to a fork, right toward the village's ancient medieval gates, or straight to continue north toward Foxwood Hall. Lady Phoebe prepared to turn the vehicle to the right.

"Don't," Mrs. Corbyn said. "Keep driving."

"What do you mean?" Lady Phoebe looked over, leaning a bit to see around Eva. "The school is that way, through the village."

"I know good and well where the school is. I said drive."

An icy, slithery sensation of dread crept up Eva's spine.

Lady Phoebe's brows converged and her chin came up. "I don't understand."

Mrs. Corbyn shifted, freed her hand from Eva's, and in the next moment something hard, cylindrical, and cold poked against Eva's ribs. Her limbs turned to liquid and her core threatened to dissolve.

She swallowed. "My lady, please do as Mrs. Corbyn asks."

"I'm not asking," the woman corrected her. "I'm demanding. Keep driving, Lady Phoebe, or my husband's gun might accidentally discharge into your maid's side."

"What?" Lady Phoebe's question was merely instinctual; Eva had every assurance that her mistress had heard Mrs. Corbyn perfectly. Without another word Lady Phoebe made the necessary correction to the steering wheel to keep the Vauxhall on its northerly course.

They rode for some moments in silence. Phoebe turned several possibilities over in her mind. They would pass Foxwood Hall shortly. Could she turn onto the drive, gun the motor, and reach the house before Elaina Corbyn made good on her threat? The open gates with their stone pillars came into view, and beyond the treetops, the chimneys of the house beckoned like stalwart friends for Phoebe to turn in.

She didn't dare risk it. And yet, even with the decision made, she involuntarily slowed the Vauxhall as if to make the turn.

"Don't even consider it, Lady Phoebe," the woman holding the gun warned. "You should understand by now I don't make idle threats."

"No," Phoebe agreed. "I shall take you at your word." Why shouldn't she? By her actions in the past several minutes, Mrs. Corbyn had revealed herself to be a cold-blooded killer. Phoebe pressed the gas, half tempted now to crash into the nearest tree or rock wall. But to what end? She could kill them all.

"No one need be hurt so long as you both cooperate. I want only to leave Little Barlow behind me. Far, far behind."

"What about your boys?" Eva asked.

"They're not my boys," the woman snapped. "They're merely stepsons, Fred's from his first marriage. I have no boys, no children at all, and I never shall. The war saw to that. Fred cannot . . . ever again."

"I'm sorry," Eva whispered, and Phoebe heard sincerity in her voice. "I didn't know."

"Of course you didn't know. It's not the sort of thing one goes about discussing." She chuckled grimly. "It's his army sidearm pressed up against you."

"But you must care for them, for the boys." Phoebe's hands tightened on the steering wheel. "You've been their mother since before the war. You've made their clothes, fed them. . . ."

"Don't remind me. Cloying, demanding little leeches. They've sucked my youth away, my life. I'll be glad to be rid of them, and of my husband. Marrying him was an impulsive act I've regretted ever since. And as for that blasted farm, sheep are smelly, dirty, disgusting creatures. I don't care if I never see another one again."

"You'll have to leave England, then," Eva said drily.

"I just might at that." Phoebe could hear the smile in the woman's voice.

"But where can you go? And with what?" Phoebe squinted as the road turned and the afternoon sun hit them head on. "You can't live on nothing."

Mrs. Corbyn patted her coat pocket with her free hand. "I won't live on nothing. I've been saving a few shillings here, a pound or two there, for years now. I've got enough laid by to see me comfortably if modestly settled, until I can find employment. My sewing skills are of the highest quality. It's not what I was hoping for, but I'll get by. And it won't be in some backwater village, I can promise you that."

"It was you," Phoebe said, with sudden insight. "You must have learned of Horace Walker's desire to buy land in Little Barlow, and you contacted Stephen Ripley about it."

The woman nodded, a little half smile persisting. "I knew Keenan was having problems paying his bills, and it presented an opportunity I couldn't ignore. I hate this village, everything about it. I'm sick of dirt and worse on my shoes, tired of village gossips, of our mean little church, never having anything interesting to do. . . . London— now there's a town. I suppose London won't be far enough away now, not unless I kill you both." She laughed, a throaty, menacing sound that sent a shiver through Phoebe and convinced her the woman meant her words.

"Killing us won't save you," Eva said defiantly. She sat stiffly upright against the seat, and Phoebe could only imagine the terrifying sensation of the pistol barrel pressed against her ribs. "The police will figure it out and they'll come looking for you. They'll close the ports."

"For one farmwife? On account of a shiftless gardener and a scheming land developer? I hardly think so. Perhaps I'll go to France, or Brussels. Who knows?"

What to do? How to disarm this woman? While stone walls, hedgerows, and undulating fields blurred on either side of the motorcar, Phoebe agonized over options that each promised to bring harm to Eva, to both of them. She could only encourage Elaina Corbyn to talk, with hopes of distracting her until some opportunity presented itself. Phoebe said, "What could you hope to accomplish with the sale of the Ripley land? It's not as though the money would have found its way into your purse."

"I thought it would solve everything, force my husband to sell the farm and try his luck at something else. There've been years he was this close to doing so anyway. Do you realize how much more a man can make working in a factory? Foremen make princely sums compared to farmers, especially since the demand for wool isn't what it was during and before the war."

That might be so, but Phoebe didn't bother pointing out that city living also cost more than village life.

"I thought this would finally force his hand." The woman pushed air through her lips, making a sound as though she spat. "And you're wrong about the money. Ripley and Walker both promised me a handsome payment once the sale went through. But then my interfering husband convinced Mr. Walker he needed sheep roaming the land around his resort, that it would be picturesque. Stephen thought it a grand idea and laughed when I demanded he dissuade Mr. Walker of the idea."

"And you killed him for that?"

"No, not for that alone." The woman tilted her head, allowing the incoming breeze to ruffle her fringe of bangs. "It was his sudden refusal to pay me my share. When I met him that morning at Foxwood Hall to discuss how and when I wanted my payment, he laughed and told me I could expect nothing."

"And that was when you pushed over the ladder and stabbed him with his own shears." Eva gave a disgusted shake of her head. "And Mr. Walker?"

The woman scoffed. Before she answered, she pointed

at the road ahead. "Take the eastbound road." She sat up straighter, watching the rutted, packed-earth road disappear beneath the bonnet of the motorcar. Once Phoebe had made the turn, she relaxed again. "Mr. Walker . . . He also refused to honor his promise to me. Said circumstances became too complicated and he likely wouldn't be buying the land after all."

Phoebe compressed her lips. Had she and Eva not been in such a predicament, she might have smiled or even laughed out loud. What Mrs. Corbyn didn't know was that the "complication" Mr. Walker had spoken of involved Phoebe's grandfather deciding to bid for the land himself.

Instead of revealing that morsel of information, she asked, "Where are we headed? Oxford?" That would make sense. From there Mrs. Corbyn might board a train to London. Or she could continue south and book passage across the channel. Then there were the eastern ports, but even if Mrs. Corbyn had been putting money away these past years, Phoebe doubted she'd wish to part with enough ready cash for passage to Bruges or beyond. No, Dover to Calais made the most sense. How long before anyone in Little Barlow thought to come after them, much less figured out in which direction to go?

And where would Mrs. Corbyn leave them behind? Phoebe knew the answer. She and Eva would not be left behind. At some point, the woman would demand Phoebe stop the motorcar, perhaps in some wooded area, somewhere deserted. She would order them out of the Vauxhall, away from the road, and kill them both. Could Elaina Corbyn drive a motorcar? She probably could. Many farm wives had experience driving their husbands' lorries.

Eva must have been entertaining similar thoughts, for as Phoebe looked over at her, she noticed Eva casting sideways glances at the door latch. Was she considering reaching across, opening the door, and shoving their captor out?

Too dangerous. Phoebe nudged Eva and gave a slight shake of her head. If Eva couldn't implement her plan fast enough, Mrs. Corbyn would pull the trigger.

Mrs. Corbyn would dispatch them both, unless a solid opportunity for escape came their way. Again Phoebe considered simply swerving and crashing the car. That might give them a fighting chance, but the impact could also cause the gun to fire directly into Eva's side. Phoebe couldn't risk it.

What to do then? Phoebe didn't know. Her throat tightened around a sense of helplessness, and she prayed for a miracle.

CHAPTER 19

Damn and blast. Eva could have kicked herself for the many clues she had missed concerning Elaina Corbyn. How blind she had been. How foolish. And now she and Lady Phoebe were to pay the price.

If only she hadn't hesitated—if she had only reached and opened the vehicle door the instant the notion had entered her head, she and her beloved mistress might at this moment be safe. But she *had* hesitated over the wisdom of such an action, and Lady Phoebe had recognized her intention for the flawed act of recklessness it was.

But what else was to be done? How to outwit a heartless, calculating killer with no conscience whatsoever?

"Do you know what I find most appalling?" Eva said aloud, not particularly caring if Elaina Corbyn answered her or not. "I find it inconceivable that after murdering Stephen Ripley in cold blood, and with such violence, you went to his brother's house to enjoy tea and scones." Eva turned her head to scrutinize the woman's profile. "That was you at Keenan's that same morning, wasn't it?"

"Eva," Lady Phoebe said, "please don't antagonize her."

Mrs. Corbyn turned to meet Eva's gaze, her expression bland. "I haven't the faintest idea what you're talking about. I've never had tea and scones nor anything else at Keenan Ripley's home. If I wish myself free of one farmer, do you suppose I'd take up with another?"

Eva turned to exchange a glance with Lady Phoebe and saw her own surprise reflected in Lady Phoebe's hazel eyes, along with a belief that, in this instance, Elaina Corbyn was telling the truth.

Could Keenan have been sincere when he said both teacups had been his, one from that morning and the other from the night before? Could all of Eva's attempts to identify his "guest," and believing it to be Alice, have sent her on a wild goose chase? No wonder she had missed clues about Elaina Corbyn's behavior, being as focused as she had been on her sister's actions.

That wasn't all. She thought back to the day the villagers had gathered to bring in the pear harvest. Almost every other farmwife had gone with her husband to the orchard, but Mrs. Corbyn had stayed away. And when Eva met her in the pasture, the woman had been wearing her tweed jacket. Again, Eva had missed the clue. True, she hadn't seen the flat cap left near Stephen Ripley's body before the chief inspector had taken it as evidence, but shouldn't she have asked more questions about it and compared Lady Phoebe's description to Mrs. Corbyn's homemade jacket?

And—good heavens!—the short, wavy auburn hairs left in the cap? Even now, Mrs. Corbyn's cropped bangs rippled in the breeze like mocking flags being waved in Eva's face. Didn't they perfectly fit the description of the hairs the police had discovered?

And finally, there had been William, who had seen the

killer. He'd described a slim, wiry figure in baggy clothing. Why, Mrs. Corbyn had worn her husband's clothes along with his cap.

"You left it there on purpose, didn't you?"

"Left what?" the woman snapped. By her tone, she was growing weary of Eva's and Lady Phoebe's questions. But Eva wanted an answer.

"You husband's flat cap. You left it there on purpose to incriminate him."

"It was a good idea. It worked, didn't it?"

"And that day in the gardener's cottage. That was you who ran me down."

The woman chuckled. "Sorry about that. But you didn't give me much choice. I couldn't very well have let you recognize me. If you had, you and Lady Phoebe would already be dead."

"Why were you there?" Lady Phoebe's grip on the steering wheel tightened as the car bumped its way over deep ruts in the road.

Those ruts resulted in Mrs. Corbyn's gun digging deeper into Eva's side, but she resisted the urge to wince. Mrs. Corbyn said, "To find the letter I'd written Stephen about Mr. Walker's plans. I did find it, you know, and everything would have been just fine if not for the pair of you. I wish I *had* killed you both that day."

The motorcar rumbled up a low hill. At its crest, sprawling fields opened up on either side of the motorcar. To the right, a frothy sea of sheep poured into sight, herded by several enthusiastic, shaggy, black and white dogs, with two men following in the rear. At first the livestock seemed intent on running parallel to the road, but as Eva watched they took a sudden turn.

"They're heading this way," she said. "They're going to cross the road. There must be a break in the stone wall up ahead."

"They'll either wait or move out of the way," Mrs. Corbyn said dismissively.

Judging by the herd's distance to the road, and the rate at which the Vauxhall was moving, Eva estimated they would reach the same crossing at the same time. Lady Phoebe apparently made the same calculation in her mind.

"We've got to slow down," she said, and changed gears as she applied the brakes.

"Keep going," Mrs. Corbyn commanded. "I told you, they'll move out of the way."

"Or we'll hit them. Is that what you want? Do you think I'll be able to keep this vehicle moving after plowing into a half dozen or more full-grown sheep?"

"Speed up then." The woman craned her neck, leaning her head out the window as she scanned the distance. "Hurry. We can pass them before they reach the road."

Lady Phoebe was shaking her head. "We won't. I don't want to hit them."

They reached a decline and the sheep dipped out of view. Mrs. Corbyn brought her head back inside the motorcar and jabbed her gun painfully into Eva's side. "I said hurry up. If you attempt to slow this motorcar again I'll shoot your friend. And you'll be next."

"And you'll be caught," Eva reminded her.

The woman shrugged. "And you'll be dead. Now go, Lady Phoebe."

The Vauxhall lurched ahead, the thin tires burning up the road even as the sheep made short work of the field. Their herders couldn't have noticed the motorcar yet, especially not over the noise of barking, bleating, and hooves tramping over the turf. The road curved frequently, and now they caught only fleeting glimpses of fluffy white bodies in motion. The shepherds might not spot them until it was too late.

Lady Phoebe began pounding the button on the Vauxhall's Klaxon horn, sending its blaring *a-rooga* cry into the afternoon air. Would the warning be enough to stop a swarming herd?

"We're going to collide with them," Lady Phoebe shouted as she maneuvered with one hand and continued thumping the horn's mechanism. *A-rooga* filled Eva's ears and blocked out other sounds while the oncoming sheep filled her vision. They were almost at the crossing point, and the first of the sheep had already streamed through the gate in the low stone wall and were descending the verge between the field and the road.

"We won't make it!" Lady Phoebe stopped sounding the horn in order to clutch the steering wheel with both hands. "I don't want to hit them."

"They're just sheep," Elaina Corbyn shouted back.

"You're detestable," Eva said, and once again contemplated reaching over, opening the door, and pushing the farmwife out.

Before the thought had wholly formed in her mind, Lady Phoebe shouted, "I won't!" and twisted the steering wheel. The Vauxhall swerved and skidded, sending up a shower of dust and pebbles. As the sky tilted in the windscreen, Eva felt herself thrown against Elaina Corbyn's side—and against the barrel of her gun, which stabbed cruelly into her side. The motorcar began to spin, turning full around as it shimmied sideways across the road away from the oncoming sheep. Road and fields streaked past as the car slid toward the verge, the rock wall, and the sturdy gatepost at the entrance to the second field.

A blast exploded in Eva's ears, setting off a deafening ringing. Before her face, the windscreen shattered outward. Shards sprinkled into the air, clattered onto the motorcar's bonnet, and slid off to shower the ground on either side. The Vauxhall came to a jarring stop at a tilt, giving Eva the sensation it might at any moment tip onto its side.

Even through the ringing, she heard the frantic bleating and running of sheep, the desperate barking of the dogs, and the urgent shouting of the shepherds.

"Eva?" Lady Phoebe shouted.

Eva barely heard her through the high-pitched whistle that pulsated in her ears, and yet the sound of her mistress's voice filled her with relief. It took her a moment to comprehend exactly what had happened. The gun. The bullet. The windscreen.

Whatever happened in that final moment before the car crashed—running off the road, climbing the grassy verge to hit the gatepost—had dislodged the gun barrel from Eva's side and sent its discharging bullet wildly into the air. It had hit the windscreen and shattered it.

Eva wasted no time. Even as she yelled to assure her mistress she was unharmed, she twisted, seized Elaina Corbyn's trigger hand, and pinned it to the seat. Then she pried the weapon from the woman's stubborn fingers, resorting to stomping on her foot when she proved uncooperative. That did the trick. Mrs. Corbyn shrieked, and Eva whisked the gun from her possession and handed it to Lady Phoebe, who in turn tossed it out of the Vauxhall.

Sheep surrounded the automobile, while the dogs stood on their hind legs, their front paws propped on the frame. They raised a ruckus of barking. Lady Phoebe opened her door and stumbled out. "Help us, please. This woman with us, the redhead—she's dangerous."

Eva used the distraction to reach around Elaina Corbyn, open the door as she had wished to do during the ride, and shove her out. The woman tumbled over and collapsed onto the ground on her side, to be overrun by panicking sheep and barked at by the dogs. Speaking of sheep and dogs . . .

Eva took a quick look about her as she slid out of the Vauxhall after Lady Phoebe. She saw no animals strewn across the road, no blood, no tufts of fur floating through the air. It seemed the motorcar had missed the animals altogether. She came around the vehicle and thrust out her forefinger. "That woman kidnapped us. This is Lady Phoebe Renshaw, granddaughter of the Earl of Wroxly, and this woman endangered her life."

"Both of our lives," Phoebe corrected her. She wrapped an arm around Eva and pulled her to her side.

The two men were clearly having difficulty grasping the situation; little in their experience could have prepared them for such a sight or such accusations. They hesitated, then moved slowly around the nose of the Vauxhall to glimpse the woman who lay moaning on the other side.

"She's wanted in Little Barlow for the murders of two men," Eva told them in a firm voice. It wasn't precisely true, but it would be soon enough.

"Yes, and I know my grandfather will want to reward you for your assistance," Lady Phoebe added, and that made up the men's minds for them. One on each side, they hauled Elaina Corbyn to her feet while Eva went to collect the discarded weapon.

Eva spent that night at her parents' cottage, sleeping in one of the two beds in the room she and Alice had shared as children. Miles had driven her out there last night, after taking her and Lady Phoebe's statements and assuring himself they were both all right. He'd been fiercely protective, sweetly solicitous. He would be coming by later that morning to drive her back to Foxwood Hall.

She and Alice had talked late into the night, airing grievances as sisters will do, but finally finding common ground and even forgiveness. In the morning, Eva once again awoke to aching bones, not to mention a couple of bruised ribs. But she was alive. Lady Phoebe was alive. Keenan Ripley had been released from jail, Elaina Corbyn having taken his place, and by nightfall yesterday Lord Wroxly had gone to visit Keenan with an offer to help him save his orchard.

Her sister's bed lay empty, the covers neatly in place, the pillow fluffed and angled just so against the iron head-board. A glance at the bedside clock let Eva know she had slept later than usual, while the sounds of voices from across the small house beckoned to her. She quickly donned the same frock she had arrived in last night, pinned up her hair, and made her way to the kitchen.

What she saw from the doorway both took her aback and made her grin. A bouquet of flowers—roses, peonies, baby's breath—sat in one of Mum's earthenware pitchers in the center of the table. And the person who had brought them? He stood with his hat in his hands, his head slightly bowed, a remorseful look on his slightly lined face. He was speaking in a low murmur, for one pair of ears only, and Eva couldn't make out the words. Whatever they were, however, she knew they were sincere. Beyond the window that overlooked the garden, Eva spied her parents walking slowly away from the cottage, looking as though they wished to appear industrious but in fact were only putting a discreet distance between themselves and the occupants of the kitchen.

Alice, on the other hand, sat at the table and stared into her coffee cup, her expression shuttered and her posture conveying the impression that she had little interest in the words her husband was speaking to her.

For all Eva yearned to remain and witness the events unfolding, she backed away from the doorway and moved out of sight. Oliver and Alice hadn't seen her. She tiptoed to the front door with every intention of slipping outside, when she heard a cry.

"Oliver, you've been the worst kind of idiot."

Eva stopped with her hand poised on the door latch.

"Yes, I admit that. But your leaving me has knocked sense into me, Alice." Oliver said more, but his voice dropped again and Eva couldn't quite hear.

Then Alice said, more calmly, "I didn't leave you, Oliver. I merely came home to think things through."

"And?" Oliver's voice rang with eager hope.

Eva held her breath, crossed her fingers, and joined him in those hopes. Unlike Elaina Corbyn, Alice had loved her life on the farm she and Oliver had built together in Suffolk. She took pride in their work and gained a sense of value from it. She and Oliver had always been partners—until recently, when he'd made bad decisions and then compounded them with reckless behavior.

"And . . ." Alice said slowly, "if you'll mend your ways, I believe we can mend things between us and on the farm."

"I've already mended them, Alice, I swear."

"Don't swear, Oliver, it's vulgar. But promise me, no more drinking—at least no more than a person should—and no more gambling. At all."

"Yes to both, Alice. I sw—that is, I promise. My solemn promise. Your father said he has some ideas that'll help us get back on our feet, not that I intend to take a penny from him. Alice, just come home. The children miss you. *I* miss you. What do you say?"

A long pause ensued. Finally, Alice said, "We've faced worse, I suppose. That summer there was almost no rain, the war, the influenza. . . ."

"That's true," Oliver was quick to agree.

"So then, yes. I suppose I'll come home."

"Alice . . ."

Abruptly, Alice said, "There's something you should know."

Sounding wary, Oliver asked, "Yes? What is it?"

"Another mouth to feed, I'm afraid."

"Alice . . . Alice . . ." His voice hitched. He coughed, cleared his throat, and spoke her name again.

Eva's eyes suddenly burned and a lump that might have been joy pressed against her throat. The last thing she heard from the kitchen was the scrape of a chair—presumably Alice getting up from the table to embrace her husband—before she opened the front door and stepped out.

Phoebe came into the morning room expecting to find her grandparents having their breakfast. She didn't at all expect to see, instead, Julia sitting at the table enjoying a mound of eggs, fruit, and toast. This was the first time Julia had chosen not to breakfast in her room in months—since before her wedding.

"You're looking chipper today," Phoebe commented, then regretted it. Calling Julia things like *chipper* was just the way to sour her mood. And yet, once again, Julia surprised her.

"I'm feeling chipper, actually. Not quite sure why. I slept well, I suppose."

"Where are Grams and Grampapa? It's awfully early for them to have eaten and gone about their business. Or aren't they up yet?"

"They're up." Julia stabbed a perfectly formed melon ball with her fork and popped it in her mouth. With uncharacteristic enthusiasm, she chewed and spoke at the same time. "They've gone to telephone Mr. Peele. They're going to beg him to come back to Foxwood Hall. And I can't tell you how glad I am. I want him to help me plan a garden for the baby, a rather extensive one. I want lots of blue hydrangeas and delphiniums as well as pink roses and such. If we plan it all out now and decide what we'll need to order, we can start the planting as soon as the spring thaw comes in the New Year. I simply don't trust it to anyone but Alfred Peele."

"That's a lovely idea." Phoebe went to the sideboard and filled a plate of her own. Perhaps Julia's voracious appetite was catching. Perhaps nearly being killed yesterday had increased her appreciation of simple things, like breakfast. Or, perhaps it was hearing Julia speak of the prospect of having a boy or a girl with equal enthusiasm, if her choices of flowers gave any indication. "If I can help, please let me know."

"Would you like to?"

Phoebe turned to face her sister. "Of course I would."

"All right then." Julia reached for the coffeepot. "There's something else I could use your help with, too. It's for Grams and Grampapa's upcoming anniversary."

"That's not for months yet."

"I realize that. I wish to order something special in honor of their fifty-fifth year together. We might even need to take a secret trip, you and I. And Amelia. I suppose we couldn't leave her out."

Phoebe carried her plate to the table. "Where to?"

Julia took on a positively mischievous and conspiratorial grin. "Sit, and I'll tell you."

Good heavens, Phoebe thought as Julia launched into her idea for their grandparents' anniversary, did a new Julia sneak into the house to replace the old one? Had she come to her senses and stopped blaming herself for her husband's untimely death? Stopped agonizing over whether she would have a boy—Gil's heir—or a girl?

Had past resentments between Julia and Phoebe simply dissipated into the autumn air? And would this surprising accord between them last? That was a question Phoebe had asked numerous times in the past. Would this time be any different?

Yes, so many questions. She let Julia talk, nodding her head in full agreement with all of Julia's plans, and wondered whether they should take another ride to Cheltenham, this time for Phoebe to consult with the fortune-teller to see what their future held.